NEW ARRIVALS AT THE LOCH

LOCH LANNICK BOOK 9

HANNAH ELLIS

Published by Hannah Ellis
www.authorhannahellis.com
Postfach 900309, 81503 München
Germany

Cover design by Katherine Newton

NEW ARRIVALS AT THE LOCH

CHAPTER ONE

Lexie batted her eyes open when Nick announced they were home. She hadn't been asleep, just pretending she was to avoid having to make conversation.

"Thanks for driving," her mum said, patting Nick's arm when they all stepped out into the pub car park.

Her dad nodded solemnly. "You're a good, safe driver."

Nick came over to Lexie and slipped an arm around her waist. He lowered his face to her ear. "Did you hear that? Your dad gave me a compliment."

"He must be going soft." Lexie shifted her weight and rubbed a hand over her rapidly expanding middle.

"Is she kicking?" Nick asked eagerly.

"No. The drive lulled her to sleep. No doubt she'll wait until I want to go to sleep and then start kicking like crazy."

"You've been asleep for the past two hours," Nick pointed out, leaning into her so she got a whiff of his aftershave. He'd removed his jacket and tie for the drive home and had undone the top button on his white shirt.

"I wasn't sleeping," she said quietly.

"Thanks a lot. You just left me to deal with your dad going on and on."

"He's upset," Lexie said. "Apparently he deals with that by blethering on about inane stuff. The trick is to pretend to be asleep."

Nick quirked an eyebrow. "I haven't figured out how to do that while driving."

"Are you coming in for dinner?" Angus called as he ambled towards the pub.

"Yeah," Nick replied, taking Lexie's hand and following her parents.

Inside the pub, Leana was pulling a pint and gave them a sympathetic smile over the beer tap. "How was it?" she asked.

Lexie adjusted her stretchy black dress as she perched on a bar stool. "It was okay, I suppose. As far as funerals go."

"Has everything been all right here?" Angus asked.

"All quiet." Leana set the pint of ale in front of the regular at the end of the bar.

"Good." Angus poured himself a whisky and wearily scanned the pub.

"Why don't you go upstairs?" Mary said to him. "I'll bring some food up. You look worn out."

"Aye. I might do that." He thanked Nick again for driving and wandered away.

"Do you think he's okay?" Lexie said, looking to her mum.

"It's difficult for him. I'm just thankful they sorted things out before Wesley passed."

"It seems cruel that Angus reunited with his brother after all those years and then he lost him," Leana said.

Mary sighed and slipped her coat off, then went to the kitchen to organise food for them.

"Were there a lot of people at the service?" Leana asked Lexie.

"Quite a few. Grandad had a lot of friends from the social club. His friend Bill was really upset. He'd been with him when he died and thought he should have been able to do something."

"Not much you can do for a massive heart attack," Nick said. "But at least he wasn't alone."

Leana reached across and squeezed Lexie's hand. "Was Stephanie there today?"

"Aye." It was the first time Lexie had seen her birth mother in almost ten years.

"Did you talk to her?"

"Yes. It was weird. She stood and made polite conversation with us for a while. That will probably be the last time I see her. Which is a good thing, I guess."

"It must be so hard to process," Leana said, distracted by a group of people walking in and approaching the bar. "I'll be back in a minute," she said as she moved to serve them.

Lexie turned to face Nick. "I hate that Stephanie knows I'm pregnant."

"She's not worth worrying about," Nick said. "Like you said, you'll probably never hear from her again now."

Lexie swiped at the tears that spilled down her cheeks. "I should be happy about that. But part of me still wishes she cared enough to want to be in contact. And I really can't understand what sort of person has no interest in their grandchild."

Nick slid a hand onto her stomach. "This little one will have plenty of doting grandparents. She'll be loved to bits and spoilt rotten."

"I know." Lexie put her hand over his. "I keep telling myself that I don't want someone like her in our child's life anyway. But my hormones are a mess and my emotions are all over the place. Everything's confusing."

Nick nodded. "It would be weird if you made it through your grandad's funeral and seeing your birth mother again without it being difficult."

"I'm so glad I've got you," she whispered, pulling on his shirt collar to draw him closer. "You look really hot in your suit, by the way."

A smile crept over his face before he kissed her. "How about we eat quick and go home for an early night?" he murmured against her lips.

~

As Elspeth and Rory approached the Old Inn, the door swung open and Lexie and Nick walked out. Their formal attire reminded Elspeth that it had been Lexie's grandad's funeral, and she felt a pang of regret that she'd forgotten to message her.

"How did it go today?" she asked.

"It was okay," Lexie said with a shrug. "I'll tell you all about it another time. I'm really tired now."

"I'll bet." Elspeth stepped closer and laid a hand on her bump. "You're getting big. Has she been kicking a lot?"

"Yeah. Usually when I sit down or want to sleep."

"I remember that. Arran was the same. He used to wedge his feet under my ribs until I felt like they were going to break. It's such a weird feeling."

Nick smiled at Rory. "Friday night date night, is it?"

"Aye." Rory grinned. "A wild night at the Old Inn."

Elspeth curled her fingers around his. "I said we could go somewhere else if you wanted."

"I just want a pint and an early night," he replied through a yawn.

"Have a good night," Lexie said. They all called goodbye as they set off in different directions.

"I can't wait until the baby arrives," Elspeth said as they walked into the pub. "It'll be so nice having a tiny baby to cuddle."

"How long has she got left?" Rory asked.

"Three months." She thought for a moment. "Maybe a bit less. She's due in January."

Rory yawned again once they were settled at a table with their drinks.

"Our Friday nights out are becoming less and less imaginative," Elspeth remarked. When the weekly date nights had started up six months previously, they'd spent their time trying different restaurants and bars. Once, they'd even done a weekend trip to Inverness. The alone time had been good for them as they slowly repaired their relationship, but inevitably they'd slipped back to the easy option of a few drinks in the local pub.

"Next week we can do something different." Rory rubbed at his neck. "Work was hectic this week. I'm done in."

"I wasn't complaining. I'm happy whatever we do." She squeezed his hand, and they spent an hour chatting about their respective weeks over food and a couple of drinks.

They'd just decided to go home when Rory's phone buzzed with a message. "It's Chris," he said as he read it. "Asking if I want to go out with them next week. It's his birthday."

Elspeth presumed he was referring to his old colleagues from Portree High School. "Where are they going?"

"The Merchant Bar. It might be a laugh to see all my old co-workers. I've been saying I'll go over and catch up with them one Friday ever since I left."

"Instead you've been stuck on boring dates with me," Elspeth said lightly.

He smiled at her. "Can we switch date night to Saturday next weekend?"

"Yeah, okay."

"You can come out on Friday too if you want?"

"With your old workmates?" she mused.

"Is that a problem?"

"No." She was sure he could read her mind and knew she was wondering if one ex-colleague in particular would be there. "I just don't know them very well. It's probably best if you go alone."

"Are you going to be annoyed with me for going?"

She gave a small shake of the head. "No. You should go if you want to."

"I feel as though you're going to be weird about it."

"Why would I be weird about it?"

"Because Jess will probably be there."

"Should that be an issue for me?"

"No." He leaned on the table. "But that doesn't mean it won't be."

"It's not an issue," she said, hoping she sounded convincing. Rory had sworn that there was never anything between him and Jess. They'd been good friends in the time he and Elspeth had broken up but that was all. Elspeth's flicker of jealousy at the mention of Jess was completely irrational. "You should definitely go out with them," she said, reaching for his hand. "I promise not to be weird about it."

"Why don't you come too? We haven't had a night out in Portree in ages."

"I'll think about it," she said, then stood and pulled her coat on.

Stepping out of the pub, Elspeth glanced over at the bunkhouse and felt a flutter of nerves. "Where are you staying tonight?" she asked. Their arrangement of living separately had made sense when they first got back together, but now Elspeth saw it as an indicator that their relationship still wasn't quite on track.

"I'll come back with you if that's all right?"

The relief was instant. Tonight, she wouldn't have to pretend she was fine with them going back to separate houses, to sleep in different beds.

"Of course it's all right," she said, as they set off home. "It's always all right."

CHAPTER TWO

"You may as well go home."

Lexie paused in tapping her pen against the desk and looked up at her boss at the activity centre. "Can't you find something for me to do?"

"You've been far too efficient in whipping the office into shape," Tim said, perching on the opposite edge of the desk. "You have everything running so smoothly that you've pretty much done yourself out of a job."

"I was thinking I could take over with cleaning the cabins."

"You're volunteering to clean?"

"I've never had a problem with cleaning, and I need something to keep me busy. If you won't even let me out on the kayaks any more, what exactly am I supposed to do?"

"I think you're supposed to put your feet up and relax until the little one arrives."

"I've got another ten weeks to go. I'll be bored out of my brains by the time the baby arrives. Taking over some cleaning shifts is a good idea."

"Not happening," Tim said.

"Oh, come on. I'm perfectly capable of cleaning."

"If you want to carry on with office duties, you're very welcome to. But that's all I can offer you from now on."

Lexie dropped her chin to her chest. When it had taken them a little while to get pregnant, she had been adamant she wouldn't complain about any aspect of the pregnancy, but if there was one thing she had a problem with, it was having to slow down. "I'm going to go crazy. The only bit of excitement I have left is my hikes with the old bids."

Tim cleared his throat, and Lexie looked up to find him shaking his head.

"Don't tell me you're taking that away too? It's only a couple of hours walking. I'm not ill, I can still walk. The exercise is good for me."

"Sorry," Tim said. "I'll take over until you're ready to come back after the baby's born."

"I can at least do it for a few more weeks," Lexie pleaded. "Where's the harm in it?"

"The harm is you're out in the middle of nowhere, roaming around the countryside. If anything happens, I'll have to live with the guilt, not to mention the wrath of Nick and your dad."

"Nothing's going to happen."

He shook his head firmly. "I can't let you. It's not only you I have to consider. The old bids might feel like friends, but they're also paying customers. I can't have them feeling responsible for the guide."

Lexie mock cried. "Being pregnant is no fun. Everyone is treating me as though I'm ill."

"You only need to take it easy for a little while. Slowing down a bit isn't such a bad thing. Enjoy it."

"I don't like being idle." She shifted the chair back and stood up. "If office work is all you can offer, I'll continue with that for now. There's not much admin to do, though, not at this time of year. I'll go and speak to my parents about increasing my shifts in the pub."

Tim snorted a laugh. "Good luck with that."

"If anyone tells me I'm not capable of pulling pints, they're going to have an argument on their hands."

"Close the door behind you then so I won't hear the shouting drifting from the pub."

~

Lexie greeted her mum cheerfully when she walked into the pub.

"I didn't expect to see you today," Mary said. "I thought you were working at the activity centre."

"I was, but there isn't much for me to do. Tim's as much of a worrywart as Nick is. I'm on office duties only. Which means he doesn't need me there much. I was thinking I could pick up some more shifts here to make up for it."

Mary paused in wiping down the bar and cast Lexie a rueful smile. "I'll let you argue that one out with your dad, but I'd guess you're not going to win that battle." She tipped her chin towards the window, where Angus was sitting opposite a young woman with a bunch of papers on the table.

"What's he doing?" Lexie asked.

"Interviewing for a new member of staff," Mary said, continuing her cleaning.

"Why?" Lexie said on a sigh.

"You'll be out of action for a while. We need someone to help out."

"I don't intend to take much time off. And it's quiet in the winter. You can manage with the staff you've got. Leana won't mind taking a few extra shifts."

"Your dad wants someone else around. It makes sense. Especially since I might like to take some time off to help with my granddaughter."

"That's a good point," Lexie conceded. "I really want to keep working for as long as I can though."

"I haven't put you down for any shifts after this weekend."

"Well, you can change that."

"Change what?" her dad said, appearing behind her.

Lexie turned in time to see the woman he'd been interviewing heading for the door. "Mum said I'm not down for any more shifts, but I'm fine to keep working."

"You need to be taking it easy now," Angus said.

"I've still got ten weeks, and Tim isn't letting me work at the activity centre except for a few measly admin tasks. I'm fine to keep working behind the bar."

"You shouldn't be on your feet for so long."

"There's plenty of opportunity to sit down. We're not exactly rushed off our feet at this time of year. And if it makes you feel better, you can give me shorter shifts."

"Fine." Angus perched on a stool and looked to his wife. "Put her back in for a couple of shifts a week. Shorter shifts, and I don't want her on her own at all."

"Hello!" Lexie waved in front of his face. "I'm here. You're basically giving me charity shifts. Half of the time you only need one member of staff behind the bar. So there'll be no point in me being here."

"Aye. It means that you can always go home if you're tired or not feeling up to working."

"It's pointless arguing about this, isn't it?"

Angus nodded firmly.

"How was the interview?" Mary asked him.

His forehead wrinkled. "She's very shy. I don't think she's cut out for working in a pub."

"Maybe she wouldn't have been so shy if you hadn't been scowling at her the whole time," Lexie said.

"You need some backbone to work in a pub. If the interview makes her nervous, how will she cope with rowdy customers?"

Lexie scanned the room. "It's not exactly a party scene. How often do we get rowdy customers?"

"That's not the point."

"What about that young lad who you spoke to earlier?" Mary said. "He seemed eager."

"He's only young," Angus grumbled. "He doesn't have any experience."

"It'd take you one shift to train him up," Lexie pointed out.

"Aye, but he might decide bar work isn't for him and then I've wasted my time training him."

"The middle-aged woman you saw first had a nice vibe," Mary said. "A motherly type is always good."

"She's got two small kids," Angus said. "No doubt she'd call in sick more often than she'd actually be here."

Lexie slapped a hand to her forehead. "I hope you're not serious. You realise that's discrimination? Presumably she has childcare lined up. Her kids probably have a very capable father to look after them while she's at work."

"Kids get sick a lot, and they need their mum when they're ill."

"Dad!" Lexie snapped. "You can't say stuff like that."

"It's the truth."

"It's absolutely not the truth – it's your opinion. And it's very outdated. Mum, will you tell him?"

"Maybe you should give her a try," Mary said.

Angus shook his head. "I had a bad feeling about her. I've got a couple more people to interview next week. Best not to rush into a decision about these things."

"Especially not since I'm quite capable of working still," Lexie said. "I don't intend to take too much time after the baby arrives either. I'll work a bit less, but I'll definitely still work."

Angus rolled his eyes. "Who exactly is going to look after the baby?"

"Nick!" Lexie said. "At least when he's not working. I realise you think only women are capable of caring for their children, but it's not true."

"I feel sorry for the modern man," Angus said. "They're expected to do it all."

Lexie's shoulders shook as she laughed. "I give up! There's no point in talking to you about this stuff." Slipping off her stool, she smiled at her mum. "Send me the rota when you've put me in for some shifts."

"Take care," Mary called.

As she strolled down the road, Lexie reminded herself that her dad meant well. He was stuck in his ways but that wasn't about to change, so there wasn't any point in getting worked up about his annoying comments.

She called hello as she arrived home. Nick shouted back to her from the living room.

"I thought you'd be a while yet," he said as she wandered through to find him sitting on the floor surrounded by piles of baby clothes.

"I ran out of things to do at the activity centre. Tim won't let me do anything that involves me moving from the office chair."

"Good." Nick checked the label of a white all-in-one sleepsuit before setting it aside. "You should be taking it easy now."

"So everyone keeps telling me. What are you doing?"

"Kerry from work gave us a bunch of baby clothes. I'm sorting them into sizes. I'll wash the newborn stuff and pack the rest of the stuff away until we need it." He reached for his laptop, which was in the middle of the coffee table, and moved it in Lexie's direction. "I've narrowed the car seat down to a choice of two. Can you have a look and see what you think so I can order it?"

"Elspeth said she has Arran's old car seats that we can have."

Nick frowned. "It's safer to get a new one. They lose their integrity after a while. I read about it."

Smiling sweetly, Lexie picked up the laptop and looked at the two near-identical car seats. "Either is fine with me."

"Just pick one."

"The blue one."

Nick looked up at her and blew out a breath. "The other one has slightly better ratings."

"That one then!"

"Good. I'll order it later. I was thinking I'll paint the nursery this weekend. And put the crib together."

"There's still loads of time."

"I like to be prepared."

"It's something I've noticed about you," Lexie said, sinking back onto the couch cushions and pulling out her phone as a message came through.

Nick picked his way through the piles of baby clothes to sit beside her, giving her a quick kiss on the cheek. "You look tired."

Her focus was on her phone and she didn't register his words. "What?" she asked, dragging her gaze from the screen.

"I said you look tired. Are you okay?"

"Fine." She tilted her phone in his direction. "Stephanie messaged me. For a moment, I thought she might have developed some maternal instincts, but she was just asking for my bank details for the money Grandad left me. She didn't even bother to ask how I am."

Nick flashed a sympathetic smile. "Did you think of anything you want to use the money for?"

"I already have everything I need. It's nice to have a bit extra in the bank though." She sighed and rested her head on Nick's shoulder. "It bothers me that Stephanie is the executor of Grandad's will. And that he left her the house."

"She is his daughter."

"I know. And it's not as though I wanted anything from him. I just have this feeling that she might be happy he's dead. It's quite a windfall for her."

"She seemed pretty upset at the funeral." Nick rubbed her upper arm. "I know she was a terrible mother, but I got the impression that she and Wesley were quite close."

"They were," Lexie said sadly. "Maybe that's what really bothers me. She cared about him, but not me. I can't help but take it personally. Grandad always used the excuse that she had me so young and wasn't ready for the responsibility of a child, but she's a grown woman now and she's still not interested in having a relationship with me."

"You know there's something wrong with her and not you, don't you?"

"Yes." She shifted so her cheek rested against his neck, savouring the warmth of his skin and the comforting scent of him. "Logically, I know that. It still hurts though."

"I know." He kissed the top of her head. "What can I do to take your mind off it? Do you want me to rub your feet or something?"

"No!" She grinned. "I'm going to make dinner while you sort out this mess."

"I can cook."

"I'm quite capable of cooking."

"You should put your feet up."

She rolled her eyes and gave him a quick peck before standing up. "I can't spend the next two and a half months sitting around doing nothing. Stop fussing over me."

"I'll try."

She smiled as she went to the kitchen, not believing him for a moment.

CHAPTER THREE

Elspeth didn't know many of Rory's colleagues from Portree High School. Their relationship had begun to fall apart soon after he'd started working there, and they'd split up not long after that. Now that he was working at Lannick High School, there wasn't as much socialising with the other members of staff. Elspeth wasn't sure if that was because he didn't get on with them or if he felt he should be spending his free time with her and Arran.

When they'd arrived at the Merchant Bar, Rory had sat beside her at the end of a long table and introduced her to the people nearest them. After half an hour, he'd gone to say hello to someone on the next table, then continued to mingle until Elspeth had completely exhausted polite conversation with the people around her.

Spotting a familiar face at the bar, she muttered that she'd be back in a minute to no one in particular.

"You're looking even more cagey than usual tonight," she said to Gary, who was staring into his pint. As Logan's best friend, she'd known him for about as long as she could remember.

"Have you seen Logan? He told me to meet him here. I knew it was a bad idea."

"As far as I know, Logan's going to the Isles Inn. Alasdair's playing a gig. I'm probably going to head over there myself soon." Sitting with Rory's old colleagues wasn't exactly her idea of a fun night.

"He told me he was coming in here for a drink first, then going to watch Alasdair afterwards. I should have gone straight to the Isles Inn."

"Why? What's the problem with this place? I didn't think you'd be bothered about sitting at the bar on your own for a bit."

"I'm not. But there's a woman here who I've been avoiding. She's usually here on Friday nights, so I've taken to avoiding the place."

"What did you do now? She's not married or something, is she?"

"No! I didn't do anything wrong. We went on a couple of dates and then she blew me off. It's all a bit embarrassing."

Elspeth shuffled onto a stool beside him. "I don't see the problem."

"The problem is I really liked her. But it obviously wasn't mutual."

"That sucks."

"Yeah."

"Which one is she?"

"Her name's Jess. You probably know her. She used to work with Rory."

Elspeth had never actually met Jess but knew her by sight and had spotted her as soon as they arrived. As she turned to glance at her, Jess stood to greet Rory with a hug. Rory caught Elspeth's eye just as he sat down with her and another woman. Elspeth swore under her breath. Now he'd think she was jealous.

"Do you know her?" Gary asked.

"Yeah. She has a thing for Rory. Or *had* at least."

Gary stared at her for a moment. "That makes sense. She

always seemed distracted when I went out with her. Like she was forcing herself to be there."

"Sorry."

He shrugged. "You win some, you lose some. I really liked her though." After finishing his pint in a long swig, he asked if she wanted a drink.

"Do you feel like going to the Isles Inn already?" Elspeth asked. "We can tell Logan to meet us there. I can't cope with any more small talk with Rory's old co-workers.

"I'm up for anything," he said, straightening up. "And I'm definitely happy to get out of here."

"I'll just tell Rory I'm going."

She crossed the room to Rory. He was mid-conversation but smiled up at her when she rested a hand on his shoulder.

"Hey!" He took her hand and gave it a quick squeeze. "Sorry. I didn't mean to abandon you."

"It's fine." She smiled awkwardly at the two women at the table.

"Sorry," he said again, then introduced Jess and Ava.

"Grab a seat before someone else nabs it," Ava said, nodding at the stool beside her.

"Thanks," she said, sitting. "I was actually going to head over to the Isles Inn," she told Rory. "Gary and Logan are going to watch Alasdair play."

"I thought we were going to head over there together later."

"I can just meet you there."

A guy at another table called to Rory. "I'll be right back," he said as he stood. "One sec."

Elspeth smiled at the two women, wishing she had a drink just so she had something to do.

"He's leaving," Ava whispered, nudging Jess. "It's now or never."

Jess shook her head and shot Ava a warning glance.

"Who's leaving?" Elspeth asked, curiosity getting the better of her.

"Gary," Ava said. "You know him, right? Jess has a crush on him. I told her to go and chat to him, but she's a chicken."

"He's not interested," Jess said. "So there's no point."

"He said you'd been on a couple of dates," Elspeth said, as all three of them watched him walk out of the door.

"Ages ago. Both times were a disaster and he's been avoiding me ever since."

"No!" Ava said adamantly. "You said you'd call him and you didn't."

Elspeth nodded. "He thinks you're not interested."

"I told you to be proactive," Ava said.

"There's no way he's interested in me," Jess said. "When we went out I was terrible company. The dates were painful both times."

"How long ago was that?" Elspeth asked, fairly sure she could guess.

"About six months."

Just as she'd thought – it was the same time she and Rory had got back together. "Maybe it was bad timing."

"Maybe." Jess offered her a weak smile. "I wasn't in a very good place at the time."

"But you like him?" Elspeth asked.

"I think so. I don't know him well. We only went on two dates, but he seemed sweet."

Elspeth wasn't sure she'd describe Gary as sweet, what with his womanising tendencies, but if he was still pining for Jess six months after they'd been out together, she supposed he might have changed.

"You should call him," Elspeth said. "Didn't you tell him you were going to call?"

"I think it's a bit late now. When people say they'll call, they don't generally mean in six months."

"I'm with Elspeth," Ava said. "Pretend you lost track of time."

The three of them cracked up laughing as Rory reappeared and sat beside Elspeth. "What are you three giggling about?"

"That's classified information," Ava said.

"I'm going to head over to the Isles Inn," Elspeth said, giving Rory a quick peck. "If I don't see you there later, I'll see you tomorrow."

"I'll come and find you in a bit."

"I don't know how long I'll stay, but Gary and Logan will probably be there all evening." Her gaze flicked to Jess, checking she'd got the message.

Ava sat up straighter. "Did you say there's live music? I love live music, don't you, Jess?"

"Can you both leave me alone please?" Jess said, her cheeks pinking.

"I feel as though I missed something," Rory said, looking quizzically at Elspeth.

She shrugged and said goodbye to them all, then smiled to herself as she walked out of the pub. Gary was leaning against the wall with his hands in his pockets.

"I was giving you two more minutes, then I'd have abandoned you."

"I'm surprised you waited at all," Elspeth said, falling into step with him. "That was unusually gentlemanly of you. Did you want to find out what I was talking to Jess about, by any chance?"

"Were you talking to her? I didn't notice."

"Yeah, right!"

"What were you talking about then?"

"*You*, as it happens. She likes you."

"If you'd have been a fly on the wall for either of our dates you wouldn't say that. I don't think I've ever felt so stupid in my life."

"Why?" She cast him a sidelong glance. "What did you do?"

"I didn't *do* anything. But she's super brainy. She's a chemistry teacher. I fix cars for a living. When I talked about my job she looked bored, and when she talked about her job I nodded and pretended I had a clue what she was talking about. I don't think I was very convincing."

"She wasn't bored. She was hung up on someone else. Maybe you should give it another go."

"And embarrass myself again? No thanks."

They turned the corner and continued to the Isles Inn at the end of the road.

"There's Logan," Elspeth remarked as she caught sight of his back disappearing inside.

"I messaged him and told him to come straight here."

They caught up with him at the bar. Elspeth waved a greeting to Alasdair, who was playing in the corner. The place was reasonably busy, but they managed to get a table and sat chatting while Alasdair played in the background.

"Are you sure you don't want a drink?" Logan asked her when he set off for the bar for the third time.

"I'm driving," she told him, sounding like a broken record.

"Leave the car and pick it up tomorrow. Get a lift home with Alasdair."

"I don't feel like drinking. I'm going home soon." As Logan wandered away she glanced at the door, hoping to see Rory arriving. She'd half expected he might bring Jess and Ava with him, but they were obviously enjoying themselves at the Merchant Bar. "I'm going to go home," she told Gary as she stood. "But I really think you should get in touch with Jess."

"That's not going to happen. If she'd wanted to go out again, she'd have called."

"Maybe she will," Elspeth said, flashing him a smile. She said a quick goodbye to Logan and waved to Alasdair before she left.

"Where are you going?" Rory asked happily as she stepped out into the fresh air to find him approaching the pub.

"Home. I got sick of waiting for you."

"I'm here now." Grinning, he slipped his arms around her waist. "Stay and have a drink with me."

"I'm driving."

He glanced in the window of the pub. "Stay and have a dance with me then."

"You don't dance," she reminded him.

His eyes twinkled. "I'd dance with you."

"Only when you're drunk." She gave him a quick kiss. "I'm going home."

His arms tightened around her waist. "Let's stay for a little bit. I promised I'd watch Alasdair play."

"You can stay. Logan's in there, and Alasdair will drive you home. It's not like we're going to the same place anyway."

"I thought I'd stay at your place. If that's okay."

Elspeth's heart felt heavy. She hated that she never knew when he'd stay over, and that when he did, he had to ask if it was okay.

"It's always okay," she said. "But I'm tired and Mum's looking after Arran. I need to get back so she can go home."

Rory nodded. "I'll come with you then. We can dance at home instead."

"I'm fairly sure you'll pass out by the time we get home." She took his hand and led him to the car, then smiled when he fell asleep five minutes into the drive. At home, she nudged him awake and watched in amusement as he muttered a greeting to her mum before stumbling up the stairs.

"Looks like someone had fun," Christine remarked.

"Yeah." Elspeth kissed her mum's cheek. "Thanks for looking after Arran."

"Any time. Did you have a good night?"

"It was okay."

"Have you got any plans for tomorrow?"

On Saturdays Isla helped their mum in the cafe so Elspeth could have a day with Rory and Arran. "Probably just go for a drive and a walk or something. We'll see what the weather's like."

"Sleep well," her mum said, rubbing her arm before slipping outside.

Upstairs, Elspeth stopped short at the sight of Rory sitting on the edge of the bed.

"I thought you'd have passed out straight away," she said.

"I was waiting for you to come and dance with me."

Elspeth smiled. "There's no music. And you're only wearing your boxer shorts."

"Yeah, I know." He reached out and pulled her onto his lap.

"What kind of dancing were you thinking of?" she asked, brushing his hair from his temple.

"The kind where you talk less and kiss more." He flashed a mischievous grin before his lips landed on hers. She laughed loudly when he manoeuvred her onto the bed and crawled on top of her.

~

"We can probably still make last orders in the Isles Inn," Ava said to Jess as they wandered down the road.

"I might be tipsy, but I'm still not brave enough to face Gary. I'm mortified about the way I left things with him."

"So don't leave things like that. Why don't you send him a message now?"

"Because I've been drinking and that's never a good idea."

"It's a great idea. You'll never be brave enough when you're sober."

"For a good reason. My rational, sober brain will tell me it's a bad idea. Anyway, it's been six months. For all I know, he's seeing someone else."

"No way. Elspeth would have said something if that was the case. She's quite sweet, isn't she?"

"Yes. Not what I expected at all."

"How did you imagine her?"

"I didn't imagine she'd be nice. It makes the whole situation easier, to be honest."

"How so?"

"When I thought she was this cold-hearted, horrible person, it felt quite depressing that Rory would choose to be with someone like that."

"When he could have you?" Ava asked cheekily.

"Yes!" Jess chuckled. "But she seemed really sweet. It's easier to lose out to someone who deserves him."

Ava nodded. "And how was it seeing Rory?"

"Surprisingly easy. It was good to catch up with him."

"Does that mean you're finally over him?"

"It seems like it."

"Definitely time to give Gary a call then!"

Jess bumped her shoulder against Ava's. "I'm quite happy being single. Especially now that I feel more settled here. When I met Rory, part of my problem was that I didn't know anyone here and was clinging to the first friend I made."

"But now you have me," Ava said, slipping her arm through Jess's and squeezing her elbow.

"Exactly!" She pulled her key from her pocket as they approached the house.

"I still can't believe you told me your place was too small for two when we first met."

"I hardly knew you. I didn't want to commit to sharing a house with someone before I knew them properly. Plus, you talked a lot and I thought you might drive me mad after a while."

"I don't talk a lot," Ava insisted. "I reckon you were just intimidated by my excellent conversational skills."

"That's what you're calling it!" She laughed as she opened the door and stepped into the hallway. "I like living with you anyway." It had only been a few months, but the arrangement was working out well. "And I'm very happy that Theresa decided not to come back to work after maternity leave. I don't know what I'd do without you around."

"Probably get bored enough to call Gary!" Ava toed her shoes off and kicked them towards the rack. "So maybe I should do you a favour and leave."

"Don't you dare," Jess said.

CHAPTER FOUR

Elspeth peeled a strand of hair from her cheek that had been whipped from her ponytail by the bracing wind. Her gaze was fixed on Arran, who wandered further down the beach with his bucket in his hand and his head down as he searched for shells and sea glass and whatever else he might find.

"How's your hangover?" she asked Rory when he huddled closer to her on the blanket.

"I wasn't even drunk."

"You were pretty drunk," Elspeth argued with a smile.

"Maybe a bit." He draped an arm around her shoulders. "It was good catching up with everyone."

"Do you miss Friday night drinks with your co-workers?"

"Not really."

"You could always start something up with your new colleagues. Get them all to go to the Old Inn on Fridays."

"I'm not sure I'm interested in hanging out with them socially. It's a much older crowd of teachers at Lannick. I'm the youngest by far."

"Yeah, it might be a bit weird." Quite a few of the current teachers had also been teaching there when Elspeth was at school. "I can't imagine you out drinking with my old teachers."

"I'd definitely rather spend my Friday evenings with you."

She rested her head on his shoulder and watched a heron fly across the loch, dragging its spindly legs behind it. "I was thinking," she said slowly. "Maybe you should move back into the cottage with us." She'd been hinting at it for a while, but since the hints hadn't worked she decided the direct approach might be better.

He pulled back to look at her, searching her features. "Is this to do with Jess?"

"No." She wrinkled her nose. "Why would it be?"

"If you're jealous of me talking to Jess, that's not a good reason for me to move back in."

Elspeth's heart beat furiously and she shrugged his arm from her shoulders. "I'm not jealous."

"I knew you'd be weird about me catching up with Jess."

"I'm not being weird about it – you are. I actually liked her." That had been a surprising turn of events but it was true. "I was even thinking we could try and set her up with Gary."

"You've got to be kidding?" He dragged his hands through his hair and let out a humourless laugh. "If you're that threatened by her, then we have more problems than I thought."

"I'm not threatened by her."

"Really?" He cocked an eyebrow. "So you're not trying to set her up with someone else to make sure she stays away from me?"

"No. It was only that Gary seems to really like her and she likes him too."

"And you know that from the two-minute conversation you had with her? She just launched into how much she fancies Gary?"

"It wasn't quite like that but yeah, pretty much."

"What's your plan then? A double date?"

She bit her lip and stared at the waves which lapped the shore.

"You can't be serious?" Rory snapped. "There's no way I'm going on a double date with Jess and Gary."

"Okay, a double date's not a good idea. I just think it's a shame that they're not together when they like each other. Maybe I'll tell Logan to give Gary a nudge to ask her out again."

"Leave it alone," Rory said, shaking his head.

"So do you want to move back to the cottage?" Elspeth asked.

"We agreed we'd take things slow."

"It's been six months. Everything's good between us, isn't it?" Aside from his current state of annoyance with her, but she assumed that was to do with his hangover. She should probably have picked a better time to discuss him moving back in.

"Everything's great," he said, taking her hand. "So I'm not sure why we need to change things."

Her stomach felt like stone, but she forced herself to smile as Arran ran over to them, holding out a wriggling crab.

"We should go home soon," Elspeth said once she'd inspected it.

"Am I sleeping at Daddy's house tonight?" Arran asked.

Elspeth stood and turned her face to the wind. "Yes."

"Are you sleeping there too?"

"No." She didn't even look at Rory. "You and Daddy can have a boys' night."

"That means I can stay up late," Arran said as he released the crab onto the sand.

Rory pulled him into a hug. "Only if you're good."

"Can I have pizza for dinner?"

"I think that can be arranged." Rory stood up and wiped down the back of his jeans. "You can come too, if you want?" he said to Elspeth.

"No, thanks." She had big plans to spend the evening wallowing about him not wanting to live with them.

~

Jess told herself that she'd be concerned about any of her pupils who were absent from her lessons. The fact that Paige Richardson was Gary's niece had nothing to do with it. She wasn't in class on Wednesday morning, and she hadn't been in school all week according to her classmates, though none of them knew why.

In the staffroom at lunchtime, her ears pricked up when she heard Paige's name. Paige's form tutor wasn't discreet in telling another staff member what a relief it was not to have Paige in class for a week, then added that it was unusual to have an unexcused absence and she hadn't been able to contact Paige's parents. It played on Jess's mind for the rest of the day. After her final lesson, she waited for five minutes until the hallway had cleared, then strolled down to the main office.

"Paige Richardson wasn't in my class today," she said to Ava, resting her hip against her desk. "Do you know what the deal is?"

Ava looked up from her computer. "It's a bit of a weird one. She hasn't turned up all week. No one called to excuse her, and her mum isn't answering her phone."

"That's weird."

"Aye." She tapped a pen against the edge of the desk. "We'll have to put a call in to the education authority soon."

"What will they do?"

"Track down the family and see what's going on. I hope everything's okay. From what I hear, she doesn't have a particularly stable home life."

"She's Gary's niece," Jess said sadly.

"Can you call him and see if he knows anything?"

"I'm not going to use Paige as an excuse to call him."

"I wasn't suggesting you should."

Jess bit her lip. "Can you give me her mum's number?"

"Yes." Ava tapped on the computer keyboard, and Jess moved behind her to look over her shoulder. She picked up the phone on her desk to call.

"I've tried lots of times," Ava said. "The mobile gives a message that the number isn't in use any more, and the home phone just rings and rings."

She was right, but Jess needed to check for herself before resorting to calling Gary. For that, she pulled out her mobile and scrolled through her contact list.

"Maybe you could ask him out for dinner while you're at it," Ava said.

"Shut up!" Jess glared at her and felt her heart rate increasing as she held the phone to her ear.

"Hello?" Gary said gruffly.

"Hi …" She hadn't actually thought about what she'd say. Should she sound official like someone calling from the school or like a concerned friend?

"When you said you'd give me a call, I thought you meant in a day or two." His voice was strained and impatient. "It's been six months."

"Sorry … erm … I'm actually calling from the school … about Paige."

"Is she all right?" His voice softened. "Did something happen?"

"I was hoping you could tell us … she hasn't been in school all week, and we haven't been able to contact anyone about it."

There was a pause, and Jess wondered whether he was still on the line.

"I wouldn't normally have called you about it," she went on. "But the school will need to inform the education authority about it soon. I thought it would be better to avoid that if possible."

"She hasn't been in school all week?" he growled.

"No. Do you know if she's ill?"

"She's not ill – she's an absolute pain in the arse is what she is."

"Excuse me?"

"That ungrateful little brat," he muttered, seemingly to himself.

"Do you think she'll be back at school tomorrow?"

"Aye. She'll be there. If I don't kill her first."

"Okay … it would be good if she had a letter explaining the absence."

"What sort of letter should she bring for skiving off?"

Jess opened and closed her mouth a couple of times before she managed to formulate words. "It would go down as an unauthorised absence if she doesn't have a note."

"Put it down as that then," he snapped. "And punish her as you see fit."

"That'll be up to her form tutor. I'm glad she's okay, anyway."

He fell silent again. "Thanks for calling," he said quietly.

"You're welcome." The line went dead and she turned back to Ava. "Paige will be back tomorrow."

"You forgot to ask him when he was free for dinner," Ava replied cheekily.

CHAPTER FIVE

"I have work to do," Ava said, tapping away on her computer the next morning. "You're disturbing me, loitering around here. Don't you need to get your classroom ready or something?"

Jess took a break from staring out of the office window to check her watch. "In a minute."

"You're waiting for him, aren't you?"

"Who?" she asked innocently.

"Gary. As if you don't know."

"I'm keeping an eye out for Paige."

"Because you think Gary will be with her."

"It sounded as though he'd be the one to make sure she'd be back in school. Aren't you intrigued about why?"

"Not really, no."

"She's here," Jess said, watching Paige hop out of a mud-splattered old Land Rover. Gary got out of the driver's side and folded his arms across his chest as he leaned on the side of the car. He watched as Paige walked towards the main doors of the school. Jess took a few steps away from the window, then paced back again. "I need to find out what's going on," she said, dashing across the room.

Dodging between pupils in the hallway slowed her pace, and she panicked that Gary would have left by the time she made it outside.

"Gary!" she shouted as he opened the door to get back in his car.

"Paige is here," he said, turning back to her. "I watched her go inside. If she slips out of a back door or something there's not a lot I can do about that."

"I'm glad she's back."

He nodded at the building. "No one's going to report her, are they?"

"No. Not unless there are more unexplained absences."

"There won't be." He pushed his hands into his pockets and rocked on his heels.

"Is everything okay with Paige's mum? We couldn't get in contact with her."

"Aye. She's fine. She moved to Glasgow with her husband. They didn't seem keen to take Paige with them, so I said she could stay with me for a while."

Jess's eyes widened. "Is that a long-term arrangement?"

"Given the way things are going, probably not."

"I thought you and Paige got on well."

"We did. Until she came to live with me. Now I'm starting to see why her mum moved to the other end of the country." He leaned on the car door and winced. "I didn't mean that. But she's driving me mad. All I get is snarky comments from her. It's not as though I'm strict or anything. I told her that if she stayed out of my way, I'd stay out of hers. Pretty much all I expect from her is that she goes to school. Apparently she can't even manage that."

"It sounds like attention-seeking," Jess said. "Her mum's left her, and you tell her to keep out of your way. I imagine she's feeling pretty lonely."

"She begged me to let her stay with me. You'd think she'd

appreciate the fact that I'm doing her a favour and be a bit grateful."

"Yeah," Jess agreed. "If she was a fully grown adult. But she's a teenager. Of course she's not going to be grateful. Look at it from her point of view … her mum left and you don't really want her around."

"Well, I obviously didn't say that to her."

"You don't have to. She'll know without you saying it."

His eyebrows drew together. "I thought you were a chemistry teacher, not a bloody psychologist."

"Sorry, I was just trying to help."

"By lecturing me?" His eyes flashed with anger. "If you think Paige has such a terrible home life, maybe you should call social services or something. You'd probably be doing me a favour."

"I don't think—" Jess flinched as Gary slammed the car door. The engine rumbled and she stepped out of the way as he reversed out of the parking space.

Back inside, Ava loitered in her office doorway with a smirk on her face. "From the view through the window I'll go out on a limb and say you didn't manage to score yourself a date?"

"With that arrogant arse? Definitely not." Jess had to take deep breaths and force herself to relax before walking into her classroom where her form group were waiting for her. By lunchtime her annoyance had subsided, but she kept remembering flashes of her conversation with Gary. She'd only been trying to offer advice and he'd bitten her head off. It was no wonder Paige was acting out if she was dealing with him being so grumpy with her.

"Are you listening to anything I'm saying?" Ava asked through a mouthful of sandwich. The two of them were sitting on a couch at the back of the staffroom.

"Yes." That was a lie. Jess had no idea what she'd been talking about. "I'm a bit distracted, that's all. I can't stop thinking about Paige. I thought about having a chat with her form teacher, but it's Mrs Miller and I'm a bit scared of her."

"She's definitely not the most cheerful teacher," Ava said. "No wonder Paige decided to take a few days off."

Jess dropped her sandwich back into the Tupperware box and shoved it into her bag. "I think I'll go and find her, check how Paige is doing. She does pretty well in my classes, but I often hear other teachers complaining about her."

"You know she's not your problem?" Ava said seriously.

"Yeah. But I get the feeling everyone feels that way about her."

"There's got to be an easier way to get yourself a date."

Standing, Jess flashed her a look of impatience. "This is nothing to do with my feelings for Gary. Especially not since they evaporated after the way he spoke to me this morning."

Ava slouched back on the couch. "Sure they did."

After striding determinedly down the hall, Jess paused outside Mrs Miller's classroom and pulled her shoulders back. She gave a crisp double-knock on the door before opening it.

Jane Miller pushed her reading glasses up her nose as she looked up from the papers she was poring over.

"Sorry to bother you." Jess pasted on a professional smile. "I was hoping to have a quick word with you about …" She trailed off at movement at the back of the room. Paige had her head propped on her palm as she stared into space with a look of pained boredom.

"Sorry." Jess's confidence melted away. "Could I speak to you in the hall for a moment?"

Mrs Miller stood and shuffled out of the classroom, pulling the door behind her.

"I wanted to ask about Paige," Jess said. "She wasn't in my chemistry class yesterday and I wondered about giving her the work she missed so she can catch up."

"Do you have it?" Mrs Miller looked pointedly at Jess's empty hands.

"Erm … No … I can put something together. I just wanted to check what the situation was. I don't want to pile on the work if she's still not feeling great or something." She swallowed hard as her throat went suddenly dry.

"She wasn't ill," Mrs Miller said. "When I asked her where she'd been, she said she couldn't be bothered to come to school. Then she made some offensive comment about having to look at me every morning. She's on lunchtime detention for the rest of the week.

'I'd hoped she might use the time to catch up on the work she's missed, but she told me exactly what she thought of that idea. Some kids are too stupid for words. If she thinks it's me who's going to suffer because she won't do the work, she's going to get a shock when she gets out into the real world having failed all her exams." Finally, she stopped talking and inhaled what appeared to be a much-needed breath.

"I heard that her home situation isn't particularly stable," Jess said.

"No one at home seems very interested in her education. There's only so much I can do. She also appears to be on a mission to antagonise me, which doesn't help the situation."

Jess forced a smile. "I'll put together the work that she missed in my class. It's up to her whether she does it or not." She took a few steps away, then turned on her heel. "I'm pretty snowed under with marking at the moment. I'll probably be holed up in my classroom over lunchtime a lot, so if you ever want to send Paige my way at all you're more than welcome."

Mrs Miller's shoulders sagged and her features softened. "If only more of my colleagues were like you. That's a very kind offer."

"No problem," Jess said.

Mrs Miller opened the door of her classroom and called to Paige. "Get your things together and go with Miss Gibson.

You'll be spending your lunch break today and tomorrow in her classroom." She reached back and touched Jess's arm. "Thank you so much."

"Sure," Jess murmured, taken aback by how quickly Mrs Miller had taken her up on the offer.

"Thank you," Paige said, swinging her backpack onto her shoulder as she set off down the corridor with Jess. "I can't stand looking at that dragon any longer."

"If you're in my classroom, you need to work," Jess said, hoping she sounded more authoritative than she felt.

"I will, I promise." She hurried to keep up as Jess strode along. "Mrs Miller is always rude to me. She hates me. Whatever I do, she always has a go at me anyway, so I may as well do nothing."

Jess pushed at the door to her classroom and held it for Paige. "If you ruin your education, it's you who'll suffer, not Mrs Miller."

"Not really. My career prospects are limited anyway."

"What do you mean?" Jess moved behind her desk while Paige pulled out a chair on the front row.

She dropped her backpack on the floor. "I'll probably just work in a bar or a restaurant or something. I don't need good grades for that."

"You do really well in my classes," Jess said. "With a bit of effort you'll be able to do whatever you want."

"I do well in your classes because you explain things in a way that makes sense. Not all teachers have that ability."

Jess shuffled papers on her desk. It was only her second year of teaching and getting a compliment from a student made warmth spread through her whole body. "Thanks," she murmured. She had her pen poised to start marking when she paused and looked up at Paige, who was pulling books from her bag. "I hear you're living with your uncle for a while …"

"Aye." She slammed her books on the desk with such force that it made Jess jump. "It's a nightmare."

"Really?"

"He's awful. The house is such a state. He won't even do my washing. I thought my mum was pretty useless, but at least I had clean clothes. Gary tells me to do it myself. I don't know anyone else my age who has to wash their own clothes."

"I'm sure he's doing his best," Jess said.

Paige mumbled something that Jess didn't catch.

"Pardon?"

Paige's cheeks flushed and she shuffled in her seat. "I just think you shouldn't stick up for him," she said quietly. "Not after what he said about you."

After opening her mouth to ask, Jess clamped her lips shut and tried to focus on the papers in front of her. It only took a moment for her head to shoot up again. "What did he say about me?"

Paige paused for a moment, looking thoughtful. "He called you a stuck-up snob."

Maybe her feelings for him hadn't dissipated quite as much as she'd thought, considering how much the comment made her stomach twist. "He said that about me?" she asked with disbelief.

"Do you remember that time I was with him and we bumped into you?" Paige finally looked up at Jess. "Well, I kept teasing him about liking you … eventually he snapped and said there was nothing between the two of you and I should credit him with having more taste than to be interested in a stuck-up snob."

Jess forced a tight smile. Presumably Gary had said that after their disastrous dates. But had he said it because he was annoyed that she didn't call him, or had he genuinely thought she was a snob? There was a possibility he'd mistaken her disinterest for snobbishness.

"I told you he's awful," Paige added.

"You should probably get on with your work," Jess said. "What are you working on?"

"Maths. I don't really get it though, to be honest."

Jess pulled up a chair beside her and spent the remainder of her lunch break talking her through the work she'd missed that week.

CHAPTER SIX

"Did you ID the kid at the end of the bar?" Lexie asked Leana on Thursday evening.

Leana glanced along the bar as she poured glasses of wine for the two women in front of her. "No. He must be eighteen though."

"You reckon?" Lexie said. "He looks about fifteen to me."

Leana looked suddenly uncertain. "No one underage comes into the pub on their own. And he ordered too confidently to be underage."

"He keeps staring at me," Lexie murmured. "It's giving me the creeps."

"You've got me worried now. Can you ask him for ID? And quick, before your dad comes down and finds out I didn't check before I served him."

Lexie walked the length of the bar. "Hi," she said, giving the fresh-faced blonde kid a curt nod.

"Hi!" He grinned at her.

"I'm afraid I need to see some ID."

His eyebrows shot up. "That other girl already gave me a beer."

"Yeah, I know. She should have checked. How old are you?"

"Eighteen," he said as his cheeks flushed.

"Can you prove that?"

He stared at her for a minute, then shifted on the stool and pulled out a black leather wallet. Lexie took his driving licence when he offered it and scanned it for his date of birth before her eyes flicked to his photo and name.

"Thanks, Dale," she said as she passed it back.

"Lexie!" her dad boomed behind her. "Doesn't it make more sense to find out how old customers are *before* giving them alcohol?"

"It makes a lot of sense," Lexie agreed, raising her eyebrows at Leana, who offered an apologetic grimace in return. "It must be baby brain. I'm all over the place."

Angus frowned. "I knew you shouldn't be working. It's too much for you in your condition."

"I'm fine. He's eighteen anyway, so there's no harm done." She glanced at the lad and flashed him a half-hearted smile.

"Don't take it personally," Angus said to him. "It's her job to check. Obviously she should have done it before she served you."

"It's fine," he muttered.

"Are you from around here?" Angus asked, leaning on the bar.

He shook his head. "Just visiting."

"Where are you from?"

"Leeds."

"Pretty far from home then," Angus remarked. "How do you like Skye?"

"I love it. It's really pretty with all the mountains and lakes."

Lexie rolled her eyes. "Lochs."

"Yes! Lochs. That's it. I was in Portree yesterday and that's nice. People are so friendly."

"I suppose it's not like that down in England. People making time to chat to each other. I'd say everyone keeps their heads down and avoids eye contact."

"Not really. People in Leeds are pretty friendly too."

Angus grunted, looking slightly disappointed. "It's a funny time of year for a holiday. Are you with your family?"

"No, it's just me. I'm travelling around for a bit while I figure out what to do with my life, you know?"

"In my day we had to get a job, not go off gallivanting." Angus's brow creased. "Anyway, enjoy yourself. I'm going back upstairs," he said to Lexie. "Try and remember to check how old the customers are *before* you give them alcohol."

She managed a tight smile as he walked away.

"I'm sorry!" Leana said, wincing as she sidled over to Lexie.

"Don't worry about it."

"Why did you take the blame?" Dale asked.

Lexie shrugged. "He's my dad. I can get away with more."

"You could have said it was me," Leana said. "I can deal with Angus's lectures."

"I know you can." Lexie sighed. "But I really couldn't be bothered listening to him rant at you."

"Is he a difficult boss?" Dale asked.

"No," Leana said. "He's a softie, but he's set in his ways and he likes to grumble about stuff."

"Do you want another?" Lexie asked, eyeing the almost empty pint on the bar.

He shook his head. "I should probably go."

"Are you staying nearby?" Leana asked.

"Yeah. It's not far." He slipped off his stool and put his coat on. "I like this place. I might come back again." He smiled at them before wandering away.

"Strange kid," Lexie remarked.

"I wish I'd taken a gap year at that age," Leana mused. "Travelling on your own is character-building. The best thing I ever did was get out of Lannick and go and find myself."

Lexie raised an eyebrow. "As I recall, you found Alasdair… then came straight back home."

"Yes." She laughed. "But even a short time away broadened my horizons."

"Oh, Aye! You're worldly wise, you are!"

"Shut up!" Leana gave her a shove. "I'm just saying I admire people who get out and see something different from the place they grew up."

"So what you're saying is that you don't admire any of your friends or family?"

She squinted. "You've got a point. We're all home birds, aren't we?"

"Aye, because we live in the best place in the world. Where would we go?"

"You make a good point." Leana chuckled and wandered away to collect empties.

~

"I can't believe he called me a stuck-up snob," Jess complained, between mouthfuls of noodles. A perk of living with Ava was having someone to sound off to at the end of the day. That and having someone to share meals with.

"I think he summed you up perfectly," Ava said.

"I'm not stuck-up! Or a snob! The cheek of him."

"To be fair, he was probably upset that you gave him the brush-off."

"Just because our dates didn't work out, that's no reason to go around bad-mouthing me."

"I thought you didn't like him?" Ava held her bowl close to her chin as she slurped her noodles.

"I don't. He's an arse with caveman tendencies. He won't even do Paige's washing. I suppose he thinks it's women's work. I wouldn't be surprised if he has her doing his washing as well. Apparently the house is a complete mess too."

"This all seems to be bothering you a heck of a lot considering you don't even like him." Ava finished her food and put the bowl down on the coffee table. "You're going to have to give him another call anyway."

"Why?"

"I need you to get him to come into the office so I can get his details. If Paige is staying with him, we at least need him down as an emergency contact. If it's a permanent arrangement I need to update her file."

"I'm happy to give you his number, but there's no way I'm calling him." They were interrupted by the doorbell. "Are we expecting anyone?"

"I don't think so." Ava uncurled her leg from under her and jumped up to look out of the window. Slapping a hand over her mouth, she moved quickly back again. "It's him," she said, her eyes sparkling with amusement.

"Who?"

"Gary! He's at the door."

"As if I'm falling for that." Jess went to the window, then darted out of the way before he could see her. "What the hell is he doing here?"

"Answer the door and find out." Ava took her arm and pulled her in the direction of the hallway.

"I'm not answering it," Jess said, peeling Ava's hand away. "You answer it."

"Don't be ridiculous. He's come to see you, not me."

Jess's heart rate cranked up a notch when the doorbell rang again, and she moved slowly to the door. When she opened it, Gary was pacing the front path, looking as though he might be about to leave.

"Hi," Jess said, drawing his attention.

"Hi." He whipped around. "How are you?"

"I'm okay," she said, clipped.

"I wanted to apologise for this morning. I was in a bad mood and took it out on you. I'm sorry."

Jess nodded. "You need to go into the school office sometime, so they have your details on file."

"My sister was supposed to do that."

"Well she didn't, so now you need to." She wanted to tell him it was also his responsibility to make sure Paige was properly cared for, and that involved providing a decent place to live and doing her washing, but she bit her tongue.

"I'll go in tomorrow morning when I drop her off," Gary said.

"Please do. If you agree to take in a minor you should take the responsibility seriously."

He glared at her. "You really don't like me, do you? I came to apologise, and you talk down to me."

"Oh, I'm sorry," she said sarcastically. "Apparently I sometimes come across as a bit stuck-up. A stuck-up snob, some might say." She heard Ava's snort of laughter from the living room.

Gary looked towards the road, where Paige was in the passenger seat of his car. "She told you I said that?"

"Yes." Jess folded her arms across her chest.

Gary threw his hands up. "Whatever," he grumbled. "I don't have time for this."

"So you're not even going to apologise?" she spat as he set off down the path.

"For something I said behind your back? No, I'm bloody well not!"

Jess let out an audible breath. "You're unbelievable."

"Me?" He turned and walked back to her. "You really are stuck-up if you're demanding an apology for something I said behind your back."

"You could at least say you didn't mean it!" She stood up straighter as he came towards her. His height was slightly intimidating.

"But I did mean it! You *are* a stuck-up snob. Now I've said it to your face as well. Don't try and make out you've never said anything bad about me behind my back."

Ava's voice drifted from the living room. "She called you an arse and compared you to a caveman."

"Well that's not very nice," Gary said. "I think you should apologise."

"There's no way that's happening!"

"So you're a hypocrite now as well?"

She held his gaze as she scowled at him. "I actually think what I said about you was bordering on complimentary. It was only offensive to arses and cavemen!"

"Stuck-up snob doesn't seem to adequately sum you up any more either."

"I think you should leave," Jess snapped.

"With pleasure!" He turned and stormed back down the path.

Jess banged the door shut as she went back inside.

"How much fun was that?" Ava said.

"No fun at all. He's an absolutely awful specimen of a man. And why the hell did you tell him what I called him?"

"It only seemed fair really. Plus, the flirty banter was so entertaining I couldn't help but throw a bit of fuel on the fire."

"I don't think you understand what flirty banter is." Jess flopped onto the couch. "That was neither flirty nor banter."

"It was sexually charged though," Ava said, beaming. "I could feel the sparks from a distance. You really should have asked him out on a date."

"You're insane." Jess launched a cushion at her but missed her head by a centimetre.

CHAPTER SEVEN

On Saturday, Lexie was working at the pub in the afternoon. She was chatting to Douglas at the bar when the kid from Thursday evening wandered in and took the same seat at the bar.

"You can't stay away, can you?" Angus said.

"The owner of the youth hostel was telling me how great the food is here," he said. "I thought I'd give it a try."

Angus smiled and handed him a menu. "Janice, I presume?" The hostel owner was a regular at the Old Inn.

"Yeah." He opened the menu. "She's really chatty."

"That's an understatement," Angus said. "It's a wonder she doesn't lose her voice with how much she yaps on."

"She seems nice. Can I have the bacon burger and a Sprite, please?"

"Coming up!" Angus said happily.

Lexie smiled at Dale as she gave the bar a quick wipe down.

He shifted on the stool. "Is it weird working with your dad?"

"Nope. It's pretty good."

"I'd hate to work with my dad," he said, with a hint of bitterness that made Lexie stop and look up.

"Don't you get on?"

He gave a quick shake of the head while Lexie grabbed a glass and filled it with Sprite.

"Your burger shouldn't be long," Angus said, wandering back from the kitchen. "Sorry, did I interrupt you?"

"Just talking about families," Lexie said, grinning at him. "Telling him what a nightmare you are to work with!"

"She doesn't know how easy she's got it," he said lightly. "I'd say your parents are missing you. I remember when this one went off on a gap year. We did nothing but worry."

Lexie tilted her head. The time she'd run off to live with her biological mother definitely hadn't been a gap year. As far as she understood it, a gap year was a carefree time of finding yourself. When Lexie had finally come home with her tail between her legs she was broken and completely lost. There'd been nothing carefree about it.

"They won't be worried," Dale said, breaking her thoughts.

"As a father, I can assure you they will be. Make sure you call home often. Your mother will appreciate it. My Mary was a wreck the whole time Lexie was away. She lived for her occasional phone calls."

Lexie's stomach plummeted as a wave of guilt washed over her. "I'd better just …" She trailed off and wandered away, doing a lap of the room to collect empties before heading back to the bar to pour another pint for Douglas. Her dad was still chatting animatedly to Dale and she zoned into their friendly discussion about the Scottish and English rugby teams. They kept up a steady stream of chatter until his food was ready and Angus left him to eat in peace.

"Janice was right about the food," he called across to Angus as he set his knife and fork on the empty plate. "That's the best meal I've had in ages."

"I'll let the chef know," Angus said. "Can I get you anything else?"

"I better not. My funds are starting to run low."

"Does that mean your travels are coming to an end?" Angus asked. "Will you be heading back home soon?"

"I'm not going home. I just need to find a job."

"Around here?" Angus asked.

"Maybe." He swirled the last of his drink in the bottom of the glass.

Lexie went over and took his plate, noticing the twitch of her dad's cheek as she passed him.

"I don't suppose you have any experience working in a pub?" Angus asked.

He smiled shyly. "I don't have a lot of experience in *any* job."

"I suppose you can't help that. Did you say you're only eighteen?"

"Yeah. I just had my birthday last month."

"I'm actually looking for a new member of staff around here," Angus said, making Lexie stop short on her way to the kitchen. "If working in a pub would interest you?"

"Dad!" Lexie hissed. "He just said he doesn't have any experience."

Angus waved a hand in front of his face. "It wouldn't take me long to train him up."

"It's hardly worth training him, if he's not even planning on staying long," Lexie said.

"If I had a job, I might decide to stay longer," he said eagerly.

Angus nodded. "There you go then. I could only offer minimum wage to start with, but we throw in meals too. If you're interested, we could chat it over."

His eyes lit up. "That would be brilliant."

Shaking her head, Lexie continued to the kitchen and loaded the plate into the dishwasher, having a quick chat with the chef while she was there.

"Are you seriously going to interview him for the job?" she

asked her dad when she returned behind the bar in time to see Dale walking out of the pub.

"No," Angus said, amusement evident in the rumble of his voice. "I offered him the job. He starts tomorrow."

"You can't be serious!" Lexie screeched. "You had lots of suitable candidates and you've given the job to someone who hadn't even applied?"

"I've got a good feeling about him."

"You don't know anything about him."

"I know he rates the Scottish rugby team highly."

Lexie rolled her eyes. "Usually you'd say that's just a fact."

"Aye. It is. Not easy for an Englishman to admit though, I'm sure. They get very shirty whenever we're better than them at something."

"You realise your 'us and them' mentality isn't politically correct. It is the *United* Kingdom after all."

"I'm all about unity. I've just employed an Englishman, haven't I?"

"I've no idea why," Lexie said. "The other day you were adamant you wanted someone with experience, and someone who'll stick around for a while."

"I think Dale will be a good employee."

"Based on what?"

"Gut feeling." He scratched at his beard. "Plus, he doesn't have any friends or family around. The pub will be his life."

"Well that's a bit sad." Lexie rubbed at her bump when the baby kicked. "And I'd like it on record that I think hiring him will end up being a disaster. That's *my* gut feeling."

CHAPTER EIGHT

When Lexie arrived home from the activity centre on Monday afternoon, Nick's car was parked in its usual spot, but there was no sign of him in the house. As she wandered up to the pub she unzipped her coat. The baby acted as her own central heating system, and she was constantly too warm, even when the temperature was only hovering above freezing.

In the pub, she crept up behind Nick at the bar and planted a kiss on his cheek.

"I was looking for you," he said. "Have you only just finished work?"

"Aye. Though I wasn't really working – just hanging around, chatting with Tim."

"Hiya, love," Mary said, appearing from the kitchen with two plates of food.

Lexie said hello to her mum, then waited while she took the food to the customers. "Are you on your own?" she asked, glancing around. It wasn't busy, but with her mum's bad back, she rarely worked an entire shift any more and was never on her own.

"Your dad's taken Dale down to show him how to change a barrel."

"He's really working here?" Lexie asked.

"Yes." Mary walked back around the bar. "He'll work your shift tomorrow evening so you don't need to come in. Angus wants to make sure he knows the ropes."

"Great, so he's taking my shifts already?"

"He seems really nice," Nick remarked.

"I think so too," Mary agreed. "He's ever so eager. Angus has taken a real shine to him."

Lexie shook her head. "Dad's so inconsistent. Last week he was adamant he wanted someone with bar experience, and this week that goes completely out of the window."

"I think it's doing Angus good," Mary said, lowering her voice. "Giving him something to focus on and take his mind off Wesley. He's been chirpier today than he's been in a while. A bit of young blood around the place will be a good thing."

"Excuse me!" Lexie said, amused. "What am I?"

"You're a boring old housewife," Nick said, then flinched when Lexie aimed a playful slap at his arm.

They were still chuckling when Angus appeared with Dale.

"Hi!" Dale said, beaming at Lexie.

"I heard you're stealing my shifts?" she joked.

"Sorry." His face fell. "Angus said you wanted to work less."

"It wasn't really a choice. That's not your fault though."

"Maybe we can work together some shifts. I heard you grew up here and know everything there is to know about the place."

Angus gave a gentle eye roll. "I think you've already learnt something from Lexie … make sure you check people's age *before* you serve them alcohol!"

"Get over it, Dad," Lexie said lightly.

"It wasn't even Lexie," Dale said, his cheeks pinking as he looked at Angus. "The other girl served me. Leana, is it?"

"What?" Angus looked to Lexie.

Her jaw tensed. "Does it even matter? We both know about checking people's age."

"Why didn't you say at the time that it was Leana?" Angus asked gruffly.

"Because I knew you'd give her an unnecessary lecture. She made a mistake and she knew it. Sometimes, all you need to say is 'don't do it again', but instead you give out these massive lectures as though we're completely incompetent."

Nick slipped an arm around Lexie's waist, resting his hand on her hip. "So don't forget to check people's ID," he said to Dale, a lightness to his voice.

"I don't think any of my staff are incompetent," Angus said, ignoring Nick's attempt to dispel the tense atmosphere. "But now I'm wondering how often you cover for Leana."

"Don't be ridiculous. Leana's great at her job and you know it." Peeling Nick's hand from her hip, she tipped her chin towards the door. "Let's go."

"Aren't you staying for dinner?" Mary asked.

"No, we'll eat at home." She forced a smile before leaving.

"What was all that about?" Nick asked as he caught up to her outside.

She explained what had happened previously and how she'd let Angus think it was her mistake rather than Leana's. "I can't believe Dad hired that kid without so much as an interview. I can't stand people who cause drama."

Nick slipped his hand into hers. "I'm not sure he was trying to cause issues. I guess he thought he was sticking up for you or something."

"As if I need someone to stick up for me against my dad!"

"Anyone who knows you knows that, but if you look at it from a stranger's point of view …"

"If you don't understand the dynamics of people's relationships, you should really keep your mouth shut."

Nick stopped at the front gate and grinned at her. "I like it when you get all fiery."

She hooked her arms around his neck as the tension left her.

"And I like how you call me fiery when I'm angry. It sounds way better."

"I only call it fiery when it's directed at other people. It's cute then. There's nothing cute or fiery about it when you're angry with me."

"I never get angry with you," she said cheekily.

"Of course not!" He smiled widely. "Why would you? I'm the perfect husband."

"Exactly." She gave him a soft kiss before they went inside.

Lexie greeted Leana cheerfully when she arrived for a shift at the pub on Wednesday evening.

"Are you on your own?" she asked, slipping behind the bar.

"No. Dale's here somewhere and your dad keeps coming down to check on things."

"What's Dale like to work with?" Lexie asked quietly, assuming he was in the kitchen and would appear at any moment.

"I like him. He's sweet. He seems to be getting the hang of things quickly too."

"That's good," Lexie said with a frown. "I kind of got a bad vibe from him."

"Really?"

"You know he told Dad that it was you who served him without checking his age?"

"Yeah, I heard about that. He apologised to me. Apparently it just slipped out. I wouldn't hold that against him." Her lips twitched to a hint of a smirk. "You just don't like him because you think he's stealing your jobs. You hate having to take things easy, and now there's this energetic kid taking over your roles. Of course you're going to hate him. That was fairly predictable."

"I don't hate him. I barely know him. And you make it sound as though he's taking over my life. It's only a few bar shifts."

"And the activity centre," Leana said.

"What are you talking about?"

"I presumed you'd know. Angus spoke to Tim about Dale helping around the activity centre in exchange for staying in one of the cabins. I think they only arranged it this morning."

"Okay, so he *is* taking over my life!"

"I think he'll be fun to have around. He livens the place up."

"I'm not lively enough for you any more?" Lexie asked, taking a deep breath as the baby pushed up into her lungs.

"You're really boring!" Leana said with a teasing smile.

After giving her a friendly nudge, Lexie turned to find Dale standing stock still with a plate of food in his hand, looking as though he'd drifted into a daydream.

"Watch out!" she gasped as the plate tilted.

His eyes snapped back into focus and he righted the plate, but not quickly enough. The battered fish and half the chips slid to the floor.

Lexie let out a low groan as she moved to help him.

"I'm sorry," he said in a rush.

"Who was it for?" Lexie asked, stopping when she realised she couldn't easily bend far enough to help him clear up the mess.

"The old guy by the fire," he told her as Leana came over to help him gather up the scattered chips. "I'm really sorry."

"It's not so bad." Lexie looked over at Douglas, who was humming and swaying beside the fire. "There's going to be a delay on your dinner," she called to him when she caught his eye. "I'll bring you a pint on the house to keep you going."

"No bother, hen."

"I'll explain to the chef," Dale said, standing with the plate of ruined food.

"Let me." Lexie took it from him. "You really don't want to get into Charlie's bad books in your first week on the job. And telling him you dropped a whole plate of his food is a sure way to get in his bad books."

"But it was my mistake."

"Just get Douglas a beer. I'll deal with Charlie."

"Thanks. I really am sorry."

"These things happen," Leana told him with a friendly pat on the shoulder. "I'm going home."

Lexie told her to have a good evening, then went to put in a fresh order of Douglas's food. She blamed the mishap on her baby bump, saying she'd lost all sense of spatial awareness and had knocked into Dale and sent the plate flying. When she went back to the bar, a group of three couples had just walked in, then another group arrived shortly after, so she was busy for a while.

"You didn't need to cover for me with the chef," Dale said, when there was a lull.

"I know." She moved to the end of the bar and shuffled onto a stool to give her legs a rest. "But I've known Charlie for years. He'll overlook mistakes from me, but with you he'll assume you're incompetent and the atmosphere will be uncomfortable. I like to keep my working environment as stress-free as possible."

"Is that why you took the blame for Leana the other day too?"

She sat up straighter, trying to give her lungs more space. "That wasn't even an issue. You really shouldn't have said anything to Dad about it."

"It didn't seem fair that Angus kept having a go at you about it."

"That's just the way Dad is. I've got very good at ignoring him. You made it more of an issue by telling him the truth."

"I was only trying to help."

"Next time don't bother." She sounded grumpier than she intended and felt bad when he looked so forlorn.

"Is there anything I should be doing?" he asked, rocking on the balls of his feet.

At a quiet clatter behind her, Lexie reached across for a set of cutlery wrapped in a paper napkin. "Take this to whoever just dropped theirs," she instructed.

Dale's eyes scanned the pub. "How did you know they—"

"I grew up here, remember. Just take it, quick."

"I don't think she needs a fresh one. She's picked the other one up."

"Take it!" Lexie snapped, thrusting it at him.

A moment later, she heard a woman thanking Dale profusely.

"How did you know she'd want a new one?" he asked when he returned behind the bar.

"They always do," she said, then pulled a face as she glanced at the patterned green carpet. "They should as well. But people often can't be bothered to ask. If you see someone drop their cutlery, bring them a clean one, whether they ask or not."

"Okay. Thanks."

Lexie glanced behind Dale's legs. "Did someone show you how to restock the fridges?"

"Yeah." He turned to look.

"Grab a few more bottles of wine," she told him, sending him scuttling for the cellar. It was a nice way to work – sitting at the end of the bar, throwing orders around. Her dad often did the same and it drove her crazy. Being the one giving orders was pretty nice though.

Surprisingly, there was no sign of her dad over the course of the evening. She'd expected him to come down and send her home early. Not that she was keen to admit it, but she wouldn't have complained too much if he'd insisted on her leaving. She was uncomfortable and tired by the time she asked the last customers to leave and locked the door behind them.

"Can you wipe the tables down and put the chairs up on them?" Lexie said to Dale. "Then tidy and wipe down the bar." He'd worked a long shift and was still full of energy and enthusiasm, so she hoped her initial reservations about him were ill-founded.

She'd just finished counting the cash in the kitchen when she heard him in the doorway.

"Sorry," he said quickly. "I didn't put you off, did I?"

"No. I'm all done."

"Where do you keep the money?"

She glanced down at the wads of cash. "In the safe," she said slowly. "But you'd need to work here for about ten years before Dad would trust you to cash up, so I wouldn't worry about that."

"Okay. What else should I do?"

"I think we're all done. You can get off home."

"Right … okay … I can hang around until you leave if you want?"

She shook her head. "I'm fine, thanks."

"I could walk you home?"

"No. I'm good thanks," she said, depositing the cash into bags. "Goodnight." He lingered in the doorway and Lexie felt a chill run across the back of her neck when she looked up to find him staring at her. "Are you always this creepy?" she asked, pulling her shoulders back as she straightened up.

"Sorry. Angus told me not to leave you alone."

"Bloody hell," she muttered. "Wait for me at the front door then. I need to put the cash away and have a quick word with my dad."

She chuntered to herself as she padded upstairs to lock the money away in the office. When she went into the living room, she found her dad fast asleep on the couch. It didn't seem the best time to give him a lecture on over-protective parenting, so she just nudged him awake to say she was leaving and would lock up behind her.

The fresh air was welcome when she stepped out of the pub with Dale.

"When's the baby due?" he asked.

"Middle of January."

"I take it this is your first kid?"

"Yeah." She was too weary for small talk and attempted to quicken her pace to avoid it. Unfortunately, speed wasn't currently a virtue of hers.

Dale glanced around as they wandered across the pub car park. “I bet it was cool growing up in a pub.”

“Everyone seems to think so. I don’t know anything different, so it just seemed normal to me.”

“Angus and Mary are really nice. I can’t believe they just gave me a job and helped me with a place to stay too. It must be great to have such cool parents.”

She nodded. “I can’t complain.”

“I think I’m going to really like working in the pub. Everyone’s so friendly.”

“Lannick’s a friendly place.”

“Seems like it.” As they reached the front gate, he bounced on his heels. Lexie had no clue how he still had any energy left. “I wanted to ask you something …”

“Make it quick. I really need to get to bed.” As she glanced around, the light came on in the kitchen and flooded through the front window. The door opened and a bleary-eyed Nick appeared.

“I was just coming to escort you home.”

“You look like you just woke up,” Lexie remarked. “Did you pass out on the couch too?”

“Yep. Are you coming in? It’s freezing.”

“Yeah.” She moved down the path, then turned back to Dale. “What did you want to ask?”

He shook his head, rocking on the balls of his feet. “It doesn’t matter. I’ll let you get to bed. It was fun working with you tonight.”

“You too,” she said automatically, then flashed him a quick smile before he called goodnight and strode away down the road.

“Has he grown on you then?” Nick asked as he closed the kitchen door behind them.

“Not really. I find him slightly creepy, but everyone else seems to like him and he seems as though he might be okay at the job. I’ll give him the benefit of the doubt I suppose.”

“You’re never good with new people,” Nick pointed out.

"I'm not sure that's true, but can we please not psychoanalyse me so late at night?"

"Sure, we'll do it in the morning instead." Grinning at her, he moved his hands to her belly. "How's my little princess doing?"

"Kicking a lot."

"That's because you took her to the pub for the evening. She thinks it's party time."

Lexie leaned forwards and rested her head on Nick's shoulder. "I think it's bedtime."

He kissed her forehead and rubbed her shoulders. "It seems as though working at the pub in the evenings might be getting too much for you."

"I'd argue with you if I had any energy. Let's go to bed."

Nick took her hand and led her to the stairs. "It's perfectly fine to take it easy, you know?"

"Don't talk crazy," she said, hating to admit that he might have a point.

CHAPTER NINE

Elspeth was mopping the floor of the cafe on Saturday afternoon when she paused. The sound of laughter outside drew her gaze. Logan was lying on the ground clutching a rugby ball while Arran and Rory stood over him looking thoroughly amused. Jasper stood nearby and barked a few times until Logan stood up and petted his head. Smiling at the sight of them having fun, Elspeth got back to work cleaning up the cafe.

Over the past week, she'd avoided the subject of Rory moving back in. She tried not to overthink his insistence on them living apart. He was right that they were happy as they were and that was what she should focus on.

The playful shouts and laughter from outside continued as she worked. It was only when she stepped out of the cafe that she realised they'd fallen quiet. Rory was on the ground while Logan crouched beside him, frown lines etched on his face.

"What's going on?" Elspeth called.

"Logan tackled Daddy," Arran replied.

Elspeth looked down at Rory's pained expression. "Are you okay?"

"I went over on my ankle." Sitting up, he pulled his trouser leg up, then winced as he moved his foot.

"Please tell me you haven't broken your ankle chasing around the garden with Logan."

"I don't think it's broken." He gave Logan his arm to help him up.

"Sorry," Logan said. "I might have got a bit carried away. You tripped me up first though."

"You're like a pair of kids." Elspeth moved beside Rory. "Can you walk?"

"I think so." He grimaced as he tried to take a step, then slung an arm around Logan's shoulders and hobbled towards the cottage.

"Is Daddy okay?" Arran asked, sticking beside Elspeth.

She ran a hand over his hair. "He'll be fine. Don't worry."

"Logan gets too rough," Arran said in a tone that sounded almost identical to Isla when she told Logan off.

"It was an accident," Logan said. "And I apologised."

"You hurt Daddy. Next time be more careful."

"I will, I promise."

"It's not so bad," Rory reassured him. "I'll probably just need to lie around for a few days while you and Mummy bring me anything I need."

"Okay," Arran said seriously while Elspeth flashed Rory a look of mock annoyance.

"Go and lie on the couch," she instructed, opening the door to the cottage. "I'll get you an ice pack." She went to the freezer, then joined them in the living room.

"It's pretty swollen," Logan said as Rory peeled his sock off. "Are you sure you haven't broken it?"

"I dunno." Rory winced when Elspeth lifted his foot and put a cushion under it. "It's probably just sprained."

"Do you want me to drive you to the hospital?" Logan offered. "It might be worth getting an X-ray."

"No. I'll see how it is tomorrow, but I don't think it's that serious."

"Shall I hang around?" Logan asked.

Rory shook his head. "I'm fine."

"Sorry again." Logan patted Rory's shoulder before he left.

"Do you want painkillers?" Elspeth asked Rory.

"Aye. Please."

After she'd brought him some, she left him and Arran watching TV while she made dinner.

"Daddy?" Arran said while they ate from their laps. "Will you stay here until your leg is better?"

"No. It's fine."

"If you stay here, me and Mummy can bring you things so you don't have to move."

Rory smiled. "I was joking about that. I can manage. I'm quite good at hopping."

"You should stay here," Elspeth said, setting her empty plate aside and moving to inspect Rory's ankle. "It's pretty swollen. If it's sprained, you'll need to rest it."

"I'll manage," he said with a curt shake of the head.

"Stay here and let us look after you."

He rolled his eyes. "Stop fussing. It's not a big deal."

"I like to fuss over you." She gave him a chaste kiss, then took his plate from him and went to the kitchen to tidy up. When she'd finished, she hustled Arran upstairs for a much-needed bath before settling him in bed.

"Why doesn't Daddy live with us?" Arran asked as Elspeth switched off the lamp by his bed.

"Not all mummies and daddies live together," she replied, hoping that would be enough of an answer. They'd had the conversation lots of times, and it only got more difficult to answer. Mostly because she couldn't think of a good reason.

"I think that if mummies and daddies don't live together, it's because they don't like each other any more. But you like Daddy."

She looked down at him. "I do. I love Daddy. We just decided not to live together for a while."

"Daddy loves you too," Arran said. "But he told me he likes living next to the pub."

"I bet he did," Elspeth said lightly. "Go to sleep now."

She wished him goodnight and slipped out of the room. When she was halfway down the stairs, the front door opened and Logan wandered in.

"Back to check on the patient?" Elspeth assumed he must be feeling guilty.

"I'm off to meet the old rugby crowd in Portree. I said I'd give Rory a lift home on my way."

Elspeth stopped on the last step.

"Are you okay?" Logan asked.

Shaking herself, she continued down the stairs. "I thought he'd stay here tonight."

Logan flashed her a sympathetic smile, then trailed into the living room with her.

"Why don't you stay here?" Elspeth asked, sitting beside Rory as he eased his sock on over his bloated ankle.

"It's not so bad."

Logan hovered over them. "If I were you I'd milk it and let Elspeth wait on you."

"I'm fine." He eased himself up from the couch and tentatively took a step. It looked painful, but he managed to limp to the front door.

"I'll talk to you in the morning," Elspeth said, giving him a soft kiss. "Call me if you need anything."

After he'd gone, Elspeth went and sat in the quiet living room. Considering she was in a relationship, she spent a lot of time feeling completely alone.

~

When she'd finally calmed down after her spat with Gary, Jess found herself tempted to message him and apologise. The incident had left her with a vague feeling of anxious anticipation.

Maybe a quick message would clear the air and she'd be able to put the whole thing behind her. But she also thought he should be the one to make a move, since it was him who had started with the name calling.

The problem with living in a small town on a remote Scottish island was that she was bound to bump into him eventually. Two weeks after their argument she was in the Merchant Bar with Ava on a Saturday evening, having not bothered with the usual work drinks the previous evening.

Jess had gone to the bar and had just ordered drinks when a figure caught her attention in her peripheral vision. Gary was standing a couple of metres away from her. He was looking the other way, so he either hadn't noticed her or was pretending he hadn't. It was tempting to run away, but with the barman heading back with the drinks that would be awkward. As she paid, she glanced to the side at the exact moment that Gary turned in her direction. From the sharp rise of his eyebrows, it seemed he was only then noticing her.

"Hi," he said.

"Hi." She tapped on the bar, willing the barman to hurry up with her change. As Gary took a couple of steps towards her, she shook her head. "Let's not speak," she said, forgetting any ideas about apologies and clearing the air. "It'll inevitably end in an argument, and I think it's better if we ignore each other from now on."

"Fine by me," he said, his expression neutral. He bordered on looking bored, which annoyed Jess immensely.

After shoving her change in her pocket, she picked up her drinks. She was all set to walk away when she hesitated. "I'll just say one thing. It's been bothering me and I'd like to get it off my chest. Then we can never speak again."

"What is it?"

"You should wash Paige's clothes. I'm sure you think you're teaching her valuable life skills, and obviously it's not a bad thing for her to know how to do her own washing. But she's fourteen. She's still a kid, which means someone should be looking after her. Let her be a kid." She took a breath and braced herself to have her head bitten off. Strangely, Gary just stared at her, his features impassive. Then he turned and ordered a pint.

After staring at his back for a moment, Jess walked quickly over to Ava.

"I just did something stupid," she whispered as she put the drinks down.

"What did you say to him now?" Ava asked, looking in Gary's direction.

"I had a go at him for not washing Paige's clothes. Which is absolutely none of my business. But I honestly don't see how it's that much effort for him to do a couple of extra loads of washing a week."

"Did he tell you to mind your own business?"

"No. That was the weird thing. He didn't react. Which was quite unnerving. I think I'd rather he'd have told me to keep out if it."

Ava sipped her drink, then widened her eyes. "He's coming over! Maybe he was just biding his time, coming up with the perfect angry retort."

"Why didn't I just keep my mouth shut?" Jess mumbled before turning in Gary's direction. He stopped abruptly and glanced around as though he was lost.

"Are you all right?" Ava asked in a tone that would have been appropriate for a small child.

"Yeah." Gary took a step away, then stopped again and looked directly at Jess. "You don't know the full story."

"What?"

"I know we agreed not to speak to each other again," he said, his brow furrowed. "But in case you want to report me to social services or something, I think you should at least have your facts straight."

"What are you talking about?"

He moved closer. "The washing."

"You can forget what I said," Jess said. "It's none of my business and I shouldn't have commented on it. I have no intention of reporting you to anyone."

She'd expected that might have been an end to the conversation, but he sank onto the stool beside her. "I'm not trying to teach her a lesson about looking after herself," he said slowly. "I just don't know how to do it."

"How to do what?" Jess asked. "The washing? You don't know how to wash clothes?"

"Obviously I know how to wash clothes. Just not women's clothes."

Jess blinked a few times, searching his face for signs that he was joking. "They're the same as men's clothes."

He tilted his head. "What about delicate stuff?"

"I doubt Paige wears much that has special washing instructions. You could ask her, but I imagine you're pretty safe to wash most of her clothes at forty degrees."

"I'm worried I'm going to ruin her stuff."

"If you're not sure, just look at the washing instructions." When his brow creased, she rolled her top up at the seam and showed him the tag. "See how it says forty … that tells you how hot you can wash at."

He rolled his eyes. "I know how to read washing instructions. I just feel a bit weird about reading the labels on her delicate things. It's kind of creepy."

Ava leaned her elbows on the table. "Are you talking about underwear?"

"Yes. Can you put bras and stuff in the washing machine?"

A smile crept over Jess's face. "You can put them in the washing machine. It's fine. Better not to put them in the tumble dryer though."

"Thank you." He picked up his pint and stood up. "Sorry to interrupt you. Have a good night."

"Thanks," Jess said, then leaned in to say something to Ava when he turned and came back.

"Sorry," he said again. "I have another question … if you don't mind." When they both shrugged, he sat down. "When I tried to do Paige's washing once – before I realised I didn't know what to do with it – I noticed that her … erm … some of her underwear is the lacy, frilly variety."

It was an effort for Jess not to laugh at how uncomfortable he looked talking about women's underwear. "So?" she prompted.

"Well, I wondered if that's normal for a fourteen-year-old?"

"I'd say so," Ava said.

"Right …" He stared into his drink. "Does it mean she's …" He swallowed hard. "I mean, I'd assume that if she's wearing lacy underwear it's because someone's going to be seeing it … I was thinking maybe I should have a chat with her about being safe or something."

Jess couldn't contain her laughter. "I'd love to be a fly on the wall for that conversation." Considering he was squirming at the mention of underwear, she couldn't imagine him having a sex talk with a teenager.

He rubbed at his forehead with the back of his hand. "It'd make her uncomfortable, wouldn't it?"

"Yes." Jess swallowed hard. "Sorry, I shouldn't tease. But I don't think you need to have a talk with her. She doesn't even have a boyfriend, does she?"

Gary shook his head. "Not that I know of. To be honest, she doesn't go out a lot, so I guess she's not getting up to much … I just wasn't sure why she'd have lacy underwear."

"Some women just like nice underwear," Jess told him. "It doesn't have to be for anyone else. And at her age, she'll just be experimenting. I'd say it's perfectly normal."

"Okay. That's good to know." He took a swig of his drink and didn't seem to be in a hurry to leave.

"Any more questions?" Ava asked brightly.

He scratched the side of his head. "Do you think it's weird that she doesn't have any friends? I was constantly meeting up with friends at her age. Sometimes she goes out on Saturdays, but as far as I can tell she only wanders around the shops on her own."

"It's pretty unusual," Jess said. "She doesn't seem to have any particular friends in my lessons. I'm not sure there's much you can do about it though."

"She used to have this one best friend, Claire, but she moved away a while ago. I feel a bit sad for her that she's got no friends. She reckons that her form teacher doesn't like her, so she's not a fan of school. If she doesn't have friends it really won't be much fun for her, will it?"

Jess offered a sympathetic smile. "I can try and keep an eye out for her at school. See if there's anyone she hangs about with."

"That'd be good. Thanks." He glanced around as a group of lads walked into the pub. Jess recognised Logan among them. "I'll leave you to it," Gary said. "Thanks for the advice."

"You're welcome," Jess said, then watched him walk over to the group who'd just arrived.

"He's kind of sweet, isn't he?" Ava said.

"Yes." Jess dragged her eyes away from him. "I think it would probably have been easier if he'd kept on being grumpy and annoying."

"So you like him again now?"

"Yeah," she said sadly. "But I'm not sure what I'm supposed to do about it."

Ava's shoulders slumped. "Just ask him out. It's not that difficult."

"Five minutes ago I told him we should stay out of each other's way and not speak to each other. So asking him out would be a bit awkward."

"Not really. He came over to chat to you immediately after you told him you shouldn't speak to each other, so it didn't seem as though he took you very seriously."

"I don't know," Jess said. "I have the feeling that things aren't destined to work out between the two of us."

"Not if you don't make a bit of effort! All you have to do is ask him out for dinner."

"Yes. But I'm a chicken, so that will require more than a bit of effort."

"Do you want me to ask him for you?"

Jess laughed. She could imagine Ava striding across the pub and asking him out on her behalf. "No, thanks. I'll think of a way to ask him that I'm comfortable with."

"You know I'm going to nag you until you go on a date with him, don't you?"

"Yes. But I promise I'm going to ask him."

CHAPTER TEN

An unusually sunny spell brought an increased number of hikers to the cafe on Wednesday afternoon. Hot chocolate and cake were in high demand as walkers broke up their trek in the warmth of the cafe. Looking out over the still water of the loch with the bright blue sky overhead, you could be forgiven for thinking it was mid-summer rather than November. Until you stepped outside, anyway.

There were two tables occupied when Isla wandered in with Arran.

"How was school?" she asked as he climbed up onto a chair at a free table.

"Good. I'm hungry."

"You're always hungry." Elspeth rolled her eyes and looked to Isla. "Thanks for picking him up."

"No problem. How's Rory? Have you heard from him yet?"

Elspeth frowned. "Last I heard he was waiting for an X-ray."

"Is Daddy at the hospital?" Arran asked.

"Yes, but he's fine," Elspeth reassured him. After spending a few days hobbling around, he'd decided to go and get his ankle checked out.

"Are you okay?" Isla asked.

"Fine." Elspeth's throat thickened as her sister flashed her a sympathetic smile. "He didn't even tell me he was going to the hospital. I only know because I happened to message him earlier to ask how he was doing. Logan had already driven him over there."

"He probably didn't want to worry you," Isla said.

"Maybe." Elspeth swallowed the lump in her throat. "I'm going to get Arran a sandwich. Do you want anything?"

"Just a coffee, but I'll get it."

A couple asked for their bill and Elspeth went to take the payment. When she went back to the kitchen, Isla was making Arran his sandwich.

"Is everything all right with you and Rory?" she asked, looking up from spreading butter on the bread.

Elspeth slumped against the counter. "I don't know," she said honestly.

"I'm sure he just didn't say anything about going to the hospital because he didn't want you worrying or offering to take him to the hospital. He knew you were busy with the cafe."

Elspeth pulled her phone from the pocket in her apron. "He could have at least messaged me to let me know what was going on." She scrolled to his number and hit dial.

"Hi," Rory said after a couple of rings.

"Where are you?"

"On the way home with Logan. It's not broken. Just sprained."

"That's good. Are you coming to our place for dinner?" He usually did on Wednesdays.

"I think I'll just head home."

She nodded through the clenching of her chest. "Arran and I can come up to your place after I close the cafe if you want?"

"Yeah, okay," he said cheerfully. "We can have dinner together."

She told him she'd see him later and turned to Isla as she ended the call, filling her in on his hospital trip.

"I can close up the cafe," Isla offered. "If you want to go and see him."

"Rory and I are fine," Elspeth said, trying to sound convincing and realising she wasn't quite sure which of them she was trying to convince.

Isla picked up the plate of sandwiches and her mug of coffee. "I know. I just thought you might want to go and see him."

"When you're nice to me, it worries me. And you don't need to be concerned about me when there's nothing wrong."

"Good." Isla smiled sweetly. "Get me a slice of that chocolate cake then!"

Chuckling, Elspeth followed her back into the cafe.

When the remaining customers left, Elspeth closed the cafe a quarter of an hour early. As she walked up the drive with Arran, Logan was arriving back. Elspeth waved at him and was grateful that he didn't stop to chat. She was irrationally annoyed at him for being the person Rory called when he'd needed help.

As they approached Rory's place, Elspeth half-heartedly smiled at Arran, who was blethering away about a game he'd been playing with his friends during breaktime at school. He didn't seem to have a clue that she wasn't really listening.

She knocked on the door of the bunkhouse before opening it and stepping inside, shouting hello as she went.

Arran ran into the living room and Elspeth followed in time to watch him jump on top of Rory, who was stretched out on the couch with his foot up on a pillow. Rory laughed and hugged him to his chest as he asked how school was.

Arran gave his standard answer of "good", then jumped down and prodded the ice pack on Rory's ankle.

"Does it hurt?" he asked.

"Yes. I'll be going slow for a few days. No running around for me."

"Hi," Elspeth said, sinking beside him and giving him a quick kiss. "How are you feeling?"

"I'm all right," he said. "It's more annoying than anything."

"I'm going upstairs," Arran announced before running out of the room. As much as he asked why Daddy didn't live with them, the fact that he had another bedroom which was increasingly filling with toys made it completely bearable for him.

"How was your day?" Rory asked.

"Pretty crap," she whispered, looking directly at Rory. Even as tears blurred her vision she could see the concern on his features. Moving his foot off the couch, he wrapped his arms around her.

"What happened?" he asked in a panic.

Elspeth couldn't reply and took comfort in the warmth of his embrace. With her cheek resting on his shoulder, she inhaled the heady scent of him.

"Tell me what's wrong," he said, stroking her hair.

Pulling back, she wiped her tears away and inhaled a cleansing breath. "Why didn't you tell me you were going to the hospital?"

"That's what you're upset about?" he asked, squinting.

"Yes. I don't understand why you didn't call and let me know. If I hadn't messaged you, I'd have ended up finding out from Isla."

"There was no need to call you. Logan had already offered to drive me. I knew you'd worry and there wasn't anything to worry about."

"But I'm your girlfriend. Why don't you want me to worry about you? If it was the other way around you'd want to take care of me, wouldn't you?"

"Yes. But you've got enough on your plate without looking after me as well. And I knew you were working. There wasn't anything you could do."

"I could have got someone to look after the cafe. Or close for the day. And even if you don't need me, I'd still like to know what's going on."

"Sorry," he said, keeping an arm around her shoulders. "I'm fine though."

"I don't understand why you won't come and stay at my place?"

He laughed. "Because you'll insist on running around after me unnecessarily."

"I don't know why that's a problem. If you're worried about me doing too much and having another breakdown, you don't need to. I'm fine now."

He pushed her hair behind her ear. "I know."

"I feel as though you don't believe me. You walk on eggshells around me and it drives me crazy."

"No, I don't."

She sighed heavily; as much as she tried not to be bothered by the fact that they didn't live together, it was always there, niggling at the back of her mind. "Then move back in. It's weird that we don't live together. Everyone thinks we have relationship problems." She looked at him sadly. "Will you please move back in? It would be better for Arran too."

As he pressed his lips together, she knew without a doubt that he was trying to find a way to let her down gently.

Her throat burned and her eyes stung. "Is it just that you don't want to live with me, or do you not want to be with me at all?"

"I want to be with you," he said, taking her face in his hands and touching his forehead to hers. "That's never in question. I love you."

"But you don't want to live with me?"

"I don't want us to rush into anything. And I definitely don't want to move back in because of what other people think. Or because Arran wants me to. It needs to be the right thing for us."

Abruptly, she stood up. Having the same conversation over and over was pointless. "Are you hungry? I can make you dinner. Arran had sandwiches and I'm not really hungry, but I'll get you something."

"I didn't mean to upset you," he said. "I just think it might be better if we wait a while. Things are fine as they are, aren't they?"

"I don't like things as they are. But if you don't want to move back in, I can't force you." She inhaled deeply, fighting her emotions. "I'll get you something to eat."

"Wait a minute," Rory called as she walked away. "It's not fair of you to walk out when I can't follow you."

"I'll be back in a minute," she muttered.

In the kitchen, she clutched the edge of the counter and sucked in air as she tried to calm herself down. It didn't work and eventually she let the tears come. Her shoulders shook as she silently cried.

"Elspeth?" Rory said, startling her.

She didn't turn around as she hastily wiped at her cheeks. "You're supposed to be resting your leg," she said, her voice breaking on the words as she tried to sound stern.

"That would be easier to do if you didn't walk away from me when I want to speak to you." He hobbled over and pulled her into a hug. "I'm sorry," he said, holding her tightly.

"I don't understand," she sniffed. "Are you trying to get back at me for breaking up with you?"

He pulled back to look her in the eye. "No. Do you really think I'd do that?"

"I don't know why you don't want to live with me."

"It's not that I don't want to … I'm only worried about us rushing things and messing things up again."

"So you think you'll move back in one day?"

"Yes."

"I miss you," she whispered.

"You see me all the time," he said with a smile.

"It's not the same as living with you. I hate never knowing when you'll stay at our place. And I really hate that you're fine with this arrangement."

He tilted his head and looked thoughtful. "If you really think it's a good idea for me to move back, I'll think about it and we can talk about it some more."

Elspeth shook her head. "There's no point in you moving back in just to keep me happy. You need to want to live with me."

"Daddy!" Arran shouted as his footsteps thundered down the stairs. "My Transformer broke again. Can you fix it?"

"Probably," he said, taking it from him. "I really hate this toy. Who bought it for you?"

"Grandad."

"Maybe we should keep it at Grandad's house so he'll be the one to deal with it when you try and transform it. There's a reason these things are for ages ten and up."

Elspeth gave him a stern look. "Go and sit down. And keep your foot elevated and iced."

He gave her a quick peck, then set off slowly back to the living room.

While Rory was eating the pizza she'd made for him, Elspeth went and tidied up the kitchen, then returned and told Arran it was time to go home.

"Can I sleep here?" he asked.

"No," Elspeth told him. "Daddy needs to rest his leg, not run around after you."

"You could both stay here," Rory suggested, looking to Elspeth. "If you want?"

"I'd rather stay at home, unless you need me to stay …" If he wanted her to stay and look after him she wouldn't say no, but otherwise she was keen to sleep in her own bed.

"I don't *need* you to."

Elspeth perched on the arm of the couch. "I don't really like staying over here. I just want to have one place where I sleep. You're welcome to come home whenever you want." Staying at the bunkhouse felt as though she was saying the situation was okay with her when it wasn't.

"Are you going to live with us again?" Arran asked, climbing onto Rory's lap.

"I don't know," Rory said.

"Don't you like our house?"

Rory smiled. "I really like your house."

"Don't you like Mummy?" he asked seriously.

"I love Mummy." Rory ran a hand over his hair. "And I love you."

"Why don't you live with us then?"

Elspeth gave Rory a quizzical look, interested to see how he'd answer that one.

"It's complicated. And this place is cool, isn't it?"

"Yes," Arran agreed.

Elspeth held a hand out to him. "Come on. Let's leave Daddy to rest." Bending to Rory, she laid a hand on his cheek as she kissed him. "Love you."

"Love you too," he said wearily. "I'll think about it."

"It's not a great sign if you have to think about it so much."

"That's not fair." He caught her hand and looked deep into her eyes. "I do love you."

She squeezed his hand before releasing it. "I'll talk to you tomorrow."

CHAPTER ELEVEN

Friday night was a complete washout for Elspeth. To start with, Rory cancelled their date night to rest his ankle. He'd wanted her and Arran to go over to his place but she'd told him they'd just see him on Saturday instead. Then, she was woken several times in the night by Arran coughing. Each time she checked on him he was fast asleep, though she wasn't sure how he managed to sleep through the coughing fits. In the morning she was awake before him, which almost never happened. His cheeks were red when she looked in at him and his forehead felt warm to her touch.

She sat in the kitchen, enjoying the peace for an hour before Arran finally padded down and joined her.

"How are you?" she asked.

He responded with a cough, then snuggled into her chest when she lifted him onto her lap.

"Are we going to Daddy's house today?" he asked, his voice thick.

"Not if you're not very well. We'll stay here and have a quiet day."

"I want to go to Daddy's house."

"Daddy will probably come here if I call him."

His chest hitched as he began to cry. "I want to go to Daddy's house."

"Okay." She rubbed his back. "Do you want breakfast first?"

"No."

She made him drink water, then laid him on the couch while she went to get ready. For the quick drive to the bunkhouse, she left him in his pyjamas and bundled him in a blanket.

"Morning!" Rory called as she walked inside with Arran in her arms. He was in the kitchen, standing by the toaster.

"Arran's got a cold." He was heavy and she took him straight to the couch. He immediately snuggled down under his blanket.

"Is he okay?" Rory asked when she joined him in the kitchen.

"Yeah, I think so. Just needs to rest."

"I would've come to your place."

"I know," Elspeth snapped, irritated by the stupid arrangement of them living separately. "But Arran wanted to come here."

Rory rubbed her back. "Are you okay?"

"Just tired," she said, leaning against his chest. "Arran was coughing a lot in the night."

"Leave him here and go back to bed if you want."

"I'm okay." She looked down at him balancing on one leg. "You shouldn't be standing around. Go and sit with Arran."

"I'm only getting breakfast."

"I'll do it."

His hand slipped to the small of her back and he pulled her to him. He tasted of coffee when he kissed her. Instead of pulling away he deepened the kiss, making her insides flutter. When he drew back he wobbled, and she took his arm to balance him.

"Go and sit down," she told him firmly.

. . .

They spent the entire day lying on the couch watching Disney films. Arran fell asleep for a couple of hours in the afternoon – a sure sign that he was under the weather.

"Arran's fast asleep and we're still watching kids' films," Elspeth pointed out, lifting her head from Rory's chest to glance over at Arran.

Gently, Rory laid a hand across Arran's forehead. "If we change it, he'll wake up."

"That's true." She snuggled back down, enjoying the leisurely afternoon. It wasn't often they had a whole day of doing nothing.

Elspeth made them pasta for dinner, then tried to coax Arran into going home.

"I want to sleep at Daddy's house," he said, setting himself off coughing.

After being adamant that she wasn't going to sleep there any more, Elspeth gave up on her conviction. It wasn't worth it.

"I guess we'll both stay here." She flashed Rory a questioning look and he nodded in reply. "I'll need to go home and grab some clothes. I don't think I've got anything here." The fresh air would be good too.

Halfway home, Elspeth paused on the path beside the loch to watch an otter running along the rocks at the shore. It had just splashed into the water and disappeared below the surface when Elspeth's phone buzzed with a message from Leana asking how Rory's ankle was. Quickly, she tapped out a message to say he was okay, then asked if Leana was at home. She could walk a bit further and call in for a chat.

Leana made her a cuppa when she arrived, and they got comfy in the living room.

"Where's Alasdair?" Elspeth asked.

"Upstairs. He's in a bad mood because he wants to go out and I can't be bothered." She set her steaming mug down and covered her mouth as she chuckled to herself.

"What's so funny?"

"I didn't want to go out, so I told him we could stay in and have sex all evening." She beamed. "He accused me of manipulating him to get my own way."

"You'd think he'd just agree to that offer."

Leana pulled her legs under her on the couch. "He knows we'll end up in front of the TV for the evening."

They fell silent at the sound of footsteps in the kitchen.

"Leana?" Alasdair shouted.

"Yeah?"

"I changed my mind. We can stay in and have sex all evening if you want."

She looked at Elspeth in amusement and put a finger to her lips. "Thank you. That's very generous of you."

"Just trying to be a good fiancé." The sound of the fridge opening drifted through. "You just need to remember that I did this for you next time I want something. Okay?"

"I'll totally owe you one!"

"We're actually having sex though," he shouted. "Don't think you can lure me into staying home on a promise and then end up falling asleep in front of the TV."

Leana grinned at Elspeth. "He's going to be mortified when he realises you're here."

"What?" Alasdair called.

"I was talking to Elspeth, not you."

"Are you on the phone?"

She snorted a laugh and Elspeth finally released a giggle too. "No!"

Alasdair wandered in, then stopped short and raised his eyebrows. "Hi, Elspeth!"

"Hello." She laughed loudly. "Don't worry, I'm not staying long. I heard you have plans for the evening!"

Alasdair rolled his eyes as he sat beside Leana with a beer in his hand. "You could have warned me that Elspeth was here."

"I could have done," Leana told him cheekily. "But that would have been a lot less fun."

"It's pretty mean of you after I've just agreed to go along with your plans for the evening."

Elspeth blew on her tea. "You're very kind to agree to an evening of sex."

"Just call me Saint Alasdair!" He sank back into the couch. "Unfortunately, Leana uses sex as a code word for drinking endless cups of tea in front of dodgy romantic films."

"One day I might surprise you," Leana said, patting his leg.

"I live in hope." He took a long swig of his beer, then looked to Elspeth. "How's the invalid? Did you come over here for a break from playing nursemaid?"

"He's all right. Arran's got a cold so we've all been on the couch for the day. I just nipped out to get some clothes for tomorrow."

"Are you staying at the bunkhouse tonight?" Leana asked.

Elspeth nodded. "I'm really sick of living apart now. It makes no sense."

"Why doesn't he move back in?" Leana asked.

"I'm not sure." Elspeth frowned as she stared into her tea. "He doesn't want to."

"I don't get it," Leana said.

"You and me both." Elspeth looked at Alasdair. "Rory talks to you, right?"

"It would make going out for drinks awkward if he didn't."

"You know what I mean," Elspeth said. "Does he ever say anything about me?"

Alasdair grimaced. "Please don't interrogate me."

"She only asked you a question," Leana said.

"I don't want to get involved in other people's relationships."

Elspeth put her drink down and rested her elbows on her knees. "Has he said anything about why he doesn't want to move back in?"

"No." Alasdair tensed. "Surely if he was going to talk to someone about it, it'd be you."

"I have no idea what's going on in his head. He says he

doesn't want to rush into moving back in, but it's been ages now. Every time I try and talk to him about it he fobs me off with some excuse. Last week he thought I wanted him to move back in because I was jealous of him chatting to Jess. Then he said he wouldn't move back in just because Arran wanted him to or because other people think it's weird that we live apart. I think he just doesn't want to."

"To be fair," Alasdair said, "I think he's got a point. I know he was concerned about you jumping back into living together and it not working out again. It probably wouldn't be a good idea to move back in just because Arran wants him to or for the sake of appearances."

"They're not the only reasons," Elspeth argued. "I love him and we're a family. I think we should live together."

Alasdair took a long slug of his beer. "What are your long-term plans?"

"How do you mean?"

"Are you going to get married? Have more kids? Will you stay in Lannick?"

Elspeth drew her chin to her chest and shrugged. "I don't know."

"What does Rory want? Is he happy living in Lannick?"

"I have no idea."

"It's good to talk about this stuff." He gave an exaggerated grimace as he looked at Leana. "Trust me on that."

Elspeth tilted her head to one side. "We've never really planned anything. I got pregnant a week after we met … everything after that has been a little haphazard. Maybe you're right that we should think about the future more."

"That was actually good advice," Leana said.

Alasdair poked her in the ribs. "No need to sound so surprised."

"I'm going to go and leave you to enjoy your evening."

"Make sure you don't forget anything," Alasdair said. "We'll be naked the second you're out of the door, so you won't want to come back in. Isn't that right, Leana?"

"Pretty much. I just need to check something on the TV."

Elspeth finished her drink and stood up, flashing Leana a playful smile. "I watched a good film last week if you want a recommendation?"

"No!" Alasdair glared at her. "I gave you relationship advice and this is how you repay me? Get out!"

"Have fun," Elspeth said, grinning as she made for the door.

When Elspeth arrived back at the bunkhouse Arran was asleep, and she carefully carried him up to his room and tucked him up in bed. Returning downstairs she got an ice pack from the freezer and took it to Rory, who was lying on the couch with his eyes closed. An arm was hooked under his head and had caused his T-shirt to rise up. Elspeth automatically touched the ice pack to his exposed midriff.

"Sorry," she said when he jumped. "Couldn't resist."

He watched her intently as she adjusted his foot on the pillow and laid the cool pack on it.

"What are you grinning at?" Rory asked.

She moved to lie beside him. "I was going to go home and get clean clothes, but I completely forgot."

"Where've you been?"

"Leana and Alasdair's place."

"What are they up to tonight?"

"Staying in to have sex," Elspeth said with a smirk.

Rory raised an eyebrow. "Watching TV then?"

"I think so." She snuggled up to him, resting her cheek on his chest and listening to the gentle thud of his heartbeat. "Do you ever think about moving back to Edinburgh?" she asked after a moment.

Rory tensed beneath her. "No. Why?"

"I just wondered." She propped her chin on his chest to look at him. "Are you happy living in Lannick?"

"Yes. I'd never leave you and Arran. Why did you ask? Are you trying to get rid of me?"

"Definitely not. I didn't mean just you. I wondered if you've ever thought about the three of us moving?"

"I've honestly never considered it. You and Arran are happy here. I'd never ask you to move."

"What if I was happy to move?"

He squeezed his eyes closed and shook his head. "This is a weird conversation. Do you want to move?"

"I don't think so." She chewed her bottom lip. "Alasdair said something that made me realise that we don't ever plan anything. I have no idea what you want out of life. I don't think I even know what I want. We never discuss this stuff."

Rory hooked her hair behind her ear. "I can't imagine you wanting to move away from your family."

"But if you wanted to, we could at least discuss it. I feel as though you always fit in with me and Arran. You'd tell me if you weren't happy, wouldn't you?"

He nodded vaguely, and she panicked that he was secretly miserable and only put up with her for Arran's sake. Shaking the paranoia away, she reminded herself how loving and caring he was with her. He never acted like someone who was with her out of a sense of duty.

"Do you want to have more kids?" she asked.

His features crumpled. "What?"

"Do you ever think about having more kids?"

He shifted his weight, nudging her off him and sitting up. "What's with all the questions?"

"I'd like to know if it's something you think about."

"I'm happy as we are," he said, repositioning the ice pack on his ankle.

"That's not what I asked." With a hand on his shoulder, she coaxed him to look at her. His eyes flickered with panic and his whole body seemed tense. "You've thought about this, haven't you?"

"Maybe." He entwined his fingers with hers. "Recently, when I see Lexie, I can't help but think that there was a time when you were wandering around here pregnant and I had no idea."

She smiled sadly. "If it makes you feel any better, I wasn't usually wandering around Lannick. I was mostly hiding away in my bedroom."

"Sorry," he said, frowning.

"It wasn't your fault."

"I know but I feel guilty that you went through all that on your own."

"I could have called you." They'd had this conversation so many times and it never got easier. She'd always regret not telling him she was pregnant.

"I feel as though we both missed out," Rory said. "But I also know that it probably put you off having more kids."

"I'm not sure that's true," Elspeth said. "I always feel a bit jealous when I see Lexie and Nick. They're so excited about becoming parents. That's how it should be. I was so embarrassed and ashamed when I was pregnant. And terrified. But if I think about doing it again, and it being planned and wanted, it feels so different."

"So, you'd want to?" His features softened and a hint of a smile played at his lips.

"Yeah. I think so. Would you?"

He nodded eagerly.

"We should have talked about this earlier," she said, stroking his hair. "How many kids would you want?"

"Another one would be great." The smile broke over his face. "Or maybe two … Or three?" He winced as though he might be pushing his luck.

"Are you serious?" Elspeth said, wide-eyed. "You'd want a big family?"

"It's not a deal-breaker," he said quickly. "Nothing is a deal-breaker. If it's only ever us and Arran I'd be perfectly happy."

A lump formed in Elspeth's throat. "You always just go along with what I want, don't you? Or whatever you think I want. I had no idea you wanted more kids. You've never even hinted at it."

"Because I knew you'd feel pressured and I'd never want that. You went through so much. I would hate to put you through anything else."

Elspeth stared into his eyes as his words sunk in. Slowly, she shook her head. "It almost sounds as though you think you owe me …"

He puffed out a gentle laugh. "I got you pregnant when you were sixteen, then left you to deal with it on your own."

Elspeth's chin pulled back. "That's not what happened. For one thing, you didn't *get me* pregnant. As far as I'm aware we were both involved in that."

"You were sixteen," he said, as though that made her exempt from responsibility. "And I told you it would be okay to not use contraception."

"We've talked about this. I could've said no. It was as much my fault as yours."

"But you were the one who had to deal with the consequences, not me."

"Because I chose not to tell you. It was my decision to deal with it alone. If anything, you get to be annoyed with me for shutting you out of your child's life."

He shook his head, dismissing the idea.

"You should never feel guilty," Elspeth said. "And you definitely shouldn't feel as though you have to go along with whatever I want and feel as though you're not entitled to have a say in what we do with our lives."

Gently, he plucked the ice pack from his foot and set it aside.

"Will you be honest with me about what you want in future?" Elspeth asked.

He shuffled further up the couch and propped himself on pillows. "I want three more kids, please."

Elspeth smiled at the teasing in his eyes and settled happily beside him.

"That was a joke," he said. "And one I wasn't convinced you'd find funny."

"I'm not promising three more kids," she said. "But it's nice to know what you want. And that you think about our future. With you being so against living with us, I started to wonder whether you saw a future for us at all."

He quirked an eyebrow. "Do you seriously doubt whether I want to be with you?"

"No. I just don't understand. You want to be with me but hate the thought of living with me?" When he didn't respond, she shifted to look him in the eyes. "Oh God. That's the problem! You hated living with me before and you don't want to do it again?"

Desperately, she wanted him to argue and tell her she was talking nonsense. Instead, he rubbed at his temples and looked as though he was weighing his words carefully.

"Just be honest with me," she said.

"Last time we lived together, everything was so stressful. Logically, I know that you weren't yourself, but I really like how things are now. I like that you miss me when I'm not there, and that you're always happy to see me. Whenever I'm at your place I feel as though you want me there."

"I do want you there. If you move back in it would be different to last time."

"That's what I keep telling myself. But I also keep thinking of the way you used to look at me like you couldn't stand the sight of me, and how there was always a horrible atmosphere."

"I'm sorry."

"I wasn't trying to make you feel bad, just explain." He swept her hair from her face. "I should just move back in."

Elspeth shook her head. "I don't mind waiting if I know the reason. I keep thinking you don't love me enough or something."

"It's definitely not that." He wrapped his arms around her and held her tight. "Don't ever think that."

"Whenever you're ready to move back in you can. But I don't want you to feel pressured either."

They sat in silence for a moment before Rory spoke. "Would you really move to Edinburgh if I wanted to?"

She pondered it for a moment. "If you had your heart set on it, I'd give it a go."

"Thank you," he whispered into her hair.

"Have I just agreed to move to the other end of the country?" she asked, trying not to panic.

"No." He laughed. "It's just nice to think it would be a possibility. And that you'd do that for me. I'm happy here though."

CHAPTER TWELVE

Elspeth was lying on the couch on Monday evening when the sound of the front door opening reached her. Whichever member of her family it was, she wondered if she'd be able to persuade them to tidy up the kitchen. Making dinner for her and Arran had been enough of an effort, and now she couldn't muster the energy for anything. She collected up the tissues beside her into one damp bundle.

"Are you okay?" Rory asked as he limped in.

"Arran gave me his cold."

"Good of him to share." He lowered himself to sit beside her and draped a hand across her forehead.

"I'm fine," she said. "How's your ankle?"

"It's okay. I get a lot of sympathy at work and don't have to get my own coffee in the staffroom."

"That's nice. I'd have liked someone to bring me drinks today."

"How's Arran?"

"He made a rapid recovery after I called the school to say he wouldn't be coming in today. He's been bouncing around all day. I just sent him up to get ready for bed."

"That doesn't sound like a relaxing day off for you."

She smiled. "I'm very happy I don't only take one day off a week these days. Arran can definitely go to school tomorrow, and I can have a day of peace." She got another tissue and blew her nose for about the millionth time. "I didn't expect to see you tonight?" Usually, he came over for dinner on Wednesday evenings and then they saw him at the weekends.

"It was too quiet at my place," he said, entwining his fingers with hers. "I also wanted to talk to you about Christmas. My parents want to know when we'll go down to see them."

"When do you want to go?"

He shrugged. "I presumed we'd have Christmas Day here and then go down after. Maybe the 27th for a few days? What do you think?"

"When are we invited? What have your parents got planned?"

"We're invited whenever we want. Mum wanted us to spend Christmas Day with them, but I told her that wouldn't work out."

Elspeth sniffed and pushed the tissue to her nose, trying to stem the flow of mucus. "Why not?" she said, muffled.

"You always have Christmas here. I assumed you'd want to continue the tradition."

"We don't always have to do what I want. Besides, I quite like the idea of Christmas with your parents for a change. I'll get to put my feet up."

"Are you serious?"

She nodded. "It only seems fair. We're with my family all the time."

"Do you think Arran would be okay with it?"

"I don't see why not. He always loves it at your parents' place."

He looked at her for a moment. "Can I tell my mum already, or do you want to think about it?"

"Just tell her. She'll be excited."

"Me too." He moved to kiss her and she pulled back. "I'm full of germs and all snotty."

"Do you want me to get you anything?"

"You're supposed to be staying off your ankle, not looking after me."

"What do you need?" he asked.

She stuck her bottom lip out and felt fairly pathetic. "Could you make that hot lemon and ginger drink you used to make when I was ill? With honey."

"I can manage that." He kissed the top of her head as he stood.

"There's leftover pasta in the kitchen if you're hungry."

He murmured his approval as he headed for the kitchen. When Arran appeared downstairs they spoke to him about Christmas. As Elspeth suspected, he was fine about spending it with Rory's parents as long as they wrote to Santa to tell him where to bring his presents.

Rory wanted to put Arran to bed so Elspeth could rest, but she insisted he shouldn't be going up and down the stairs unnecessarily while his ankle was still painful. She read Arran a story, then agreed to lie down with him for five minutes and fell fast asleep too.

It was just after ten when she woke and made her way blearily to her own bed.

"I thought you'd have gone back to the bunkhouse," she said when she found Rory there.

"I didn't feel like it." He put his arms around her when she shivered beside him. "How are you feeling?"

"Tired." Snuggling up to him, she was asleep again within moments and didn't wake until morning. She must have slept through her alarm and had a minor panic until she heard Rory chatting downstairs with Arran.

"Did you turn my alarm off?" she asked when she joined them in the kitchen.

"Yes." He kissed the side of her head. "I thought you could do with a lie in. I can drop Arran at school on my way to work."

"Thank you." She looked at him wearily. "Can I go back to bed then?"

"Yes."

She told them both to have a good day and went back upstairs. A complete day of rest did her good, and she was feeling much better by the time she went to pick Arran up in the afternoon. Her mum brought dinner over for them to save Elspeth having to cook. They'd just finished eating when the front door opened and Rory wandered in.

"Daddy's here again!" Arran announced with delight, hopping off his chair to greet him.

"I can't keep away," he said, smiling at Elspeth. "Are you feeling better?"

"Yes, thank you. There's a bit of shepherd's pie left, if you want it?"

He reheated it in the microwave and chatted about his day as he ate. Elspeth decided not to comment when he stayed over again, worried that drawing attention to it might somehow jinx it. She'd just enjoy it and hope it became a regular thing.

Jess's mind was on her Tuesday morning lessons when she walked out of the staffroom and almost collided with a red-faced Paige, dashing along the corridor.

"Are you okay?" Jess asked.

"I got in trouble with Mrs Miller again and I'm supposed to be in the classroom half an hour early every day this week." She didn't stop but slowed her pace and turned, walking backwards as she lifted a section of damp hair from her shoulder. "My hairdryer blew up and Gary reckoned he could fix it, which he clearly couldn't. So now I'm late and my hair's wet."

Jess hurried along beside her to avoid making her even later.

"I swear the wiring in his house is dodgy and that's why my hairdryer stopped working."

"Is the house really that bad?" Jess asked.

"It's a complete disaster. I think it's dangerous. There's a plug socket hanging off the wall in the kitchen and Gary's solution is not to use it. I feel as though I'm risking my life every time I use anything electrical. Plus, the heating doesn't work properly so it's bloody freezing."

"Are you just staying with him for this school year?" Jess slowed as they approached her classroom.

"I've no idea. Depends what's going on with my mum."

"You must miss her," Jess ventured.

"Kind of. I didn't get on with her husband, so I'm happy to be away from him. I have to run, I'll already be in trouble."

"Have a good day," Jess called as Paige rushed into Mrs Miller's classroom.

The following day, Jess was walking across the car park with Ava when Gary's car pulled in and Paige hopped out. He gave a quick wave before driving away again.

"You made it on time this morning?" Jess called to Paige.

"Yeah. So today I'll only get into trouble for having damp hair!" She shook her head as she caught up to them. "It's as though Mrs Miller somehow thought I'd decided to come to school with wet hair for a laugh. It's not as though the state of my hair affects her or my schoolwork, so I don't understand why she had a go at me about that. She just enjoys shouting at me, I reckon."

"Well, at least you're on time today," Jess said, biting her tongue to stop herself from bad-mouthing another teacher to a pupil.

Paige flashed her a smile as they walked in through the double doors. "See ya," she said and quickened her pace, striding away from them.

"If I lend Paige my hairdryer, can I use yours?" Jess asked Ava, as they wandered towards the staffroom.

"Yeah. But I think that goes beyond your remit as a teacher."

"It must be really annoying for her to come to school with damp hair. But I may also have an ulterior motive."

"Like what?" Ava asked, stopping at the staffroom door.

"I could drop the hairdryer off with Gary. He'll see what a caring, generous soul I am, and he'll probably also want to thank me by taking me out for a drink. What do you reckon?"

"I reckon calling him and asking him out would be much more straightforward."

"Yes. But slightly scarier. He can say no if I ask him out; he can't really say no to me lending Paige a hairdryer."

"I prefer the direct approach," Ava said. "But your way might work too."

~

Jess had never been to Gary's house. If she remembered correctly, it was just outside of Portree, but that was all she knew. What she did remember was where he worked, so after nipping home to pick up her hairdryer at the end of school, she drove over to the car repair place on the road out of Portree. Parking on the road, she wandered along the pavement, peering into the yard with a variety of cars. A long stone building sat off to one side, the door at the end seeming like the obvious place to head to.

She walked slowly towards it and was contemplating chickening out when movement at the window drew her attention. A man looked out at her, then opened the door a moment later.

"Can I help you, lass?"

"I'm looking for Gary," she said uncertainly.

"He's down there somewhere," the guy said, pointing.

Jess pointed too. "That way?"

"Aye." He nodded before disappearing back inside.

Automatically, Jess set off in the direction he'd indicated, not entirely sure where she was going. At the far end of the building, a bifold garage door was partially open and she stuck her head inside. Her nose twitched at the heavy smell of motor oil and grease. Gary was standing over a tool chest with his back to her.

"Hi," she said, resisting the urge to turn and run away.

He whipped around, surprise flashing on his features. "Hey." He frowned. "Are you having car trouble or something?"

"No." She held up the hairdryer as though that should explain everything.

He walked over, wiping his grease-stained hands on his jeans before he took it from her. "I actually fix cars. I don't know much about fixing hairdryers, which Paige can attest to."

"It's not broken," she said, managing a small smile. "Paige said hers is broken, so I thought she could borrow mine."

His eyebrows pulled together and he calmly handed the hairdryer back to her. "No, you're all right thanks."

She blinked a few times as he walked away. It genuinely hadn't occurred to her that he might not appreciate the gesture. "What do you mean, no?"

"I mean we don't need your charity. I'm not quite sure what sob stories Paige has been feeding you, but she clearly neglected to mention that I'm taking her shopping on Saturday to buy her a new hairdryer and all the other stuff she keeps complaining she needs."

"I just noticed her hair was damp in the mornings," Jess said weakly.

"So you decided to play Little Miss Fix It? I'm perfectly capable of making sure Paige is looked after. I don't need you sticking your nose in and trying to make yourself feel good by looking after us little people."

Jess's eyes stung, but she held off tears as she set the hairdryer on the sideboard next to her. "That wasn't what I was trying to do."

"Yeah, right! Do you help all your students like this then? It's not just your way of trying to make me feel inferior?"

She shook her head but couldn't meet his gaze. "I was actually just using it as an excuse to see you."

He shifted his weight. "What?"

"I wanted to see you. I thought maybe we could be friends or whatever. But now I think it's probably better if we go back to the plan of avoiding each other."

She could feel his eyes on her as she slipped outside, but he didn't come after her and she managed to keep her tears at bay as she got in the car – and amazingly for the drive home too.

CHAPTER THIRTEEN

"Is Daddy coming to our house again tonight?" Arran asked as Elspeth walked him home from school on Friday afternoon. Rory had stayed over every night that week, and Arran was obviously getting as used to it as Elspeth was.

"I think we're going out for dinner and you're staying at home with Granny."

"Will Daddy be there when I get up tomorrow?"

"I think so." She certainly hoped so.

"Are you and Daddy married?" he asked, causing Elspeth to blink a few times as she looked down at him.

"No. Why?"

"Because Kylie in my class says grown-ups have to get married to get a baby."

Elspeth smiled to herself. "Kylie's wrong."

"Are you going to marry Daddy?"

"Maybe one day." She squeezed his hand. "You're asking a lot of questions today."

"Can I have cake when we get home?"

"A small slice!"

Back at the cafe he devoured a slice of chocolate cake, then followed Elspeth around for an hour, chatting animatedly about whatever random things sprang to his mind.

Once the last customers left, Elspeth set about sweeping the floor while her mum cleaned the kitchen. Arran jumped down from his seat and ran across the room when he caught sight of Rory arriving. He launched himself into his arms.

"Where are we going for date night?" Elspeth asked, when he kissed her cheek.

"I thought you might have some brilliant idea."

Elspeth leaned on the broom handle. "I do have an idea," she mused as a plan formulated.

"What is it?" Rory asked, lowering himself onto the nearest chair with Arran still in his arms.

"It'll have to be for next week. It requires planning."

"Are you going to tell me?"

"No. It's a surprise. Which means you need to pick somewhere for tonight."

"Can I come too?" Arran asked.

Rory tickled him. "I reckon that would defeat the purpose of date night."

"Please!" Arran screeched as he wriggled to get away from the tickling.

Rory looked to Elspeth, who shrugged.

"We can go to the pub for dinner," Arran suggested. "I want fish fingers and chips and ice cream."

"I suppose that saves us having to make a decision," Elspeth said, looking to Rory.

Elspeth's mum walked out of the kitchen. "Did I hear I'm released from babysitting duties this evening?"

"Yes." Elspeth smiled. "Arran's taking us up to the pub for dinner. Are you paying for us too?" she asked him teasingly.

"No! I haven't got any money. Daddy will pay."

"Fine by me," she said.

"I'm hungry." Arran hopped down from Rory's lap. "Let's go now."

"It's like you think you're the boss today," Rory said, ruffling his hair.

"I am! Hurry up please!"

When they walked into the pub, Arran went around greeting everyone he knew. First, he shook hands with Douglas, who was sitting at a table by the fire. They were very fond of each other and had a sweet friendship despite their eighty-year age difference. Next, Arran said hello to Mary who was bringing food out to the table beside Douglas's. Finally, he moved to climb onto a bar stool beside Nick and held out his curled hand for a fist bump.

"Hey, Little Man," Lexie said across the bar.

"You're very fat," Arran said in reply.

"That's not a very nice thing to say," Elspeth told him as Nick and Rory chuckled beside her.

"Were you that fat when I was in your tummy?" Arran asked.

"Your mummy was way bigger than this." Lexie walked around the bar to stand beside Arran.

"She must have been really fat."

"Arran!" Elspeth hissed. "Stop saying that. Lexie's pregnant, not fat."

"What does pregnant mean?" Arran asked.

"When you have a baby in your tummy," Lexie told him.

He seemed to consider the information for a moment. "How do you know if someone has got a baby in their tummy or if they're just fat?"

Behind them, Douglas laughed loudly. "If I knew the answer to that I'd have saved myself some uncomfortable conversations over the years."

"You can ask when the baby's due and see if you end up with a black eye," Nick suggested.

"Here." Lexie took Arran's hand. "Do you want to feel her kicking?"

With his hand on Lexie's bump, Arran's eyes widened. "I think she wants to get out!"

"She's got a little while to wait," Lexie told him.

Elspeth slipped her arm around Rory's waist, pulling him close as she thought about their conversation about having more kids. She wondered how Arran would react to being a big brother.

"Who's that?" Elspeth asked, looking behind the bar to where Angus had wandered out of the kitchen with a young lad.

Lexie rolled her eyes. "Dad's new project. He was interviewing for a new member of staff and chose this kid who has no experience whatsoever. Dad says he has a good feeling about him. That's how he chooses staff – based on gut feelings."

"He seems like a nice lad," Nick said. "And he's enthusiastic."

Lexie glanced over at him. "Eighteen-year-olds shouldn't be so smarmy. The way he sucks up to my dad is sickening."

"Angus is his new boss," Nick said. "Of course he's going to be eager to please."

Elspeth looked at Rory as he shifted his weight. "Are you okay?"

"My ankle's a bit painful. I need to sit down."

"Come on," Elspeth said to Arran. "Let's get a table and order food."

"I'll stay with Nick. I want fish fingers and chips."

Elspeth exchanged a smile with Nick before they went to the table in the corner.

"Should we be worried about how at home our son is in the pub?" Rory said as he stretched his leg out.

Elspeth picked up the menu. "Possibly."

"Are you going to tell me what exciting plans you've got for next Friday night?"

She grinned up at him. "I wish I hadn't said anything. It was only a vague idea that I had. Now you're building it up to something amazing."

"It better be. After I spend the next week wondering, I'm going to have built it up in my head to the best date night ever."

"I'll try my best," she said, her lips flickering to a smile as she mulled over the idea some more.

CHAPTER FOURTEEN

Ava went back to visit her parents that weekend, leaving Jess with the house to herself. Drying her hair with Ava's hairdryer on Saturday morning made her think of her encounter with Gary all over again. If it weren't for the fact that Paige had sidled up to her in the hallway on Thursday and quietly thanked her for lending it to her, she'd have seriously regretted giving her hairdryer away in return for a few harsh words.

She should probably be annoyed with Gary for the way he'd spoken to her, but all she could muster was a vague sadness that made her bones feel heavy and sapped her energy.

Late in the afternoon, she was engrossed in a pile of marking at the kitchen table when a knock came at the door. With her pen still in her hand, she moved to answer it.

"Hi," Gary said, standing on the doorstep and holding out her hairdryer. "I'm returning this. Paige has a new one. Thanks for lending it to her."

"No problem." Remembering their previous encounter when she'd told him she'd been looking for an excuse to see him, her cheeks heated up and she felt self-conscious when her hand brushed against his on the hairdryer. "Paige could've given it to me in school."

He shoved his hands in his pockets and bunched his shoulders up. "It seemed like a good excuse to see you."

Jess swallowed hard as she searched for something to say.

"I wondered if I could offer a blanket apology for all the times I've acted like a complete idiot," Gary said. "I don't have an excuse or anything. There's a chance I'm just a complete idiot. But I am sorry."

"I'm sorry too."

He glanced at his shoes, then back up at her. "Have you had dinner?"

"No."

"I was thinking we could … maybe … I mean if you wanted to, we could …"

"Are you asking me out for dinner?"

He let out a long breath. "Trying to, yeah."

"Now?"

"Yes. Or another time. Whatever's good for you."

"Now works for me." She opened the door wider and gestured for him to come in. "I just need to get changed. Do you want a drink?"

"Yeah, okay." He followed her to the kitchen and tipped his head towards the pile of papers on the table. "Did I interrupt you?"

"Yes. But you've done me a favour." She smiled and opened the fridge. "Beer?"

"Aye, go on then." Shrugging his jacket off, he draped it over the back of a chair.

"You look nice." The black shirt suited him. "I don't think I've seen you in a shirt before."

"Just those other two times that we went on dates," he said flatly.

More heat crept to her cheeks. "Oh, yeah. I remember now."

"No, you don't," he said with a smile, reaching to take the bottle of beer from her.

"Sorry." She really didn't remember and was annoyed with

herself that she'd been so preoccupied the previous times she'd been out with him.

After directing him to the living room, which was slightly tidier, she hurried upstairs and had a mild panic over what to wear.

Overriding the instinct to wear jeans, she finally settled on a navy-blue shirt dress. Teamed with a brown belt and matching boots, she felt comfortable but confident.

"You look great," Gary said, standing when she joined him in the living room.

"Thanks. Where are you taking me?"

"I was thinking of Scorrybreac, if that's okay with you."

"That's great." She'd never been but had passed the place often and always thought it looked cute. A white-washed house overlooking the harbour at Portree that had been turned into a fine dining restaurant. "I think you usually need to book though. Especially at the weekend."

"I just called. They have a table for us."

It was only a fifteen-minute walk and the blast of fresh air felt good after spending the day cooped up inside. Gary asked about her week and she chatted easily about work and her students as they ambled along.

When they arrived at the restaurant, the waitress greeted them warmly and seated them at a table in the bay window. A fire flickered gently at the other side of the room, the logs giving off the occasional crackle.

"I've never been here before," Gary said, looking out of the window. The sky was slowly darkening, and streaks of pink swept across the horizon and reflected on the water below.

"Me neither," Jess said. "I like it so far."

Gary turned and looked at her with an intensity that made her shift in her seat. "I do too."

"It's a set menu," Jess said, switching her attention to the menu as nerves stirred in her stomach. "You just have to choose how many courses. I think three sounds good. What do you think?"

He was still gazing at her. "I'm happy with three."

They were interrupted by the waitress bringing their drinks and taking the food order, which gave Jess a moment to breathe.

"So, you took Paige shopping today?" she asked when they were alone again.

"Yes. Not my idea of fun, but Paige enjoyed it. She's at home now, trying on all her new clothes."

"Where did you go?"

"Over to Inverness. Eastgate Shopping Centre."

"That's quite a drive just to go shopping."

"Tell me about it. But Paige has been pretty miserable since her mum left, so it was worth it to cheer her up."

"It must be hard for her. Is she close to her mum?"

He shrugged. "They used to be close. Then Donna started seeing this guy a few years back. Paige never got on with Scott, so there's always been a bit of tension since he came on the scene."

"Poor Paige." Jess fiddled with the linen napkin in front of her. "How do you …" She trailed off, shaking her head.

"What?"

"It doesn't matter. It's probably an inappropriate question."

"Just ask …"

"I was just wondering how it works financially. Does her mum give you money or something?"

"She gives me the child benefit money. Which is about eighty pounds a month."

"That doesn't sound like much."

"No. But it's fine. She's my niece. I don't mind."

A smile tugged at Jess's lips. "How much did she spend at the shopping centre today?"

He winced. "About three hundred quid. I've been trying not to think about that, so thanks a lot for the reminder."

"Sorry. I bet it really did cheer her up though."

"It better have done. And at least she seems to like me again."

"Nothing like buying your way into a person's affections," Jess joked.

He chuckled. "I don't think it's just the new wardrobe. Having a day out and doing something different probably helped too. We seemed to have got stuck in some kind of stalemate where we just weren't getting on."

"It must've been quite an adjustment for you both when she moved in with you."

"I don't think I realised how difficult it would be. We always got on great when we'd hang out every now and again. Living together is completely different. Plus, sometimes she seems so grown up that I forget she's not. When you had a go at me and told me to let her be a kid, it got me thinking."

"Sorry about that," she murmured.

"No. You were right. I'd never really looked at the situation from her point of view. Her mum essentially chose her new husband over her. They moved down to Glasgow because he'd got a job there."

"Poor kid. At least she's got you. I'm sure she appreciates you taking her in. Even if she doesn't seem very grateful."

"Sorry. I'm going on about my life and my dysfunctional family. Tell me about your family instead. Have you been back to Aberdeen recently?"

She was impressed that he remembered her family were in Aberdeen and spent a while telling him about her most recent visit to catch up with her parents and older sister. Conversation flowed easily over the course of the meal, and she found herself laughing frequently.

By the time they stepped outside the sky had turned midnight blue and a sea of stars twinkled overhead.

"Do you feel like another drink at the pub?" Gary asked.

In no rush to cut the evening short she readily agreed, and they set off in the direction of the Merchant Bar. They hadn't got far when Gary's phone beeped and he pulled it from his pocket. He slowed to a stop as he read the message.

"Everything okay?" Jess asked.

"Yeah." He gave a half-hearted smile and set off walking again. "It's Paige, asking how long I'm going to be. She does this every time I'm out in the evening. I thought it was just one more way for her to annoy me, but she made some comment the other day about finding the house creepy when she's alone, so I think she gets freaked out at night."

"Where's your house?" Jess asked as they continued walking at a slower pace.

"On the road out of Portree to the north. It's set back a bit, through some trees, so you can't see it from the road. It's pretty secluded."

"It definitely sounds a bit creepy." Jess smiled. "If you want to get back and check on Paige, we can get a drink another time instead."

"Do you mind?" he asked, a crease appearing between his eyes.

"No, of course not." She sort of did actually. The evening had been lovely, and she was in no rush for it to end.

"Sorry. I'd love to stay out, but since Paige and I have been getting on again, I'd rather not upset her."

"It's fine. I understand."

Gary insisted on walking her home and it didn't feel like any time at all until they were standing outside her door. "Can I take you out again sometime?" he asked, shifting his weight.

"I'd really like that."

He nodded and glanced around. "I was wondering about something … you know when you came to my work the other day …" Cringing at the reminder, Jess waited for him to get to his point. "You said you were hoping we could be friends?"

"Yes …"

"I just wanted to check – so we don't get our wires crossed – did you mean you only want to be friends?"

She pressed her lips together, hoping she wasn't blushing bright red. "No. I wasn't really thinking of only being friends."

"Okay, good. I was a bit confused by all the arguing and stuff."

"That was just because you called me a stuck-up snob," she said, her voice laced with mirth.

He winced. "Can we forget about that?"

"Why did you think I was stuck-up?"

"I didn't. Not really. I was mostly just put out that you weren't interested in me."

"Mostly?" She was fairly sure *he* was blushing now, but in the dim light it was hard to tell.

"The other times we went out you kept blethering about chemistry and science. I wasn't even sure what you were talking about half the time. I felt slightly inferior, and there were a few times when I thought you rolled your eyes at stuff I said."

"I'm really sorry." There was a definite chance that she'd come across as stuck-up. "I'm not sure why you were put out when I didn't get in touch again. I'd have thought you'd have been happy to be rid of me."

"Nah." He scuffed the toe of his shoe against the path. "I really liked you."

"It was bad timing for me," she said, wishing she could go back in time and shake herself. "I was hung up on someone else, and I couldn't stop thinking about him."

"I heard. At least I don't need to take it personally any more. I thought you just found me utterly boring."

"Definitely not."

"And you're over the other guy now?" he asked.

She suspected he knew exactly who the mystery guy was but appreciated him pretending otherwise. "Yes. Completely." It might have been the wine but she was feeling brave. "I think if I were to go out with anyone else now, I'd only be able to think about you."

"You probably shouldn't go out with anyone else then." As he took a step towards her, butterflies took flight in her stomach.

"I probably shouldn't," she whispered, right before his lips met hers, taking her breath away and making her heart beat erratically.

It seemed like only a moment before he pulled away again. Instinctively, Jess slipped her hands up to his neck and brought his lips back to hers. With his hands on her hips he drew her close, their bodies moulding together and making her wish he wasn't in such a rush to leave.

"I guess you should get going," she murmured when they finally broke apart.

"I suppose I should," he replied, his face still close to hers.

"Can I see you again soon?"

"Yeah." His breath tickled her cheek. "Definitely."

CHAPTER FIFTEEN

Rain was falling in a torrent on Thursday afternoon when Elspeth's mum walked into the empty cafe, shaking her umbrella before closing the door behind her.

"Have you had any customers?" she asked.

"None all day," Elspeth replied.

"Why didn't you close up and go home?"

She shrugged. "The noise of the rain on the roof here is kind of therapeutic." There was something about the view over the loch on bleak days that soothed her. The mountains, which could be so prominent, were hidden by mist and fog, but occasionally you'd still catch a glimpse of them, looming large in the distance.

"Are you okay?" Christine asked, taking a seat opposite her. "You've been very quiet this week."

"Just thinking." She tapped the mug in front of her, the remnants of her coffee stone cold. "I wanted to ask you a favour."

"You already asked me to look after Arran overnight tomorrow."

Elspeth smiled lightly. "Yeah, I know. It's another favour." Nerves fluttered in her stomach. As soon as she told someone her plan, it would make it all real. She'd spent all week chewing over the idea and she still wasn't sure if it was ridiculous.

"Don't keep me in suspense," her mum said, when the silence stretched on.

"You know that old ring in your jewellery box with the blue stone?"

"My grandmother's engagement ring?"

"Aye." A lump formed in Elspeth's throat. "Could I have it?"

Christine gazed at her intently. "What for?"

"I was thinking ..." She sucked in a deep breath as the muscles of her throat tensed so much it was difficult to speak. "I want to ask Rory to marry me."

"Is that what this big date night is all about tomorrow? You're going to ask him then?"

"I think so. I'm just scared he might say no." It was completely irrational; after their recent conversations about the future, she felt as though they were on the same page.

"He loves you. I'm sure he wouldn't say no. Didn't you say he's moved back into the cottage too?"

"Not officially. He's been staying over every night for the past couple of weeks, but I haven't dared draw attention to it in case I jinx it. That's daft, isn't it?"

"If you're nervous about proposing, you could always drop some hints. He'd probably ask you."

"I thought about that, but I want to ask him." Her gaze drifted out through the steamed-up windows to the misty rain hanging over the loch. "Ever since I got pregnant, I always feel as though I'm just stumbling through life without really making plans. I want to marry Rory. I want us to be a proper family and I want to have another baby." Her chin twitched and she flicked her gaze back to her mum, who gave her a gentle smile. "If I ask him, it'll feel like I'm in control of my life for once."

Christine reached over to hug her. "You should ask him then. It's a good idea."

"So can I have the ring?" Elspeth asked, catching a stray tear at the corner of her eye.

"Of course you can. But you don't need a ring to propose – just ask him and then go shopping and choose whatever you want."

"I really love your grandma's ring. I like that it has history." Her lips spread to a wide smile. "She had a happy marriage, didn't she?"

"Aye." Christine nodded. "I think she did. Come on. Let's close up and go and dig it out."

~

"Is this how it's going to be every weekend now?" Ava asked as she and Jess walked down to the pub on Friday night. "You're going to ditch me to hang out with your boyfriend?"

"He's not my boyfriend," Jess said, unable to keep the smile from her face. "And I'm not ditching you."

She cast Jess a sidelong glance. "You don't usually make so much effort for your colleagues."

"I haven't gone to a lot of effort. And I'm definitely not ditching you. Gary said he might call into the pub and say hi, that's all."

"I'm fairly sure you're going to sit at the other side of the pub with him all night."

"I promise I won't."

"It's fine if you do. I like seeing you cheerful. The cloud of gloom and doom hanging over you was getting tedious."

"You make it sound as though I need a man to be happy."

Ava chuckled. "That's exactly what I think."

"Okay. There might be a smidge of truth in that. But is it so bad to want a boyfriend? I realise women are supposed to be content to be alone, but that feels like going against my natural instincts. I would like to be in a relationship. If that makes me anti-feminist or something, so be it." She smiled, thinking of how much she'd enjoyed exchanging messages with Gary over the week. "I'd also like some sex," she whispered as the pub came into sight.

"That I understand! It's been a while for me too. I keep having naughty thoughts about Chris Duffy."

Jess rolled her eyes, not at all surprised that Ava was contemplating something with the sports teacher. The flirting between the two of them wasn't subtle. "I'm surprised you two haven't hooked up already."

"I can't decide if I want to go there. It could end up being awkward, since we work together."

"That's true. If you like him, I think it's worth giving it a go, but if it's just a fling you're after I'm not so sure."

"There's my dilemma. I'm not sure if I really like him or not. Usually, I'd date him to find out, but if I date him and it doesn't work out, I'm stuck having to see him every day."

"You spend enough time with him." Jess stopped outside of the pub. "You'd think you'd be able to figure out if you like him enough to date him."

Ava pulled the door open. "Maybe when you ditch me for Gary this evening, I'll hang out with Chris and pretend I'm on a date with him."

"I'm not going to ditch you."

"I don't believe you for a minute," Ava said, looking pointedly at the far end of the room, where Gary was perched on a bar stool, chatting away to the barman.

Jess's heart rate went into overdrive. "I didn't think he'd be here already."

As though he knew he was being talked about, he turned and looked. His spontaneous smile set butterflies in motion in Jess's stomach.

"Hello," she said when they went over to him.

"Hi." He stood and kissed her cheek. "How are you?"

"Fine, thanks."

He smiled at Ava, then bought them both a drink.

"I suppose I can put up with you stealing my friend if I get free drinks out of it," Ava said as she took a swig of her beer.

"Am I stealing your friend?" Gary asked.

"Yeah. She's going to hang out with you for the evening and leave me to make small talk with the boring bunch."

"I thought they were your friends," Gary remarked, following her gaze to the three tables occupied by their colleagues.

"A couple of them. Mostly they're colleagues and acquaintances."

"Why do you hang out with them then?"

"Habit," Ava told him.

Jess let her eyes roam over the familiar faces at the other side of the room. "Two of them fall into the category of friends for me. Possibly three."

"Is Chris the possible friend?" Ava asked.

"Yeah. Sometimes I think he's all right, and sometimes he annoys the hell out of me."

"I feel the same." Ava took a long sip of her drink. "I suppose I'll leave you lovebirds alone and go and see if I can figure out whether I like Chris or not."

"See you in a bit," Jess said to Ava's retreating form, then turned to Gary. "She has a bit of a crush on Chris but can't decide if she should do anything about it."

"That's the good thing about working with my dad," Gary said. "No romantic drama at work."

"You work with your dad?"

"Yes."

"So it was your dad who I saw when I came to visit you at work last week?" He nodded in reply. "I had no idea you work with your dad."

He gave her a playful smile. "I'm fairly sure I've told you that before."

"Are you ever going to let me forget how awful I was the first times we went out?"

"Maybe one day."

"That's generous of you." She took a sip of her drink to distract herself from her embarrassment about her previous behaviour. "So what's it like, working with your dad? Does he own the place?"

"We're joint owners."

"Do you get on well?"

"Yeah. We're both pretty chilled about the business, which means there's never any stress or drama, but we're probably not as profitable as we could be. Neither of us is overly ambitious. We just like fixing cars."

"It's great that you enjoy your job."

He nodded. "You enjoy teaching, right?"

"Yes. The teaching itself is great. I don't even mind all the lesson plans and marking. What I don't enjoy is the staffroom politics. There are a few teachers who really test my patience."

"Which ones?" he asked, looking in the direction of her colleagues.

"No one here," she said. "The ones who would never come out for drinks with us."

"I suppose that's something to be thankful for. You don't have to deal with them outside of work." He pulled his phone from his pocket and read a message.

"Paige?" Jess asked.

He nodded and slipped the phone away. "Telling me not to be late."

"It's almost like you're the teenager in the relationship and she's the adult."

He smiled widely. "That's exactly how it feels. Except I think I had more freedom when I was a teenager."

"How come Paige didn't move in with your parents if they're nearby?"

"Their place is about a half hour drive away – over on the west of Skye. So it wouldn't have been ideal for school. They don't have a lot of extra space either. And Paige doesn't get on too well with her gran." He shook his head when Jess gave him a questioning look. "It's not a big deal. Just that Paige wasn't keen to live with her."

"Did you ever figure out how to wash women's clothes?"

His cheeks pinked and he smiled bashfully. "Aye. I didn't ruin anything either. Paige was happy."

As she sipped at her drink, the conversation flowed so effortlessly that Jess barely registered time going by. She was on her second drink when she caught Ava glaring at her across the room.

"I reckon I'm going to be in trouble for monopolising you," Gary said. "I should probably leave you to be sociable and go and see what Paige is up to."

Ignoring the pang of disappointment deep in her gut, Jess nodded. "Have you got much planned for the weekend?"

"I'm working tomorrow but if you're free in the evening we could go out for dinner? Paige is going to a friend's house for a movie night, so I won't spend the evening being nagged about getting home before curfew."

"I thought you said she didn't have friends."

"It's a new friend, Sophie. Do you know her?"

"Yes!" Jess beamed. "I put them together for an assignment last week. Sophie's lovely. A bit cheeky but a good kid. Her parents are nice too."

"Were you matchmaking for friends?" he asked, amused.

"I realised the kids always sit with the same friends and work with the same partners. I mixed everyone up. I'm glad Paige is hanging out with Sophie."

"Me too. So do you want to do something tomorrow?"

"I'd love to."

"Great. I'll message you tomorrow to figure out the details." He leaned over and softly brushed his lips against hers. "Have a good night."

"Thanks." She smiled, even though she suspected her night could only go downhill from there.

Ava appeared beside her seconds later. "I told you!"

"I didn't ditch you. I was just about to come and join you."

"You've been chatting to him for two hours!"

"No way." Jess checked the time, surprised to find that it really had been that long. "I'm sorry. I'm a rubbish friend."

"Yeah, you are." Ava raised her eyebrows. "Buy me a drink and I'll forgive you!"

"Deal," Jess said and turned to the barman.

CHAPTER SIXTEEN

By Friday, Elspeth was buzzing with nervous excitement. She paced the kitchen while she waited for Rory to come home from work. Arran was already at her parents' house and would stay there for the night. After chatting it through with her mum, she was feeling much more confident in her decision. The flicker of nerves that he might turn her down refused to leave her, but she was doing her best to ignore it and concentrate on her excitement instead.

Finally, the front door opened and she thought she might burst with anticipation.

"I thought you'd still be at the cafe," Rory remarked.

"Mum said she'd close up so we can leave."

"Where are we going that we need to leave so early?"

"It's a surprise." She grinned as he slipped his arms around her waist. He'd been bugging her all week for clues and she was going to make him wait a little longer. "You'll find out soon enough."

His eyebrows pulled together. "What should I wear? Do I need to put a shirt on?"

"No. Wear whatever you want." She glanced down. "How's your ankle? Can you manage a short walk?"

"Yes. It's bloody freezing out, though. Where are we walking to?"

"I feel like some fresh air and exercise before dinner."

"You're being very mysterious. Can you at least give me a clue as to where we're going?"

"No. Let's just go and then all will be revealed."

"I need to have a shower and get changed."

"You can get changed quickly. Put something comfy on. You don't need to shower."

He dipped his nose in the direction of his armpit. "Are you sure?"

Elspeth put her face against his neck and inhaled deeply. "You smell great. We need to leave soon or it'll be too dark to see where we're walking."

As they strolled along the path beside the loch, Rory gave up on asking where they were going. Instead, he gave Elspeth intermittent questioning looks, which made her giggle every time. They'd just passed the Old Inn when more laughter bubbled out of her.

"Do you remember the time I told you there were dolphins in the loch and you believed me?"

"It's not *that* funny." He paused to look across the water, the mountains clearly visible in the distance. Nearby, the surface of the water was broken by a couple of moorhens, gliding effortlessly along. "The loch links to the sea, so dolphins *could* come in. And at the time I had no idea how much you like to tease."

"I was freaking out that day, trying to work up the courage to tell you about Arran."

"You didn't tell me that night." He took her hand as they continued to amble along. "If I remember rightly, we went to the activity centre and stole a rowing boat."

"I'm fairly sure we only borrowed it."

"Is that where we're going now? For a moonlit boat ride?"

"No chance. Not now I know how bad you are at rowing."

"I was being intentionally bad so you'd be all heroic and help me."

"It was a fun night." She fell silent, imagining what her life would be like if Rory hadn't come for another holiday on Skye. She pushed the thought away, refusing to dwell on it.

"Are we going to the activity centre?" Rory asked, giving her a sidelong glance.

She smiled widely. "Yes."

"Why?"

"You'll see."

After another ten minutes they came to the clearing by the loch which housed ten log cabins belonging to the activity centre. Rory had been staying in cabin number four on his first visit to Skye. He and Elspeth had spent New Year's Eve huddled together on the patio, watching fireworks go off over the loch. It was the night Arran had been conceived.

"What are we doing?" Rory asked as Elspeth led him to the same cabin and produced the key from her pocket.

"I thought a night away might be nice."

"You rented the cabin?"

She nodded as she opened the door. "Tim renovated them recently and I've been wanting to have a nosey."

"Where are we having dinner?" Rory asked, following her inside. They took their shoes off in the hallway and went through to the cosy living room with the kitchenette at the far end.

"Trust you to worry about your stomach." She moved to the kitchen area. "I brought food down earlier. There's a quiche that just needs to go in the oven. And I made salad, and there's a baguette and ham and cheese."

"Sounds way better than a restaurant." Rory put his hands on Elspeth's hips and drew her close. "This was a great idea."

"I'm glad you like it. Can you believe it's been almost six years since the first time we were here?"

"Quite a lot has happened since then." He shifted his weight and looked slightly pained.

"Sit down and put your foot up," Elspeth instructed. "Do you want a beer?"

"Are you going to wait on me all evening?"

"Maybe!" She got drinks and joined him on the couch, sitting sideways to face him.

Rory gulped at his beer and set it on the coffee table. "It's weird being back here," he said, looking around. "The renovations are an improvement. It's all modern and fresh."

"I think Lexie had been nagging Tim to redecorate them for years. Personally, I liked them as they were. It always felt very nostalgic coming back here to find nothing had changed."

Rory sank back into the couch cushions and looked at Elspeth intently. "It's nice to get you alone. I've been wanting to tell you something … but Arran's always around at home so I never find the time."

"What is it?"

A small smiled played at his lips. "Depending on how observant you are, you might have already noticed … but I moved back into the cottage."

Elspeth cracked up laughing. "I did notice you've been there a lot."

"I like being there a lot," he said seriously. "I was thinking I'd move the last of my stuff and tell Mary and Angus that I'm officially moving out of the bunkhouse. If that's okay with you?"

"It's more than okay with me." Her smile stretched wide and she moved to kiss him. "Everything's going to be different this time. I won't mess things up again, I promise."

"You didn't mess things up." He tilted his head. "We had a rough patch and we got through it. It doesn't matter any more."

"I love you so much." She gave him a lingering kiss. "I'm going to start getting the food ready."

"I'll help," he said, standing and following her to the kitchen.

"You should rest your leg."

"It's loads better. Give me jobs to do. I feel bad sitting around while you do everything."

She pulled out a chair at the kitchen table. "Sit there and I'll give you something to do."

"I have an idea. How about I sit here …" He dropped into the chair but snatched at her hand and pulled her onto his lap. "And you can sit here too … and then you can kiss me."

Laughing, she lowered her face to his. As her lips moved against his, she closed her eyes and felt a wave of happiness sweep through her. "I don't think this is a very productive way to get dinner ready," she murmured.

"You might be right," he agreed, his breath tickling her lips. He pulled back, searching her features. "What are you looking so serious for?"

"Just thinking." She raked her fingers through his hair and felt an unexpected wave of emotion. Quickly, she got up and moved to turn the oven on.

"Are you okay?" Rory asked, his eyes following her.

She nodded, swallowing the lump in her throat. "I'm great." She put him to work slicing the baguette while she arranged the rest of the dinner things on the table. Predictably, she'd made too much food, especially since she lost her appetite once it was all ready. She half-heartedly picked at it and tried not to let her mind wander as Rory chatted away.

When he complained that he'd eaten too much, they moved to the couch and lay down together.

"Is everything okay with you?" Rory asked, stroking her hair. "You've gone very quiet."

"I'm fine," she mumbled as her heart kicked into an irregular rhythm.

"Are you tired?"

"No." She pushed herself up and off the couch. "Don't move. I'll be right back."

Her overnight bag was in the bedroom where she'd stashed it that afternoon. The zip whirred as she opened the inner pocket.

She found the worn, leather ring box immediately and closed her fingers around it.

"What are you up to?" Rory said, slinging an arm behind his head as she walked back into the living room.

She perched on the edge of the couch and looked down at him sprawled out. "Close your eyes."

"Why?"

"Just do it," she said, a slight tremor to her voice.

He stared at her for a moment, then did as he was told. Briefly, Elspeth closed her eyes too, taking a deep breath as she tried to get her heart rate under control. Then she uncurled her fingers to look at the small box in her hand.

"Seriously, what's going on?" Rory asked.

"Hang on." She set the box in the middle of his chest. "Okay, open your eyes." As his eyes slowly opened, she panicked and covered the box with her hand. "Wait a second."

"Elspeth! What the heck is going on? You're being weird. What's this?" He tried to peel her fingers from his chest, but she clamped them down.

"I'll show you in a second. I need to tell you something first."

"You're making me nervous."

She blinked back tears. "I keep thinking about what we talked about the other week … about having more kids and what we want from the future. I'd never really thought about it. Since I had Arran it feels as though I just followed this pre-destined path, so I was thinking about what I really wanted for my future…" She paused, and her throat felt painfully tight.

"And?" Rory asked.

Tears filled her eyes as she laughed. "I came up with all these different ideas, but I think I just like working at the cafe and living in Lannick. I'm happy as I am."

"That's good." He put his hand over hers at his chest and gently stroked his thumb across the back of her hand. "Why are you upset?"

"I'm not."

He smiled gently. "You're crying."

"Pretend I'm not," she said, swiping at her cheeks with her free hand. "I'm messing this up."

"Messing what up?"

"I wanted to tell you that when I think about my future, all that really matters is that you're in it. I could live in a different place and have a different job … and I'd be fine … as long as I have you." Her voice broke on the final words and she drew her hand away from Rory's chest.

He plucked the ring box from his chest and sat up as he opened it. "What's this?"

"It was my great grandmother's engagement ring. I've always had my eye on it, and Mum said I can have it."

Rory stared down at it, then opened his mouth as though he was going to say something but didn't.

"Will you marry me?" Elspeth asked, her stomach completely tied in knots.

His eyebrows shot up as he looked at her.

"I know you only just moved back in," she said quickly. "And I realise you said you wanted to take things slow, but I absolutely know what I want and—"

He cut her off, taking her face in his hands. "Yes. I'll marry you." Smiling widely, he wiped tears from her cheeks with his thumbs. "Of course I'll marry you."

Elspeth pressed her lips together and tasted the salt from her tears. "Are you sure?"

"Yes!" He laughed. "I would've asked you if I'd known you were thinking about it. I've thought about asking you about a million times."

"Really?" She tilted her head, pushing her cheek into his palm.

"Yes!" He pulled her against his chest.

"I thought you might say no," she said tearfully.

"No way." He held her tightly for a moment, then pulled

back and found the ring again. "Just to be clear … you'll be the one to wear this, right?"

"Yes." She laughed and held her left hand out until Rory pushed the ring on over her knuckle.

He held her hand as he inspected the sapphire surrounded by tiny diamonds. "I love you so much," he said, his eyes meeting hers again. "I can't believe you just proposed!"

"I liked the idea of getting engaged here."

Rory chewed on his bottom lip. "If someone had told me the first time we were here that we'd end up coming back here to get engaged, I wouldn't have been a bit surprised. But I'd never have believed what would happen between then and now."

"We haven't exactly been predictable. But I'd really like it if we are from now on. Boringly predictable would be good."

Rory grinned. "How about we get married, have a few more kids and live happily ever after?"

Her shoulders shuddered as she laughed. "A *couple* more kids might have to do!"

"I guess I can live with that." He looked at her ring again and beamed as he kissed her.

CHAPTER SEVENTEEN

Elspeth sang to herself while she showered the following morning. She could hear Rory moving around the kitchen when she stepped out of the bathroom with a towel wrapped around her. When the door to the cabin opened, she stopped short and clutched at her towel as a young guy appeared in front of her. He brought a rush of cold air with him, making goose-bumps ripple up Elspeth's arms.

"What are you doing?" she asked, registering that she vaguely recognised him.

His head shot up and his eyes widened. "I'm sorry. I've come to clean. Check-out is at ten so I didn't expect anyone to still be here."

"Lexie said there was no one else booked in so we didn't need to rush to get out."

"You're friends with Lexie?"

"Yes." Elspeth tried to figure out why he was so familiar. "Do you work in the Old Inn too?"

He nodded rapidly. "I just started there a few weeks ago."

"You've probably met my sister, Leana. She works in the pub."

"She's really cool." He rocked on the balls of his feet. "I'm Dale, by the way."

"Nice to meet you. I'm Elspeth."

He pursed his lips. "Are you the artist or the one with the cafe?"

"I have the cafe," she said, smiling.

"That's so cool to have your own cafe. Leana said you make amazing cakes. I want to come and try them sometime."

"You should," Elspeth said as Rory appeared and put an arm around her shoulders. "This is Dale," she told him. "He's working at the Old Inn. And here." She beamed as she introduced Rory as her fiancé.

"It's really good to meet you," Dale said, drumming his fingers against his thigh.

"Are you new on Skye?" Rory asked.

"Yes! But I love it here already. Everyone's so friendly."

"Where are you from?"

"Leeds."

"And you just decided to move to Skye?"

Dale's smile didn't budge. "I've been moving around for a while, trying to find the right place for me, you know?"

"Do you have a lot of family in Leeds?" Elspeth asked.

"No." The bright smile faded. "Not really."

"I bet your parents are missing you," Elspeth said, her motherly instincts kicking in.

"Probably not." He managed a crooked smile. "My mum's not around and I don't get on with my dad."

"I'm sorry," Elspeth said, leaning closer to Rory as she shivered against the freezing air.

"I'll come back later to clean." Dale took a few steps backwards. "Sorry to disturb you."

Elspeth murmured that it was fine as the door closed behind him. "That was weird," she said to Rory.

"Very. He's as shady as anything."

"I thought he was sweet. It's just weird how he's on his own."

"He said he's been moving around for a while, but he doesn't look old enough to make statements like that."

"I think he's had a rough life."

"You got that from a two-minute exchange?" Rory said, chuckling.

"I got that from the fact that he's a teenager without anyone looking out for him. I'm glad Angus has taken him under his wing."

"I got a bad vibe from him." Rory shrugged. "But maybe that was just because he was checking you out. I suppose that's your fault for standing around in a towel."

"I just got out of the shower," she said, grinning. "It's not my fault he walked in without knocking."

"I bet he's glad he didn't knock." Rory pulled her close and bent his head to kiss her.

Elspeth sighed when he moved his lips to her neck. "I thought we were going soon."

"I vote we stay a bit longer," he said, walking her in the direction of the bedroom.

She laughed when her legs hit the bed and she fell backwards. "I guess a little longer would be okay."

~

Leana looked up from pulling a pint as Lexie waddled into the pub on Saturday afternoon. "You look lovely."

"Do I?" Lexie asked, frowning. "I feel like a big fat blob."

"No! You're glowing. Pregnancy suits you. How are you feeling?"

"Pretty good actually. Getting more and more uncomfortable but I can't complain. I'm just getting impatient now."

"Me too. I can't wait to have a baby to cuddle."

Lexie glanced around the room. "It's busy in here. Who's helping you?"

"Dale's around somewhere. I think he's in the kitchen."

"I was just looking for Mum, but I can help out if you need a hand?"

"No. I'm fine." Leana paused to pass two beers across the bar and take the money. "I think Mary's upstairs." She looked thoughtful. "I'm not actually sure. I've been so busy for the last couple of hours that I've lost track. Your dad's definitely out."

"I'll go up and look for her, but give me a shout if you need any help." She lumbered through to the back of the pub and up the stairs, not bothering to knock as she walked into the flat. Hearing a noise in the living room, she wandered in that direction.

She called out a greeting as she pushed the door open. It was hard to know who was more surprised: her or Dale.

"What are you doing here?" she asked as the hairs on the back of her neck stood up.

His eyes darted around the room. "I wanted to leave Angus a note in the office ... about being low on crisps and snacks."

"This isn't the office," Lexie pointed out frostily.

His cheeks flushed bright red. "I was looking for a pen."

"Did you check the desk in the office? There's a whole pot of them."

"I couldn't see any. I must have missed them."

"I take it my mum isn't here?"

"No, she's at the hairdresser."

"So you're just snooping around the flat?"

"No. Honestly, I was looking for a pen."

Angus's heavy footsteps announced his presence a moment before he walked into the room. "What are you two doing slacking off up here while poor Leana does all the work?"

"We're low on crisps," Dale said. "I was going to leave you a note about it in the office."

"I'll add it to the order. Now, go back down and help Leana, will you?"

"Yeah, okay." He scurried away.

"That was weird," Lexie said, sinking onto the couch after he'd left.

"What?" Angus asked.

"He could've just told you when he saw you. Or left a note behind the bar. Are you okay with him coming up to the flat when you're not here?"

"Aye, he's fine." He dropped into the armchair. "I gave him a tour the other day and showed him the office. He's eager to learn about everything. He had a lot of questions about the business side of things. I'd say he's got a head for business."

Lexie's eyes widened. "You didn't let Leana near the office until she'd worked here for about ten years. And you'd known her pretty much all of her life."

"Dale wants to learn. He's a good lad."

Lexie gave a quick shake of the head. "You don't know anything about him. You didn't even check his references."

"I didn't need to. I've been hiring staff for forty-odd years. You develop an instinct about people."

"My instincts say there's something dodgy about him," she admitted. "The whole gap year thing sounds fishy to me."

"How do you mean?"

"I don't know." She couldn't put her finger on it; she just had a bad feeling about him. "Does he ever talk about his family?"

"From what I've gathered he doesn't have a good relationship with his dad. But he hasn't said much and I don't like to pry."

"I presume he'll be going back home for Christmas?" Lexie asked.

Angus tutted and blew out a breath. "I'm supposed to ask him about that. Your mum's keen to draw up a roster for December and sort out who's working at Christmas and

Hogmanay. I imagine he'll be going back to his parents for a visit. Are you still planning on going down to Nick's parents?"

She told him they were, and they chatted idly until Mary arrived half an hour later with her hair freshly cut and styled.

"Leana says it's been busy this afternoon," she said, setting her handbag down beside the couch.

Angus stood and kissed her cheek. "I should probably go down and give them a hand."

"It's all calm now, but I'm sure Leana could do with a break. Send her up here and we can have a cuppa and some girlie time."

Mary had made tea for the three of them by the time Leana came up, thankful to get off her feet for a while. The conversation mainly revolved around pregnancy and babies until they were almost at the bottom of their drinks, then Mary switched the conversation to work.

"I need to sort out the roster for December," she told Leana. "What are your plans for Christmas? Will you be going down to visit Alasdair's family?"

"We'll stay here for Christmas." Leana finished her tea and set the mug on the coffee table. "I think the plan is to go to Edinburgh for a few days over Hogmanay."

"Is there any possibility you can work on Christmas Day? We'd pay you extra of course, but we'll be a bit stuck without Lexie to help out."

"I suppose I could. Alasdair would probably come and prop up the bar for some of the time." A smile broke over her face. "I wonder if I could get the whole family up for Christmas dinner in the pub. That'd be fun."

"It would," Mary agreed. "I think your mum likes to stick to her traditions though."

"Aye, but it's going to be a bit different this year with Elspeth and Arran down in Edinburgh with Rory's family. And I reckon Mum might be happy at not having to cook. I'm going to ask."

"I don't think I like that plan," Lexie said sulkily. "The first time I'm not here for Christmas and you're going to have a big Mackenzie party in the pub! It doesn't seem fair that you'll be having loads of fun while I have a sedate Christmas with Nick and his parents. His brother won't even be there. He's going to his in-laws."

"What if I promise that we won't have any fun?" Leana joked.

Mary nodded solemnly. "And I promise to be on the lookout for anyone having fun. I'll put an immediate end to it. We can make it a rule … no one's allowed to have fun in the pub on Christmas Day. Everyone has to eat their dinner and sit sombrely until it's time to go home."

"Do you think we should advertise it that way?" Leana asked Mary. "Maybe make up some flyers?"

"Shut up!" Lexie said, rubbing the top of her bump as she laughed.

They were all still giggling as they trooped downstairs and into the pub. Angus was leaning on the bar, chatting to Logan and Isla while Dale brought food out to a family at a table by the window.

"What do you think about Christmas dinner in the pub?" Leana asked Isla and Logan. "I'll be working so I thought it might be a laugh if you all have dinner here this year."

"I'm game," Logan said.

"Me too," Isla agreed. "If you're working and Elspeth's down in Edinburgh it'll feel quiet at home."

"I'll see if Mum's up for it," Leana said. "I guess Dad will be keen."

Dale wandered back around the bar, squeezing past Lexie, then standing awkwardly as though he didn't know what to do with himself.

"I can work on Christmas Day if you need me to," he said to Mary.

"I assumed you'd be heading home for a wee while," she told him.

"No. I'll be here so I'm happy to work."

Mary looked at him in surprise. "Your parents must be missing you. You should get back and visit them."

"I'd rather stay here. Is it okay if I work? I won't have anything else to do."

Lexie felt slightly uncomfortable at all the sympathetic looks he received.

"If you want to work, that's great," Angus said cheerfully. "It sounds as though we might be busier than usual if the Mackenzies are here."

"Are you sure your parents aren't expecting you?" Mary said to Dale. "Your poor mother must be missing you."

"No." Dale's cheeks flushed. "My mum won't be expecting me."

"Aren't you close?" Angus asked.

Dale's gaze darted to Angus and his jaw worked furiously before he found any words. "No. Mum's … erm … we're not … I mean …" His eyes glazed over for a moment. "She died."

Leana broke the silence by murmuring a few sympathetic words, which everyone else joined in with.

"Did you lose her recently?" Mary asked, giving his arm a rub.

"Pretty recently, yeah." He looked at Angus with wild eyes. "Would you mind if I leave early today? I've got a headache and it's getting worse."

"You get off if you need to," Angus said in his deep baritone.

"Sorry." Dale's eyes dropped to his shoes as he shuffled past them all.

Logan reached a hand out to stop him. "I lost my dad when I was about your age," he said gently. "If you ever want to chat, let me know. I know how difficult it is to lose a parent."

"I'm fine. Thanks though." He bolted for the door.

"Poor kid," Isla said after he'd gone.

"Do you think I should go after him?" Logan turned to look at the door. "I feel bad for him."

"I think he wanted to be alone," Leana said. "It might be best to give him some space."

"I wonder what the situation with his dad is," Mary mused. "You'd think he'd want to spend Christmas with him."

"If it's the first Christmas without his mum, he might want a complete change," Logan said.

"We'll have to keep an eye on him," Angus said. "Try to make sure he has a good Christmas."

CHAPTER EIGHTEEN

"Are you ever going to tell me where we're going?" Jess asked as she walked with Gary towards the harbour at Portree. All he'd told her was to be ready at 6 p.m. and dress warm. When he'd picked her up they'd set off on foot, but he still refused to say where they were going.

"You'll find out soon." He gave her a quick sidelong glance. "I hope you'll be warm enough."

"I thought we were going for dinner? Surely we're not eating outside at this time of year. It's December next week." She was wearing a winter coat along with a hat, scarf and gloves, but she still didn't fancy spending too much time outside.

He took her hand and grimaced. "I'm getting a bit nervous that you're not going to like my plans."

"If they involve eating in the freezing cold, I'm nervous too."

He stopped and raised a flirty eyebrow. "I'll keep you warm. I promise."

Smiling, she pushed on her toes to kiss him. "Dinner outside is starting to sound more appealing."

"Wait there for a minute. I'll be right back."

He nipped inside the fish and chip shop behind them.

Through the window, she saw him shake hands with the guy behind the counter, then take a bag from him before walking back outside.

"Are we eating fish and chips?" she asked.

He took her hand and continued along the harbour. "Maybe."

"If we keep walking this way, we're going to run out of land."

"That's kind of the point." He stopped at the top of the harbour steps and nodded to one of the sightseeing boats that did tours of the island. It was all lit up with fairy lights.

"This is where we're eating?" she asked, following Gary down the steps until they came level with the boat.

"Aye. A friend of mine owns it." He stepped onboard, then offered her his hand. "He said I could borrow it."

"Is it always covered in fairy lights or was this your handiwork?"

"I'd really like to take the credit." He slipped an arm around her waist and drew her close. "But the guy who owns the boat did it. He organised a romantic meal on the boat for his girlfriend's birthday yesterday."

"Cute."

"Yeah. I'm afraid you just get fish and chips, but I thought we could at least use the romantic setting."

"It's perfect," she said, giving him a lingering kiss.

"I've got wine too." He untangled himself from her and moved to the table in the centre of the deck. Beneath it was a bag containing a bottle of white and a couple of glasses. He lit a candle in the centre of the table, then set about pouring wine and unpacking the takeaway dinner.

Jess sat opposite him, resting her leg against his under the table. Closing her eyes for a moment, she registered the peaceful sound of boat masts clanging and the gentle slap of water against the harbour wall.

"What do you think about eating outside now?" Gary asked, handing her a glass of wine.

"I'm really happy you told me to dress warmly." She pulled her hat further over her ears, then tapped her glass against Gary's. "But dinner on the water was a great idea."

As usual, time slipped by unnoticed as they chatted and ate. It wasn't until she began to shiver that she realised the sky had turned pitch black. The only remaining light came from the fairy lights, a sliver of moon overhead and the faint glow of nearby streetlights. All of it was reflected on the ripples of the water.

"Do you want to go somewhere else?" Gary asked. "We've finished the wine and you look perished."

"I'm not that cold," she lied, wrapping her arms around herself. Gary looked at her dubiously. "Okay, I'm freezing, but I'm still not keen to go anywhere else. It's beautiful here."

Standing, Gary took her hand and led her to the padded seat that ran around the edge of the deck. When he sat down, he pulled her close beside him.

The heat from his body warmed her immediately, while also making her stomach all fluttery. Tilting her head back onto his shoulder, she pulled his arms tighter around her and looked up at the glittering stars overhead.

"This was a lovely idea," she said after a moment, turning to face him without putting any distance between them. "Thank you." It was a long time since a guy had gone to any effort for her, and it left her feeling a little emotional. The wine was probably to blame for that too, but everything felt utterly perfect.

"You're welcome." He pushed a strand of hair from her face before he kissed her. While her lips explored his, she forgot all about the cold. It was only when he finally drew back that she shivered again.

"You're freezing," he said. "Let's go and warm up somewhere. It's still early. We could walk up to the pub if you want?"

So long as the evening wasn't over yet, she didn't care where they went.

Gary did a quick tidy up and switched the fairy lights off before helping her back onto dry land. They were wandering past the colourful buildings which lined the harbour when his phone began to ring.

"It's Paige," he said before he answered it.

"Can you pick me up from Sophie's house?" she asked loudly.

Gary moved the phone from his ear and tapped the screen, apparently trying to turn the volume down but only making the static noise louder.

"I thought you were going to walk home?"

"I was," she huffed. "But Sophie's parents don't want me walking home alone in the dark. They said I should get you to pick me up or her dad can drop me off."

Gary frowned at the phone, apparently giving up on the volume settings. "Get her dad to drop you off then. I'm out with Jess."

"I don't want him to drop me off," she complained.

"Why not?"

"Because it's embarrassing," she snapped. "They live in a nice house with nice things and a garden. They're normal. I don't want them to see where I live. And if he drops me off he might figure out that there's no one at home and I don't know when anyone will be coming home. They'll think it's weird. They actually supervise their kids. Can you please come and pick me up?"

"I guess so." He sounded amazingly calm for someone who'd just got a dressing down from a fourteen-year-old. Jess was starting to see why some of her teachers had a problem with her attitude.

"I'll be about ten minutes or so," he told her.

"Don't bring Jess. Having my uncle turn up with his new girlfriend who's also our teacher might be more embarrassing than people seeing where I live."

Gary winced as he told her he'd be there soon.

"Sorry," he said when he ended the call.

Jess shrugged. "I take it we're not going to the pub?"

"I'm really sorry. I thought she'd just walk home."

"Does she always speak to you like that?" Jess asked, sounding more judgemental than she'd intended.

He didn't reply and the atmosphere turned decidedly frosty as they ascended the steep road from the harbour.

"Are you okay getting home alone?" Gary asked, stopping where the road levelled off.

"Yeah."

"Sorry," he said again.

"Paige was really rude to you on the phone, you know?"

"I know. But she's having a rough time at the moment. She takes it out on me."

"You shouldn't let her get away with it."

"The more I push back, the worse she gets. I've found it's best to ignore her when she's grumpy with me."

"It doesn't seem fair when you've taken her in and had your life disrupted. All you get in return is attitude and abuse."

He put his hands at her hips, standing squarely in front of her. "You're the one who reminded me that she's a kid and I can't expect her to be grateful."

"I know." She rested her forehead against his. "That was before I realised her attitude would interfere in my dating life."

He bit his lip and looked at her in amusement.

"Sorry," she said. "I didn't mean to sound as grumpy as Paige. I'm just disappointed that our evening got cut short."

"Me too." He kissed her deeply. "I'll make it up to you. Paige's mum's coming up next weekend, so I'll have a teenager-free weekend."

"Is she staying with you?"

"No. Her husband's coming too and he's not my biggest fan. They've rented a holiday cottage for the weekend. Paige will stay with them."

Jess bit her tongue to refrain from commenting on the fact that they could afford to rent a holiday cottage but couldn't give Gary more to help with the cost of having Paige live with him.

"Maybe I can finally see your house next weekend?" she asked.

He nodded. "I think it's about time."

The thought of having uninterrupted time with him made her stomach tingle with anticipation.

"The house isn't as bad as Paige makes out, by the way," he told her.

"Really? Because she seems pretty offended by the place."

"It's kind of a mess." His arms tightened around her waist. "I've got so used to it that it barely registers any more."

"You have a week to tidy it up."

"I'll see what I can manage." He licked his lips before kissing her again. "I'll talk to you soon," he said, then released her and set off in the opposite direction.

CHAPTER NINETEEN

Elspeth had just turned the sign on the door to closed, when Isla waltzed into the cafe on Sunday afternoon.

"Congratulations!" she cooed, wrapping Elspeth in a hug before backing off to inspect the ring. "It's so cool that you asked him. Were you nervous?"

"Terrified," she said, watching the light bounce off the stones in her ring. "Thank goodness he said yes."

"I'm really pleased you two sorted everything out."

"Me too." Elspeth made a start on wiping down the tables. "It's such a relief."

"Have you got any wedding plans yet?"

"No. We haven't even talked about it. I don't want to wait long though. Maybe in the spring. Something simple."

"You should have it on the garden beside the loch. It'd be beautiful. That's what I'd have done if I'd had the choice."

Elspeth grinned. "Are you ever going to forgive Logan for forcing you to have that beautiful wedding in the castle?"

"I suppose it was all right in the end! What happened to my jewellery, by the way?"

"What jewellery?" Elspeth asked, focused on removing a

coffee stain from the tabletop and thinking they were still talking about weddings.

"The revolving stand full of my jewellery that's usually beside the till. You shouldn't move it. Loads of customers end up picking something while they're waiting to pay or checking out the cakes on display."

"Yeah, I know." Confused, Elspeth looked over at the till and the empty countertop beside it. "I didn't move it."

"Well it's not here."

Moving towards the till, Elspeth glanced all around, though she wasn't sure where else it would possibly be. If it had fallen, she'd hardly have missed the crash.

"It was here earlier," she said, scanning all the surfaces. "A woman bought a pair of earrings. I remember she spent ages picking them out."

"Maybe Mum took it to clean it or something?" Isla suggested.

Elspeth shook her head. "I've been on my own all day. Mum's out with friends."

"It can't have just disappeared!"

"Of course it can't have," Elspeth said exasperated. "Do you think someone stole it?"

"No way. How could someone take it without you noticing?"

"It's not that big. I guess someone could have taken it while I was in the kitchen or something. What else could have happened to it?"

"Oh my God!" Isla screeched. "I just restocked it yesterday. It was completely full."

"Sorry." Elspeth pulled her phone from her pocket. "I'm going to call the police and report it."

Isla took a seat and stared up at Elspeth as she explained the situation over the phone. "Is someone going to come and take a statement?" she asked when Elspeth ended the call.

"Aye." She leaned on the counter, staring at the space where the jewellery stand should be. "They said an officer will be over shortly."

"Were you busy today?" Isla asked.

"Fairly. There were a few groups of hikers here over lunchtime." She racked her brain, running through the day in her head. "Dale was here for a while. I wonder if he noticed anything strange."

"Who?"

"The lad who's working at the pub. Leana had been telling him about my cakes, so he came to try them. Stayed for ages. Have you met him? He's very chatty. I had a lull in customers and he asked me about a million questions."

"He seems like a sweet kid," Isla said. "Sounds like he's had a rough time of it. He got all upset in the pub yesterday … his mum died recently. He seems a bit lost."

Elspeth took a seat beside Isla. "Today he kept going on about how lovely Angus and Mary have been. It seems as though he loves working in the pub." Her mind whirred to seeing him at the activity centre. "Did you say his mum died?"

"Yeah. Why?"

She shook her head. "He told me and Rory that he wasn't in touch with her."

"Hard to be in touch with someone if they're dead."

"Isla!"

"What?" She raised her eyebrows. "It's true, isn't it?"

"It's a bit odd to say he's not in touch with her if she's dead." She shrugged. "I suppose he didn't want to talk about it. We'd only just met him."

Her attention was drawn to the door as it opened. A uniformed police officer stepped inside.

"That was quick," Isla remarked.

"I was up at the Lannick distillery," he said, wiping his boots on the mat. "You're not going to like this, but someone stole a load of your jewellery from the gift shop there earlier today too. Along with some other stuff."

Isla dropped her chin to her chest and sighed heavily. Then Elspeth settled in to answering the officer's questions as best she could.

~

Lexie had six weeks until her due date and was getting close to admitting that working at the pub was getting too much for her.

"Are you okay?" Dale asked. He was taking a break and sitting at the bar to eat his dinner.

"I'm fine." It irritated her immensely that her dad had given Dale instructions to keep an eye on her. The way he watched her was unnerving.

"Are you sure?" he asked. "You look like you can't breathe properly."

She sucked in a deep breath. "Having a small human take up the space where your lungs should be does that to you."

"Maybe you should sit down for a while."

"I'm fine," she hissed, then moved to pick up Dale's phone from the shelf at the back of the bar when it vibrated its way towards the edge. Automatically, she checked the screen as she passed it to him, then watched while he declined the call from his dad. "You could've answered it," she said. "It might be urgent."

He took a sudden and profound interest in the food in front of him, idly pushing the chips around before popping one into his mouth.

"Do you talk to him much?" Lexie asked.

He shook his head, then stood abruptly and disappeared to the kitchen with his plate. It was another thing that made her wary of him. He'd ask her a hundred questions about her life while they worked, but as soon as she asked him anything he clammed up.

"Hi!" she called to Keith as he wandered in looking weary. "Everything okay?"

"Aye. Just an annoying afternoon. Someone stole a bunch of stuff from the gift shop at the distillery so I spent a good while with the police." He slipped onto a stool, shaking his head. "It turns out someone stole a load of Isla's jewellery from the cafe today too, so the policeman left us and went straight down there."

"Did Elspeth see anyone?" Lexie asked in surprise.

"No. She just noticed the jewellery was gone at the end of the day. She didn't notice anything unusual."

Lexie poured him a beer and set it in front of him. "What was taken from the distillery?"

"Funnily enough, it was mostly Isla's jewellery. And a few other bits and pieces. Nothing of great value." He took a few gulps of beer and let out a satisfied sigh. "They didn't go near the whisky. It was all small things. Notepads, key rings, that sort of thing. Whatever someone could quickly stash into a backpack, I reckon."

"That's terrible. And is Elspeth okay? It must have given her the creeps knowing that someone stole from right under her nose."

"She sounded all right on the phone. Isla was there with her when the officer interviewed her."

"Aren't there cameras at the distillery? Can you see anything on that?"

Keith shook his head. "I looked through it with the police officer, but the camera only covers the door. There are a few people coming in and out with backpacks, but that's pretty normal. Plus, it was raining on and off this afternoon so most of the people coming in have their heads down and hoods up. You can't make out much at all."

"I hope they find whoever did it." A gust of cold air blew in as the door opened, and she forced a smile for the police officer who walked in. She knew him vaguely. "Hiya, Tony."

He tipped his head in greeting. "Is your dad around?"

"Yeah. I'll fetch him for you." She was all set to head

upstairs but almost collided with her dad in the corridor at the back. "Tony Fields is here to see you," she told him. "There's been some thefts today at the distillery and at Elspeth's cafe. I suppose they're warning local businesses to be vigilant." She followed when he walked into the bar and greeted Officer Fields.

"I was hoping to have a quick word with you in private," Tony said.

After ushering him through to the back of the pub, Angus arrived back again a couple of minutes later. "Where's Dale?" he asked Lexie.

"There." She pointed across the pub to where he'd paused in collecting glasses to chat to a couple of regulars.

"Can you manage on your own for ten minutes?"

"Yes," Lexie replied, then watched in confusion as Angus went and said something to Dale. They both walked quickly through to the back of the pub.

"What's all that about?" Keith asked.

"Your guess is as good as mine."

Five minutes later, Leana breezed in for her shift. "I just spoke to Elspeth," she said in a rush. "I don't understand how someone can so brazenly walk into the cafe and steal jewellery. And at the distillery too," she added, resting her hand on her dad's shoulder. "What's the world coming to?"

"My dad and Dale are upstairs talking to the police now," Lexie said quietly.

"Dale was at the cafe today," Leana said, slipping behind the bar. "That'll be why they want to speak to him."

"Do you think he did it?" Lexie said in a rush.

Leana looked at her as though she'd gone mad. "Of course not. They just wanted to know if he saw anything. Why would anyone think Dale is the thief?"

"Because he was at the scene of the crime," Lexie said. Surely that was obvious.

"There's no way he did it." Leana's features tensed. "You can't actually think that?"

"I don't know." Lexie shrugged, then felt her cheeks heat up when Dale reappeared. Hopefully he hadn't heard her.

"Is everything all right?" Leana asked, putting a hand on his arm. "Did you manage to tell the police anything from the cafe today?"

"I felt really useless," he said, focusing on Leana. "I wish I'd taken more notice of what was going on around me."

"Why would you?" Leana said sympathetically. "No one expects something like that to happen. Especially not around here."

Dale pressed his lips together. "I remember a woman was looking at the jewellery right before I left. The police officer said that at least helps them with a timeline. I wish I could have been more helpful."

"It sounds as though you *were* helpful," Leana said kindly.

Lexie hung around until the police officer left and then went upstairs and found her parents in the living room.

"Is Dale a suspect in these robberies?" she asked bluntly as she sank onto the couch.

Her dad coughed on a humourless laugh. "No. What makes you say that?"

"Because Tony questioned him about it."

"As a possible witness," Mary said, "not because anyone thinks he did it."

"What if he *did* do it?" Lexie said.

Her dad rubbed his hands across his face as he sighed. "What nonsense have you got in your head now?"

"I've seen him acting suspiciously around the pub. One time he was asking about the safe, then I caught him snooping around up here."

"Right." Angus rolled his eyes. "So, Dale's committed some petty thefts at local businesses as a prelude to his big pub heist?"

"You don't seem to be taking me seriously."

"I don't think you should go around accusing Dale," Mary said, patting her hand. "He's been making such an effort to be a part of the community. He's not been here long but he's well liked."

"Perhaps that's all a plan to gain people's trust so no one will suspect him. You have to admit it's quite a coincidence that we have a newcomer in the village and a few weeks after he arrives, crimes start happening."

"Aye," Angus grumbled. "I'd say it is a coincidence. And that's all it is."

"So you won't even entertain the possibility that—"

"No. We won't," Angus interrupted her. "And you need to stop making wild accusations. You've been wary of Dale since he first walked through the door. I don't know if it's your hormones or what, but you're being very irrational."

"Oh, great!" Lexie stood up. "Everything I say is the hysterical ramblings of a pregnant woman, is it?"

Angus threw his hands up. "I didn't say that."

"You pretty much did," Lexie snapped. "I'm going home." She swung back around when her dad called out to her.

"Just so you know. Rory called earlier to say he's moving out of the bunkhouse. I thought I'd offer the place to Dale."

Lexie rolled her eyes and mumbled her disapproval as she walked away.

CHAPTER TWENTY

"When does your dirty weekend officially start?" Ava asked after dinner on Thursday evening.

Jess loaded the dishes into the dishwasher, then went to sit back at the kitchen table. "Don't call it that," she objected half-heartedly.

"Why not? Paige is away for the weekend. Don't tell me you won't spend the entire weekend in Gary's bed?"

Jess felt her cheeks burn as her lips pulled to a wide smile. "Hopefully some of the weekend."

"When does Paige leave?"

"I'm not exactly sure. Gary didn't know when her mum was arriving when I spoke to him yesterday."

Her phone began to vibrate on the table and she peered at the screen. "Speak of the devil."

"Maybe Paige is already out of the way and he wants you to go over to his place immediately."

Jess's stomach flipped at the thought. As she swiped at the screen to answer the call, she stood and wandered to the kitchen window.

"I have a small problem," Gary told her, causing her stomach to cease with its gymnastics.

"What?" she asked.

"Donna can't come up this weekend after all, but Paige is desperate to see her so I said I'd drive her down to Glasgow for the weekend."

"And you'll stay in Glasgow with her?"

"Yeah. It wouldn't be worth dropping her off and coming back."

"No." It was a long way to go for a weekend anyway.

"I'm really sorry to postpone our plans."

"It's okay," she said weakly. "When will you leave?"

"I'll pick Paige up from school tomorrow afternoon and go straightaway."

Jess nodded. There wasn't much she could say, and she was desperate to get off the phone so he might not realise how upset she was. "We can do something next week."

"Yeah. I'll give you a call over the weekend."

"Great. Talk to you soon." She ended the call and sank back onto the kitchen chair.

"What did he say?" Ava asked.

"He cancelled on me."

"No way. How come?"

"He has to take Paige to Glasgow for the weekend." Jess laid her arms on the table and rested her head on them. "Do you know what this feels like? When I liked Rory and he was constantly chasing after Elspeth."

"This is absolutely not the same. Gary isn't running around after his ex. He's looking after his niece. From what I can tell, he really likes you. There's just a lot going on in his life at the moment. He has a fourteen-year-old living with him. Of course that's going to complicate things. You need to be flexible, that's all."

"You're right." She reached for her phone. "I don't want to wait until next week to see him."

"What are you doing?" Ava asked.

"Being flexible," she replied and hit dial on his number. As it rang, it occurred to her there was probably a fine line between flexible and desperate. Hopefully she was staying on the correct side of the divide.

She swallowed hard when he answered. "I was just thinking," she said. "Since I won't see you over the weekend, are you free for a drink tonight?"

His hesitation made her think she might have crossed the line to needy and desperate.

"I'm in the middle of helping Paige with her homework … hang on a sec …" His voice became muffled and indecipherable as he spoke to Paige. "I'm really sorry," he said, his voice clear again. "I told her I'd help and I don't know how long it's going to take." Again, he asked her to wait, then sounded as though he was moving around. "I was just moving out of Paige's hearing. I don't think she actually needs help; she's just being weird about me going out."

"Don't worry about it. It was only a thought."

"I'd really like to see you. I think Paige is upset about her mum cancelling her plans to come up here. Hopefully seeing her at the weekend will help."

"I hope so," Jess said. "It's good of you to take her down there."

"Quite annoying actually. I'd much rather hang out with you." He paused. "Why don't you come over here this evening? Paige will be around, but we can have a drink and hang out."

"That sounds good."

"Oh." He sounded suddenly uncertain. "My place is kind of a mess. You'll have to squint and ignore it!"

"How about I give you an hour to tidy up?"

He laughed loudly. "You could give me a month and I'd still struggle. Come whenever you want. I'll send you the location. You can't see the house from the road and there isn't really a driveway … more of a dirt track. If you have any problems finding it, give me a call."

. . .

When Gary sent her the location she was surprised by how close it was. After some deliberation she decided to go on foot so she could have a drink and stopped at the shop to buy a few bottles of beer.

Nearing where she thought the house would be, she pulled her phone out to check she'd got the location right. After walking a few more metres, a gap appeared in the trees and an uneven dirt track threaded through them. Thankfully she was wearing trainers or the rugged terrain might have been a challenge. As soon as she walked beyond the tree line she saw Gary's car parked in front of a bright white house with scaffolding hugging one side. The step outside the front door was made up of a row of red bricks which had sunk into the muddy earth. She put a foot on them and reached up to knock on the wooden door.

"Hi," Gary said as he opened it wide. "Did you find it okay?"

"Yeah. Fine."

He stepped back and beckoned for her to come in. "Did you walk?"

"Yes. I fancied a beer." She held the bag out to him as she wiped her feet on the mat, then registered the layer of dust and dirt that covered the stone floor of the kitchen.

"Keep your shoes on," Gary said brightly. "I need to do something about the driveway one of these days so we're not constantly walking mud in. For now I've just accepted that I'll be living in a mess for a while."

"It's really nice though." The kitchen looked brand new and was stylish and homely, though the bare plaster on the walls was obviously waiting to be painted. In one corner, paint tins were stacked beside a bucket filled with assorted paint brushes. In the middle of the room was a solid wood table, where Paige sat bent over a load of papers. When Jess smiled at her in greeting, the corner of her mouth twitched but it was more of a scowl than a smile.

"The place is a dump," she grumbled.

Jess turned to Gary. "On the way over here I started to worry that maybe you were a complete slob or a hoarder or something."

"No, it's just a work in progress." He flipped the tops off two of the beers and passed her one.

"How long have you lived here?" She wandered further into the room, taking it all in. Beside the open-plan kitchen was a staircase. Beyond that, the room turned the corner and she peeked around at the living room with a fireplace on one wall and patio doors at the far end. The bare floors were as dusty as the kitchen floor and the walls were unfinished too.

"I bought it two years ago and moved in about a year ago," Gary said. "I got it for a good price, but it needed a lot of work. Some guy was trying to build it on the cheap and the building company he used had been messing him around. He ran out of money before they finished and just wanted a quick sale."

"What state was it in when you bought it then?" she asked, moving back into the kitchen.

"Obviously a terrible state," Paige said, "since Gary thinks it's all right now."

"Hey!" He leaned against the counter and grinned. "It is looking good now. The only things left to do are cosmetic. There were no windows when I bought it and the roof wasn't properly insulated. Oh, and there was no kitchen." He smiled at Jess. "I've had to do it up bit by bit. Whenever I can afford to do more, I do something else. My best friend Logan is a painter and decorator so that's handy. He's done a lot of work for me. The two of us painted the outside of the house recently."

"I bet it will be gorgeous when it's all finished."

"If it's ever finished," Paige said as she began to collect up her papers and books.

"What are you working on?" Jess asked. "Anything I can help with?"

"It's an English project. We have to make posters and programmes for a theatre production."

"How are you getting on with it?"

"Fine." She scooped up her things. "I'll go upstairs and get out of your way."

"You don't have to," Jess said. "I'm really happy to help if you want? There's got to be some perks to being friends with a teacher, right?"

Paige raised an eyebrow and shook her head before disappearing up the stairs.

"Why do I get the impression I'm not her favourite person?" Jess asked.

Gary walked over and lightly kissed her. "Don't take it personally. I get the impression she doesn't like people in general at the moment."

"Is me being here going to cause issues?"

Gary set his beer on the table and slipped his arms around her waist. "If it does, Paige is just going to have to get used to it."

Jess tilted her face to meet his gaze. "I don't want to make things more difficult for Paige."

"Honestly, she's had a bad attitude for years. It's annoying, but there's only so much I can pander to her moods. I can't give up my social life and be constantly at her beck and call." He pushed her hair from her face. "I'm glad you came over."

"Me too." She closed her eyes as he kissed her.

When they broke apart he led the way through to the living room. Jess took her shoes off and pulled her legs under her on the couch.

"Are you warm enough?" Gary asked. "Paige is always complaining that the house is cold and gets huffy with me when I tell her to put more clothes on."

"It's a bit chilly," she admitted wrapping her arms around her middle.

"I can light a fire. It'll be toasty in no time." He crouched at the fireplace, where logs were already arranged in the grate.

"It'll be lovely here once it's all renovated."

Gary nodded as he lit a match and held it against the kindling. "I'm going to get the garden landscaped and put decking all along the back of the house. You can't tell now, but the view over the loch is beautiful."

"I imagine it's nice to do the house up yourself and make everything exactly how you like it."

He chuckled as he came to sit beside her. "That's what I thought when I bought the place. It's starting to feel like a never-ending project now."

"You'll get there."

"I always have plans to get stuck into decorating in the evenings, but then I never have the energy after being at work all day. Progress has definitely slowed since Paige moved in too."

"It must feel good to own your own place. I like where I live, but renting makes it feel temporary. It doesn't really feel like home."

"Do you think you'll stay on Skye?" he asked, putting an arm around her as she snuggled closer beside him.

"I've honestly no idea. I love it here and I enjoy my job. I have no plans to leave. I'll just see what happens I suppose. Have you always lived here?"

"Aye." He took a swig of his beer. "I can't imagine living anywhere else."

"Have you travelled much?"

He nodded. "I've seen a lot of the Highlands."

Laughter burst from her. "Have you ever left the Highlands?"

"Yes. I've been to Edinburgh a couple of times, and Glasgow."

"Have you ever left Scotland?"

"I've never felt the need. Why, have you found anywhere better?"

Turning, she caught the twinkle of amusement in his eyes. "I haven't actually."

"That's good to hear. I don't have to contemplate leaving." He stretched his legs out and slouched further into the couch. "I imagine you've been around a bit?"

Amused by the teasing in his voice, she told him all about the holidays she'd been on and travelling she'd done. He seemed impressed as he asked about the various places, and she happily regaled him with stories while the logs crackled in the fireplace.

After two hours the fire was all but burnt out, and they'd switched from talking to kissing and from sitting to lying. Gary lay half on top of her with his thigh wedged between her legs. The slow kisses had been building in intensity and her skin felt hypersensitive as his hands explored beneath her top. As his hips pushed into hers, she let out a low moan, which was interrupted by Paige clearing her throat loudly.

The urge to jump apart from Gary was hindered by the fact that she was pinned under his weight and his hand was caught in her bra. Finally, he freed himself and pulled her top back into place as he sat up.

"I thought you'd be asleep by now," he said to Paige.

"*Hoped* I would, more like. Sorry to interrupt." She sounded anything but sorry.

Gary checked his watch. "Why are you still up?"

"I thought you'd look over my homework when Miss Gibson had gone home. I didn't realise she was staying over."

"I'm not," Jess said, sitting up and smoothing her hair down. "I was just about to leave."

"It didn't look like it." Paige sighed loudly, then glared at Gary. "I have to hand my project in tomorrow and you said you'd help me with it."

"I did help you," he said. "It was practically finished, wasn't it?"

"I wanted you to look at it when it was completely finished."

"I'll come and look at it in a minute."

"It doesn't matter any more. I don't even know why I put so much effort into it." She turned and stomped up the stairs. "It's not as though anyone cares whether I get good grades or not."

Gary dropped his chin to his chest and ran his hands over his face. "Sorry about that."

"It's fine." Jess pushed her feet into her shoes as she stood.

Standing beside her, Gary took her face in her hands to kiss her. "I wish you could stay."

"That definitely wouldn't go down well with Paige. And I have to be up early, so I should be going anyway."

"Thanks for coming over," he said, walking her to the door. "Are you okay getting home?"

"Yes. Fine." Opening the door, it occurred to her that making it back to the road would be the biggest challenge, but there was just enough light from the house for her to pick her way over the uneven ground. "I hope Paige isn't too annoyed about me being here. Have a good weekend in Glasgow."

He told her to have a good weekend too and kissed her again before she set off for home. Knowing she wouldn't see him over the weekend left her with a heavy feeling in her chest, and she reminded herself to be grateful that she'd met someone who she was excited about spending time with. And who seemed to feel the same way about her.

CHAPTER TWENTY-ONE

"How was work?" Lexie asked when Nick arrived home.

"Fine." He dropped his backpack and bent to kiss her cheek and run a hand over her belly as she leaned back in the chair at the kitchen table. "Did you hear about the thief striking again?"

"No. Where?"

"A couple of gifts shops in Portree yesterday afternoon. Same thing: they just swiped a bunch of stuff. Nothing of great value, just small items."

Lexie rubbed at her belly. "I don't think Dale was working yesterday," she mused.

"What?" Nick pulled a chair out and sat down.

Lexie hadn't mentioned her suspicions about Dale to Nick. After the reactions from her parents, she'd thought it best to keep it to herself. But more than a week had gone by and she couldn't get the idea out of her head. "I think it's suspicious how he was at the cafe right before the jewellery went missing. And that all this is happening since he arrived."

Nick screwed his face up. "You don't really think he'd do that, do you?"

"I don't know. I just think there's something not right about him. I went to visit Elspeth earlier and she mentioned that Dale had told her that he doesn't see his mum much … which is a different story to what he told us."

"His mum died recently. And he's clearly struggling with it …"

"Is he?" Lexie asked. "He doesn't come across as someone who's grieving to me." She thought about how he'd reacted to the phone call from his dad the other day and wondered if she was being unfair.

"Everyone grieves differently," Nick said. "Just because he puts on a brave face doesn't mean he isn't hurting. Who knows what's going on in his head? As far as I can see he's a slightly messed-up kid who's trying hard to fit into a new place."

Lexie chewed on her thumbnail. "I have a weird feeling about him. He's annoyingly cheerful and chatty one minute, then clams up and gets all brooding."

"Because he's going through a lot. You should give him the benefit of the doubt."

Lexie stared out of the window as rain began to fall in a fine mist. "I wonder if Keith would let me look at the CCTV footage from the distillery. He said it was difficult to make people out, but maybe if he knew who to look for …"

"Are you serious?" Nick asked, resting his forearms on the table. "You can't go around playing detective just because you're bored. And you definitely can't tell anyone your suspicions about Dale. Mostly for your own sake, because you sound paranoid and neurotic."

"Now you sound like my dad, blaming everything on pregnancy hormones. I have a gut feeling about this. I'm telling you there's something not right about Dale."

"Maybe I should invite him over for dinner," Nick said.

Lexie puffed her cheeks out and managed to contain a laugh, which she was sure would come out sounding completely manic. "Why would you invite him over for dinner when I've just told you I have a bad feeling about him?"

"Because I think you should get to know him better so you get over your crazy ideas about him."

"They're not crazy," she said calmly. "When it turns out he's the thief, both you and Dad are going to owe me an apology for not taking me seriously."

"Hopefully the police will catch the thief soon and we'll have some answers."

"I could get the spare key for the cabin Dale's staying in and go and snoop around a bit while he's at work. He's probably got all his stolen goods stashed there."

Nick pushed his palms to his temples and exhaled loudly. "You definitely can't do that. Besides, he's moving to the bunkhouse as we speak. I offered to help him move but he said he was fine."

"Of course he said he was fine. He didn't want you seeing his stash of stolen goods. You know what I'm going to do? I'm going to go over there now and insist on helping him move! Then we'll find out the truth."

"You're going to help him move?" The corners of lips twitched to a smile and his eyes sparkled.

"Aye. What's so funny about that?"

"You struggle to move your own body, so I'm not sure how you think you could help someone move house!"

She gave him a friendly shove but couldn't help but laugh. He made a valid point. "Please can you go and offer to help again. Snoop around a bit …"

"No." He shook his head. "You've got to let this go." Standing, he moved behind her and massaged her shoulders. "Promise me you won't say any of this to anyone else. You have no proof that Dale's done anything wrong."

"I won't say anything," she said, defeated. "But I'll be keeping an eye on him. You should too."

"I'll try to keep an open mind," Nick said, bending to kiss her neck.

"I have to talk to you about something else too," she said with a discreet grimace.

"What?" he asked wearily.

"I was thinking about Christmas. Going down to your parents' place when I'm eight months pregnant probably isn't the best idea. I'll be so uncomfortable. It'll be better for me to be at home and in my own bed."

Nick returned to his seat. "And this is just because of the pregnancy and nothing to do with the fact that the Mackenzies are having Christmas dinner in the pub and you're worried about missing out on the fun?"

"Your mum said they'd be happy to come here for Christmas. I think she's quite excited by the idea."

Nick's eyes bulged. "You spoke to my parents before you discussed it with me?"

Her shoulders rose towards her ears and she gave him a sheepish smile. "I was bored this afternoon, so I thought I'd give your mum a call. Then it just slipped out. But I knew you'd agree to whatever I wanted, so I didn't think it mattered if I spoke to you first or your mum."

He raised his eyebrows and took a deep breath. "You're really annoying, you know?"

"Yeah." She smiled sweetly. "But I love you."

"It's a good job I have a lot of patience," he said, smiling as he leaned to kiss her. "Christmas in Lannick it is!"

CHAPTER TWENTY-TWO

Jess went to the school office at the end of the day on Friday.

"Are you ready to go?" she asked Ava.

"Yes." She looked up from scrolling on her phone. "I was just waiting for you."

"I'm so happy it's the weekend," Jess remarked as they made their way out of the building.

"Have you got plans with lover boy?"

"Nothing specific." After not being able to see him the previous weekend, she was desperate to spend time with him. "He said he'd probably call into the pub this evening, then we can make plans for the rest of the weekend. I think he'll be working tomorrow but maybe I'll go out with him for the day on Sunday. I feel as though I only get brief snatches of time with him. Having a whole day together would be great."

"Or a whole night," Ava said cheekily as they approached Jess's car. "Which reminds me, I'm going back to visit my parents tomorrow and I'll stay the night, so you'll have the house to yourself."

"When did you decide that?" Jess asked as she slipped behind the wheel.

"Today. Mum messaged to say Dad's away for the weekend and asked me to go over and hang out with her tomorrow night."

"That sounds nice."

"Will you take advantage of having the place to yourself and invite Gary for a sleepover?"

Jess smiled widely as she turned the engine on. "I guess he can't stay over anyway because of Paige, but maybe I can cook for him tomorrow night and we can at least get some alone time."

"It's almost like dating a single dad, isn't it?"

"I've never dated a single dad," Jess said, manoeuvring the car out of the parking spot. "But I imagine so. I could do with figuring out a way to get into Paige's good books. Her hating me isn't exactly an ideal situation."

"I'm sure she doesn't hate you."

"I told you what she was like in my class this week." She'd been disruptive and insolent and had absolutely lived up to the reputation that she had among the other teachers. Jess almost sent her out of the class but resisted, knowing it would likely only make matters worse.

"She probably feels threatened by you and is testing you. Don't let her see she's getting to you. Eventually she'll come around."

"I hope so."

"Shall we have dinner in the pub tonight? I can't be bothered to cook."

Jess agreed to the plan and they got ready as soon as they arrived home, then headed straight out again.

"I take it you're going to ditch me again this evening," Ava said when they finished eating at their usual table by the window in the Merchant Bar. A few of their co-workers had arrived and were chatting away at the adjoining table.

"That's my plan, yes." Jess checked the door as it opened but was disappointed when it was the sports teacher, Chris. She looked back at Ava. "Just to check … when you joke about being annoyed at me for ditching you, you are joking right?"

"Yes!" She laughed. "Of course. I'm happy for you. Besides, I'm good at keeping myself amused." She aimed a flirty smile in Chris's direction and held her beer bottle aloft, gesturing for him to bring her a fresh one.

"I do feel kind of guilty when I leave you alone for the evening and chat to Gary."

"I honestly don't mind. And if I did, I'd just come over and hang out with the two of you. I have no problem being the third wheel."

"Thanks. I feel as though I haven't seen him in ages." She glanced at the door again as a group of young lads walked in.

"Did he say what time he's coming?" Ava asked.

"No." Jess pulled her phone out and registered a new message from Gary. "He's not coming," she told Ava as she read it. The disappointment felt like a lump of lead in her stomach.

"Why not?" Ava asked. "Let me guess … Paige?"

"He doesn't say, but I'd assume it has something to do with her. All he says is that he can't make it after all but would like to do something tomorrow evening if I'm free."

"That's not so bad then. You get to hang out with your best friend tonight and your boyfriend tomorrow. It's the perfect weekend."

Jess forced herself to smile, then replied to Gary's message. After spending the week looking forward to seeing him, having to wait another day left her feeling deflated and unsociable. Chris came to sit with them and then Heather who was always easy to chat to. As much as Jess tried to enjoy the evening, her mind wandered constantly to Gary.

She was contemplating going home when she received another message from him, asking how her evening was going. Her spirits lifted to know that he was thinking of her, and she kept up a steady stream of messages with him for the rest of the evening, causing a lot of mock disgust from Ava and a few comments from the others about who was causing her to grin at her phone so much.

~

By the following evening, Jess was filled with nerves about her date with Gary. She'd had all day to think about it, which probably wasn't a good thing. As she primped and preened herself on the assumption that they'd be moving their physical relationship on a level, she couldn't shift the niggling worry that he might not even turn up. Him cancelling their plans seemed to be becoming a regular occurrence. While she prepared dinner she hoped she wasn't wasting her time.

Clock watching made her nerves kick up another notch. It was ten minutes after he was supposed to arrive when nerves turned to irritation. When she was going to so much effort, the least he could do was turn up on time.

It was another ten minutes before the doorbell rang. Her enthusiasm for the evening had completely fizzled out, and she could barely manage a smile when she answered the door.

"I'm really sorry I'm late," he said, holding out a bottle of wine and a bunch of yellow roses.

"Thanks." She took the proffered items and gestured for him to come in.

"Are you annoyed with me?" he asked, hanging his coat on the rack and toeing his shoes off.

She inspected the flowers to avoid making eye contact. "I was starting to think you weren't coming."

"I've been looking forward to it all day." He cupped her cheek as he kissed her. His warm lips pressing against hers made her traitorous stomach turn a somersault and her irritation subsided. "I had to work all day," he said, following her to the kitchen. "I got home later than I thought and then …" Schooling her features to impassive, Jess waited for the inevitable mention of Paige. She was undoubtedly the reason he was late. "I just ended up rushing," Gary finally said with a quick shake of the head.

"It's okay." She decided it would be a waste to spend the precious little time she had with him being annoyed. She'd shake it off and enjoy the evening. "Are you hungry?"

"Starving," he said, smiling widely. "What are we eating?"

"Honey-roasted chicken and sweet potato fries."

"That sounds amazing."

"Don't get too excited. I'm not the best cook, and you're late so it might be dry and overcooked." She'd kept it in the oven on low but wasn't sure how it would taste now. "It looks okay," she said, pulling the roasting tray from the oven.

"Can I do anything?" Gary asked as she plated up the food. She directed him to pour the wine.

"It's really good," he said as he tucked in. Jess was actually quite proud of the simple but tasty meal and nodded her agreement as she took a sip of wine. She asked him how work was and they chatted about their respective weeks as they ate.

"How was it in Glasgow, by the way?" She'd asked him on the phone but hadn't got much of a response.

He shrugged. "It was all right. Far too much driving for one night away, but Paige was happy to see her mum."

"How is Paige?"

Another shrug. "Same as usual. She barely spoke to me this week. Although she was telling me about your lesson the other day. She loves your classes. She was saying how much fun it was this week."

Jess almost choked on her chicken. Obviously the story Paige had given Gary about that week's lesson had been slightly distorted. Paige probably knew that whatever she said would get back to Jess. She was sending a message that she'd enjoyed disrupting her lesson and acting like a teenage delinquent. It was tempting to tell Gary exactly what had happened, but she didn't want to ruin the atmosphere.

"What's she up to this evening?" she asked instead, placing her cutlery neatly on her empty plate.

He picked up his wine. "Hanging out at home." He checked his watch and swigged his drink.

"Have you got a curfew?" Jess asked lightly.

"No," he said, with what she would've sworn was an edge of irritation to his voice.

"Good." She stood up, feeling the need to move. "Let's go in the living room. It's more comfortable."

The change of scenery didn't lighten the atmosphere as she'd hoped, and Gary seemed distracted while she did her best to make conversation.

She was telling him about a particular colleague who she didn't like when she noticed his eyes glaze over. "Am I boring you?" she asked, abandoning her anecdote.

He blinked rapidly. "No. What were you saying?"

"You didn't hear any of it, did you?"

"Sorry." He ran a hand through his hair. "I had a busy week. I'm a bit wrecked. I promise I'm listening. You were talking about one of the other teachers?"

"I can't even remember what I was saying."

"We could always give up on talking," he said, raising a suggestive eyebrow and slipping an arm around her waist to pull her closer.

Goosebumps rippled over her arms as he kissed her softly. His lips trailed along her jaw, nipping at her earlobe before dropping down her neck to plant soft kisses at her collarbone. With a hand in his hair, she coaxed his face back to hers and kissed him deeply as they sank back onto the couch.

Five minutes later, Jess was breathing heavily between kisses and aching for more skin contact.

"Do you want to go upstairs?" she murmured. The drawn-out moment before he replied was enough to make her stomach lurch with fear.

"Yes," he said eventually.

She'd have preferred it if he hadn't needed to think about his reply but told herself she was overthinking it and led the way up to her room with her fingers lightly entwined with his.

His eyes swept the room, which she'd tidied that afternoon. Then his arms curled around her waist, pulling her firmly against his solid frame. Sinking her fingers into his hair, Jess closed her eyes and pressed her lips to his, working them in a rhythm that felt utterly natural.

Gary lifted her off the floor and took a few steps to lower her onto the bed. As he lay on top of her, Jess's heart rate increased and her whole body buzzed with anticipation. Pushing her hands under his T-shirt, she explored the taut skin of his back and pulled him closer in the process.

When he paused and looked deep into her eyes, she brought a hand up and stroked his cheek.

"Are you okay?" she whispered.

He pushed her hair from her forehead and gave an almost imperceptible nod before moving his lips back to hers and closing his eyes. His hand tugged at the hem of her top before his fingers teased the skin of her midriff.

The kisses stopped again and he withdrew his hand and muttered an apology.

"What's going on?" Jess asked as he sat up.

His brow wrinkled. "I can't stay over."

"Because of Paige?" she asked, sitting up and resting a hand on his shoulder.

"Yeah."

"It's okay. I presumed you wouldn't be able to stay."

He dipped his head and dragged his hands through his hair. "I'm really sorry. I need to go."

"Now?"

"Yeah." He tilted his head to look her in the eyes. "She didn't want me to go out and I just left her alone."

"What do you mean?"

"She asked me not to go out. She'd done the same last night, so I was already annoyed with her. We ended up having a big argument. I told her she was messing up my social life and I couldn't stay at home babysitting her all the time."

"That might have been a bit harsh," Jess said with a grimace. "It's also true. She's old enough to be left alone. She can't expect you to be at home all the time."

Moving to sit at the edge of the bed, he dropped his head to his hands. "I had such a go at her. She was really upset, and I just left and slammed the door behind me."

"So that's why you've been on a different planet all evening?"

"I shouldn't have left her like that, but she was being completely unreasonable. She started crying but I swear she only did it for effect."

"It sounds like she was acting more like a toddler than a teenager."

"She's having a tough time with her mum not being around, and I don't know how to deal with her. If I pander to her demands every time she throws a fit I don't know where we'll end up."

"You can't let her get her own way all the time. But maybe you can come to some sort of compromise with her."

"That's what I thought I was doing. I told her I'd stay in with her yesterday but I was going out tonight. She still flipped out today. I need to go and check on her though. I hate that I left her so upset."

"She'd have called if she was really upset."

"I muted my phone and left it in my coat pocket." He stood up and stretched his neck. "I'm a horrible person, aren't I?"

"No." Jess rested a hand at the waist of his jeans.

"Thanks for being so understanding about all of this." He hung his arms around her shoulders and planted a kiss on her forehead. "I really wish I could stay. But I'd feel really crap sleeping with you and then getting up and leaving immediately."

With her face against his chest, she could hear the thud of his heart as the scent of him invaded her nostrils. She inhaled deeply before stepping away. "You should check on Paige."

Downstairs, he fished his phone out of his coat pocket while pushing his feet into his shoes.

"She hasn't been in touch. Which feels more ominous than if I had twenty missed calls."

"I'm sure she's fine." Jess opened the door and looked out at his car on the road. "Are you driving?"

"No. I've had too much to drink. I'll come back for the car tomorrow."

"Let me know how Paige is," she said, then kissed him goodbye and watched him walk away.

CHAPTER TWENTY-THREE

On Sunday morning, Jess cleaned the house from top to bottom in a bid to distract herself from thinking about Gary. He'd sent a message late the previous evening to say Paige was fine and he'd be in touch. Jess was keen to go out for a walk to clear her head, but she knew Gary would come to collect his car at some point, and she didn't want to miss him.

After switching the vacuum cleaner off she went to the living room and glanced out of the window for about the hundredth time, then assured herself that he wouldn't collect his car without at least calling in for a quick hello.

It was the middle of the afternoon when he finally arrived, and Jess was torn between being pleased to see him and annoyed with him for keeping her waiting all day. Mostly, she was irritated with herself for being the sort of woman who waited around for a guy.

"Are you coming in?" she asked, when he hovered on the doorstep.

"I probably shouldn't." He wiped his oil-stained hands on his scruffy jeans, but it didn't do anything to remove the black smudges. "I'm filthy."

"I didn't realise you worked on Sundays."

"I don't usually. Just needed to clear my head."

Fixing cars seemed an odd way to get your thoughts in order, but she didn't comment. "How's everything with Paige now?"

"Not great. I wanted to talk to you about it actually."

"Are you sure you don't want to come in?"

Frowning, he looked at his well-worn heavy boots. "I better not. Maybe I'll go and shower and talk to you later."

"You're making me nervous. Hang on…" After shoving her feet into a pair of trainers, she stepped outside, wrapping her arms around herself against the freezing wind. "What's going on?"

Gary shifted his weight from foot to foot. "When I said Paige could live with me, I thought it'd just be like having a house-mate. I never really considered that she needed someone to look after her. Which I can see was pretty naive and kind of stupid of me."

"Okay," Jess said, not quite sure where the conversation was going but feeling nerves stir in her gut.

"She's missing her mum," he went on. "And I think she's really hurt that her mum left. This morning she ignored me completely, and when I finally got her to talk she told me how she feels like no one really cares about her."

Jess smiled tightly. "I can see that things aren't easy for her, but I also think she's quite manipulative. Her throwing tantrums like a toddler is attention-seeking."

"I know." He sighed and looked at her sadly. "And part of me thinks I should be strict with her and not put up with her trying to manipulate me. But I don't think I can do that, and I don't think it would work. Paige's problem is that no one puts her first. I don't think anyone ever has. The reason she's attention-seeking is because she needs someone to give her some attention."

"What are you trying to tell me?" Jess asked through the lump in her throat.

"I need to show her that I'm there for her. If she doesn't like being on her own in the house in the evenings, I need to stay at home with her."

"So when she says jump you ask how high?"

He pressed his lips together. "Pretty much."

"Where does that leave us?"

Pain flashed in his eyes and Jess knew exactly where that left them. "I'm sorry," he muttered. "Whenever I'm with you I feel torn. And I feel terrible any time I have to cancel on you or leave early because of Paige. It's a really bad way to start a relationship."

"You don't want to see me any more?" she asked, surprised at how even her voice was.

"I *want* to," he said, taking a step towards her. "It's absolutely not that I don't *want* to. I just can't see how it can work at the moment."

When he took another step towards her, she took one back and then another until she was inside the house.

"I'm really sorry."

"You keep saying that," Jess said with a hand on the door.

"Can you at least talk to me?"

"Why?" she asked on a sigh. "It seems as though you've already made your decision. Surely you don't expect me to beg you to change your mind?"

"No, but I feel terrible and …"

"And you want me to tell you it's fine to make you feel better?" she snapped. "I can't stand here and tell you that I understand and that it's okay … it's definitely not okay with me."

"It's not okay for me either. I just don't know how I can be in a relationship at the moment."

She puffed out a humourless laugh. "At the moment? I hope you're not implying that it's just bad timing? If you expect me to hang around while you sort things out with Paige, I have bad news for you. If you don't want to be with me, that's final. I'm not going to wait around and hope you might change your mind."

"I don't expect you to," he said sadly.

"There's nothing else to say then." She managed to bang the door shut before tears slid down her cheeks. In the living room, she watched through the window as Gary's car pulled away, then sank onto the couch and closed her eyes, telling herself they weren't even officially a couple so it wasn't a huge loss. She just wished it didn't hurt so much.

She hadn't moved from the couch when she heard keys in the lock an hour later.

"Hi," Ava called. "Is it safe to come in? Is everybody clothed?"

"It's safe," Jess replied, wishing the weekend had gone differently and Ava's concerns weren't wildly optimistic.

"How was it?" Ava asked, unwinding a long green scarf from her neck as she walked in. "Did you have a good weekend?"

"No." Jess leaned her head back and blinked away more tears. "It was a complete disaster."

Ava's eyes narrowed as she sat down. "What happened?"

"Gary split up with me. If we were even together. I'm not actually sure what our relationship status was but whatever it was is no more." She went back to the beginning and told the whole story, from the previous evening to slamming the door on him that afternoon. "Why am I always attracted to the wrong guys?" she finally complained.

"I don't think you are."

"Just bad timing?" Jess swiped her fingers under her eyes to catch her tears. "I can't spend months moping around hoping he changes his mind or the situation changes. I did enough of that with Rory."

"I don't think you should. I was only pointing out that it's not a case of you choosing the wrong people. It's more bad luck." Ava pulled her in for a hug which left Jess fighting off yet more tears.

"What's really annoying is that I think he's probably doing the right thing."

"How so?" Ava asked.

"For Paige. If I look at the situation objectively, he's probably right. He's doing what's best for her." She pressed her lips together. "Of all the reasons to break up with someone, he managed to pick one that makes me like him even more."

"So maybe you do just need to be patient," Ava suggested. "Paige is being awkward this week but she might be over it in a week or two."

"I'll drive myself crazy thinking like that. I'd rather move on." Jess shook her head, suspecting that would be easier said than done. "It's really rude to break up with someone so close to Christmas, isn't it?"

"At least you only have two more weeks of work. Then you can take some time to chill out."

"That's true. I can go back to Aberdeen and stuff myself with Mum's cooking until the New Year. Then I'll come back with lots of resolutions about forgetting about Gary and moving on with my life."

"Oh," Ava said, looking thoughtful.

"What?"

"Nothing … I was just hoping I might be able to persuade you to come back sooner and celebrate Hogmanay here. Chris and a bunch of people were talking about doing something."

"I'll think about it," Jess said.

She'd have to think about it later though. For the moment all she could focus on was how much she wanted to see Gary.

CHAPTER TWENTY-FOUR

"This will be my first Christmas that I'll be in the pub and not working," Lexie remarked as she slipped her coat on to head over there.

"Presumably the first that you're not drinking too," Nick said.

"That's true." She inhaled deeply, feeling as though she wasn't getting enough air.

"Are you okay?" Nick's mum asked, rubbing her arm.

"Yes. There's no room for her to get any bigger though."

"Not long to go," her father-in-law said as they filed out of the door.

Aileen slipped her arm through Lexie's. "I'm so excited about meeting my grandchild. The next few weeks can't go fast enough for me."

"You and me both," Lexie said.

"Enjoy it, I say," Phil said. "Make the most of being able to sleep at night."

Lexie rolled her eyes. "It's pretty difficult to sleep now, with a baby kicking around inside me."

"I'm glad we came here in the end," Aileen said as they

approached the pub. "It's great not having to worry about cooking."

Nick and Phil murmured their anticipation for their upcoming Christmas dinner so that Lexie's mouth was watering by the time they walked into the pub.

The Mackenzies were standing beside the bar and there was a bustle of hugs and greetings and cries of "Happy Christmas". Finally, Lexie made it around the bar and gave her mum a big hug. Angus gave her a quick kiss on the cheek before getting back to pouring drinks.

"Happy Christmas," Dale said, appearing beside her.

"Happy Christmas," she replied flatly, then was slightly stunned when he gave her a hug.

"I've never spent Christmas Day in a pub before," he told her.

"I think all of my Christmases have been spent in a pub."

Nick appeared and shook Dale's hand. "What would you usually do for Christmas?"

"Go to my grandparents' house."

"They'll be missing you," Nick said. "Have you called home?"

"I messaged earlier." His eyes darted around the room. "I better get back to work."

Lexie leaned close to Nick. "Do you really not see how cagey he is?"

"I see a kid who's away from his family at Christmas for the first time. Can you at least try and be nice to him today?"

"I still think he stole from the gift shops."

"Lexie!" Nick let out an exasperated sigh. "You have absolutely no proof."

"There's no proof he didn't do it either, since no one was caught."

"I don't want to talk about this again."

Lexie grabbed at his arm when he went to walk away. "Why

are you acting as though I'm the one who's done something wrong?"

"Because it's not like you to think the worst of someone."

"Sorry," she whispered, hating how disappointed he looked. To be fair, she'd never really given Dale a chance, but her gut instincts told her to be wary of him. "Maybe it's a pregnancy thing … like not trusting strangers as a protective instinct."

"He's not a stranger any more," Nick pointed out.

"Don't be annoyed with me. Please."

"I'm not." He kissed her cheek and took her hand to lead the way back over to the Mackenzies. Leana had just brought food out to a family sitting near the fire and she stopped to hug them both.

A long table had been set at the side of the room to accommodate their large group. As they took their seats, they spent a few minutes pulling crackers and reading out the terrible jokes from the small squares of paper. They were all wearing paper crowns and chatting away when the food came out. Douglas joined them and interspersed eating his dinner with singing Christmas carols.

When Lexie couldn't manage all her food, Logan and Nick kindly helped her out. She had an inkling that Logan had strategically seated himself close to people he didn't think would manage a full dinner so he could get extra.

The afternoon seemed to fly by as everyone mingled and chatted. Lexie couldn't seem to get comfortable sitting down and spent most of her time wandering around the pub. Since she was up, she ended up behind the bar pulling a few pints to help.

She'd just passed fresh beers to Alasdair and Logan when she turned to find Dale standing with his back to her. He was hunched over; she wasn't sure what he was doing and moved closer to peek over his shoulder. His phone was vibrating in his hand, the display showing a call from his dad.

"Are you going to answer it?" she asked.

Startled, Dale's head shot up, and Lexie caught the tears in his eyes before he whipped his gaze from her and wiped frantically at his cheeks.

"Are you okay?" She laid a hand on his shoulder as a sinking feeling hit her stomach. Maybe Nick was right that she'd been too quick to judge him. At that moment, she could definitely see what Nick saw. He was just a messed-up kid.

"I'm fine." There was a faint quiver to his voice as he shoved his phone into his pocket. "I just need five minutes. If your parents are looking for me, can you tell them I'll be right back?"

He didn't wait for an answer but set off towards the front door.

"Can you get me another beer?" Douglas asked across the bar.

"I'm not working," Lexie told him. "Hang on a minute and Leana will get you one."

She fought her way through the groups of people in high spirits and followed in the direction Dale had gone. Outside, she spotted him sitting on the wall at the other side of the carpark.

"Did you call your dad back?" Lexie asked when she approached and saw he had his phone in his hand.

"No." He licked his lips and swiped a hand across his cheeks. "I don't want to talk to him."

"Why not?"

"I hate him. I hate him and my mum."

Lexie's eyes widened. "It must have been hard to lose her," she ventured. "Do you mean you hate that she died?"

He tilted his head to look at her. "I hate that she left me. Everything is such a mess."

"Do you want to talk about it?" She rubbed at her upper arms in a bid to generate heat. The baby did a pretty good job of keeping her warm, but sitting outside the pub without a coat when it was a few degrees below freezing wasn't exactly comfortable.

He wiped at his face again. "You wouldn't understand. You have the best parents. They'd never do anything to hurt you."

"No. They wouldn't." Her mind flicked to Stephanie. It wasn't the first time her birth mother had popped into her head that day. A small part of her had thought she might at least send a message, but of course she hadn't. Not that it mattered. Dale was right about her having great parents. "What happened with your dad?" she asked.

His shoulders trembled and more tears filled his eyes. "I just want to hate him, but I miss him too. And sometimes I think I shouldn't even be here. I should probably go home and sort things out."

"Why don't you?"

"I like it here. I don't want to leave."

"Can't you sort things out with your dad on the phone?"

He shook his head. "Dad always said that I act first and think later. He's right; I did something stupid and now I don't know how to fix it."

"Do you want to tell me what it is?" Lexie asked. If he confessed to stealing from the gift shops, she'd be happy in the knowledge that her instincts weren't completely off. If he had a good reason and felt remorse, then Nick could also be right about him being a confused, grief-stricken teenager who needed support.

"It's hard to explain everything," he said quietly.

"Just start at the beginning," she said, hoping the story wouldn't take too long or they might both freeze to death in the pub car park. At the sound of her name, she glanced over to see Nick standing in the pub doorway.

"Are you all right?" he called.

"Yeah, fine. We'll just be a minute."

"Do you want Christmas cake?"

"Yes! In a bit."

"Angus is looking for Dale."

"Tell him he'll be back in ten minutes," she shouted.

Beside her, Dale shot up from the wall. "I better get back."

"It's all right," Lexie said, annoyed at the interruption. "Stay and chat if you want."

"No. It's Christmas. You don't want to hear my problems. I'm fine anyway."

"Are you sure?" she asked, but he was already striding across the car park. He'd disappeared inside by the time she reached Nick.

"Aren't you freezing?" he asked.

"Yeah, I am."

He raised his eyebrows. "What was all that about with Dale?"

"I'm not entirely sure. His dad tried to call him and he got upset. But he was being cryptic. He said he'd done something bad, but I'm not sure if it was to do with his dad or what?"

"That's weird."

"Yeah." She gave him a playful jab in his side as she walked past him into the pub's entranceway. "You interrupted us at the exact wrong moment. I felt like he was about to confess something important."

Nick tilted his head. "You think he was about to tell you about his life of crime and petty theft?"

"I didn't say that."

"Unfortunately for you, I can read your mind."

"Good. I don't need to ask you to get me some Christmas cake then? You'll just do it."

"I'll be glad when you're not pregnant any more so you stop bossing me around."

"I love that you think it's going to stop then!" She looked back at the door when it opened.

Gary beamed at her and called out Happy Christmas. "I haven't seen you in ages," he said, kissing her cheek. "I hate to break it to you, but I reckon you've put on weight since the last time I saw you."

She pulled a face at him before Logan sidled over and embraced him.

"I thought you couldn't make it," he said.

"I got sick of my family. Any chance I can crash at your place? My sister and her fella are at mine and they're driving me crazy. Plus I feel like getting drunk!"

"Course you can," Logan said as they all moved towards the bar.

"Where's your girlfriend today?" Leana asked as she poured him a pint.

Behind him, Isla and Logan made throat-slashing gestures, but Leana didn't even seem to notice.

"We broke up," Gary said, slipping onto a stool.

"Sorry about that," Leana said. "Plenty more fish in the sea though, eh?" It was Gary's usual response to splitting up with a woman.

"I actually really liked her," Gary said, then paused and took a couple of long gulps of his beer. "It's all pretty crap to be honest."

Isla tugged on Lexie's elbow and led her across the room.

"What are you doing?" Lexie asked.

"Saving us. I can't listen to Gary going on about Jess again. We were at his place to help him with some painting the other day and he couldn't stop talking about her."

"*She* broke up with him then?"

"No, it was him. He's got his niece living with him and she's kind of a handful. It's a long story."

Lexie was distracted by Dale clearing a table nearby. She tried to catch his eye but he was focused on what he was doing and only glanced over on his way to the kitchen.

"Can I get you two anything?" he asked.

Lexie shook her head. "We're fine. Thanks." She wanted to ask if he was okay, but he seemed to have perked up and she didn't feel like asking in front of people. Maybe Nick was right and they should invite him over for dinner sometime.

"I think my mum and Nick's mum might have had a bit too much wine," Isla said.

Lexie followed her gaze to where Christine and Aileen were huddled together in fits of laughter. "This is going to become a regular thing, isn't it?"

"I reckon so," Isla said. "Every Christmas will be spent in the pub from now on."

"Did you miss being with your family for Christmas?" Rory asked as he and Elspeth climbed into bed in the spare room of his parents' house.

"No." She pulled the covers up to her chin and moved her feet against Rory's legs to warm them. "I had a really good time."

"Really?" he asked, slipping an arm behind her head. "My family are slightly nuts."

Elspeth snorted a laugh. "They crack me up. The way your grandad kept offering Anita meat was hilarious."

"She has no clue that he only does it to wind her up. Every time we get together she explains to him what a vegetarian is in her condescending tone. She talks to everyone like they're five years old. I don't know how John puts up with her."

"He's as weird as she is though, really."

"Hey! That's my brother you're bad-mouthing." He pulled her closer. "He's a bit odd though," he admitted. "Did you get sick of all the questions about the wedding?"

"No. It made me think about it a lot though. Do you think we could get married this spring?"

"The sooner the better for me," he said, snuggling up to her. "Are you still thinking of getting married at your parents' place?"

"Unless you have a better idea."

"No," he said hesitantly.

She turned in his arms, searching his features in the dim light from the lamp. "Do you want to do something different?"

"No, it's fine. Whatever you want will be perfect."

"Don't do this again," she said on a sigh. "You get a say too. If you want to get married somewhere else tell me. Do you want to get married in Edinburgh?"

He gave a small shake of the head. "Do you remember six months ago… we'd just got back together and we went for dinner one evening at the Lochview Hotel …"

"There was a wedding happening," Elspeth said, thinking back.

"Yeah. Things seemed so uncertain between us, but I remember seeing the wedding party and hoping it would be us one day."

"You want to get married at the Lochview Hotel?" she asked in surprise.

"It just stuck in my head. But I'm happy to get married anywhere."

"We could look into it," she said, mulling it over. "It's a great venue. I don't know why I always imagined us getting married at my parents' place."

"I really am happy to do that too." He yawned and reached over to switch the lamp off.

After giving him a quick kiss, they settled down to sleep. It only took Rory a couple of minutes to drift off, whereas Elspeth's brain refused to switch off as she chewed over Rory's idea for the wedding.

The following morning, she was awake before him. Immediately, her thoughts were racing again. On her phone she went to the website for the Lochview hotel and scrolled through the wedding section. The photos were stunning and she quickly read a few of the glowing testimonials.

"What are you doing?" Rory asked groggily when he woke half an hour later.

"I want to get married at the Lochview." Setting her phone

aside she snuggled back down with him. "I sent an email asking about availability."

"Are you sure?"

"Yes. I think it's a great idea. I just hope they have availability this spring or summer. I don't want to wait too long."

"Me neither," he said, nuzzling her neck.

CHAPTER TWENTY-FIVE

The cafe was closed completely between Christmas and New Year. Elspeth enjoyed the break and the quality time with Rory and Arran. The more they talked about the wedding, the more excited Elspeth got. After all the months of being cautious and taking things slow, their relationship felt stronger than ever and neither of them wanted to wait long to get married.

On New Year's Eve Elspeth wandered over to Isla and Logan's place in the afternoon.

"Did you decide to come out in Portree with us tonight?" Isla asked as she opened the door to her.

"No. We're staying at home."

They moved to the living room where Logan was sprawled out watching TV. He shifted to make space on the couch.

"You should come out," Isla said. "It'll be a laugh. Get Mum and Dad to look after Arran."

"I think they're going up to the pub. And we're quite happy to stay in."

Logan grinned. "Isla only wants you to come out so it's not just us and Gary."

"If he starts going on about Jess again, I'm going to shake him."

"You should be sympathetic," Logan said. "It's kind of your fault."

"How on earth is it my fault?"

He rolled his eyes. "You're the one who told him to stop dating bimbos and find someone he actually cares about. He did that and now he's heartbroken."

"I think it's a shame he and Jess aren't together," Elspeth said. "Can't they sort things out?"

"He's decided to stay away from her," Isla said in a tone that suggested she was sick of the conversation. "He's worried about messing her about and hurting her. He thinks the kindest thing to do is keep his distance." She shook her head. "I might have created a monster. It was probably better when he moved from one woman to the next with no concern about who might get hurt."

"I reckon they'll sort things out eventually," Elspeth said. "But I might just be optimistic about relationships at the moment. Especially since we've started planning the wedding."

Logan sat up straighter. "Have you set a date?"

"Yes." She smiled widely. "We're getting married at the Lochview Hotel in March."

"Just over a year," Logan said, nodding approvingly. "That's a good amount of time to get everything organised."

"This coming March," Elspeth corrected him. "Ten weeks from now."

Logan's jaw hung open. "Is that a joke? Ten weeks to plan the most important day of your life?"

"Ten weeks to plan a party," Isla said, clicking her tongue. "Don't be so dramatic."

"Don't start with all that again," Logan snapped before switching his attention back to Elspeth. "I don't think you realise how much work it is to plan a wedding … there's a lot to do. Lots to think about …"

"Where are you going?" Isla asked as he wandered out of the room.

"I'll be back in a minute."

"You know he's going to have a nervous breakdown about your wedding now, don't you?" Isla said. "As though I don't have enough on my plate with listening to Gary droning on about Jess, I'm now going to have to listen to Logan panic about your wedding plans."

"He makes me laugh," Elspeth said quietly. "Why does he get so worked up about weddings?"

"I've no idea."

"I've found it," he said, walking back in with a blue notebook in his hand.

"Oh God, no!" Isla groaned and flopped back on the couch. "Not that thing. I thought I'd seen the last of it."

"What is it?" Elspeth asked.

"My wedding planner," Logan said, sitting close beside Elspeth. "Everything about our wedding is in here. You can borrow it if you want. Just don't lose it."

"Please lose it," Isla mumbled. "What on earth do you need it for anyway?" she asked him. "Are you intending to have another wedding someday?"

"It feels like a possibility sometimes, yeah." He glared at her. "It's a keepsake."

"This is a lot of information," Elspeth said as she flicked through.

"Are you sure you want to get married so soon?" Logan asked. "I'd advise giving yourself more time. You don't want something hastily thrown together for your big day."

"The hotel had a cancellation. It seemed like a sign."

"Like a bad sign … it's the day someone else was supposed to get married but called it off. Not a good omen really."

"Will you shut up!" Isla said. "Can't you just be excited for them?"

"Yeah, I am. I just don't want you to get stressed."

"We'll keep it quite small. Close friends and family for the ceremony and a meal, then invite more people for a party in the evening."

"It'll still be a nightmare to organise. Just when you think everything is under control, some wedding crashers will mess up your table plan."

Isla stared at him. "No one crashed our wedding."

"Erm … what about Nick's parents?"

"I invited them!"

"At the last minute!"

She shook her head. "I can't believe you're still not over that."

"I might invite Nick's parents to our wedding," Elspeth mused. "They're really lovely."

Isla laughed loudly. "You just want to invite them because they bought us that gorgeous crystal vase you've had your eye on. You think they'll get you a good present."

"That's not the reason," Elspeth said, trying her best to keep a straight face. "They're very nice people."

"Yeah right!" Logan said.

"It's the truth. I wouldn't invite them just to get a gift."

Logan raised an eyebrow. "So you'd still invite them if I told you the crystal vase wasn't from them?"

"It was!" Isla said.

He shook his head and took his wedding planner back from Elspeth. "I have the gift list in the back of here … I'm fairly sure the vase was from Aunt Viv."

"No!" Isla leaned closer to him. "Oh, you're right. I always thought it was from Aileen and Phil."

"What did Nick's parents get you?" Elspeth asked, leaning in.

"A set of wine glasses and some money," Logan told her.

"How much money?"

"I dunno." He squinted at the page. "It's smudged."

"Do you think it was more than the cost of having them at the wedding?" Elspeth cracked up laughing when Isla and Logan turned to look at her. "I was joking. I'm inviting them anyway." She gave Logan a nudge. "Do you reckon your Aunt Viv might like to come to my wedding?"

"You're so shallow," he joked.

"I'm going to go," she said and stood up. "I told Arran we'd bake a cake this afternoon. I just wanted to tell you about the wedding. Oh, will you be my bridesmaid?" she asked Isla.

"Of course." She grinned. "We get to go dress shopping again. It was fun last time."

"What will my role be?" Logan asked.

"I dunno." She shrugged. "Do you want to be an usher or something?"

"Not when you ask me like that! Who's the best man?"

"I don't know. Probably Alasdair."

"Why Alasdair and not me?"

"It's up to Rory," Elspeth said, rolling her eyes in Isla's direction and heading for the door. "Have fun tonight."

~

Jess had tried hard to put Gary out of her mind over Christmas. Being in Aberdeen with her family was a good distraction for a few days, but once Christmas was over and the new year approached she felt increasingly melancholy. She told herself that in January she'd put the drama with Gary behind her and get on with her life, but she had a feeling it wasn't going to be that easy.

Even her plans for Hogmanay were tainted by thoughts of Gary. She'd been all set for a night out in Portree with Ava and some of their colleagues – until she'd realised there was a good chance of Gary being out in Portree too. No doubt she'd spend all evening panicking about bumping into him. Thankfully, Ava had been happy with her idea of inviting people over to their place for drinks and nibbles, then heading out to watch the fireworks later in the evening.

It had been a good plan. Spending the evening playing hostess kept Jess occupied and cheerful. After a few glasses of wine she even managed to convince herself that the new year might be just the fresh start she needed.

"A house party was a great idea!" Ava told her, slinging an arm around her shoulders as they left the house to venture down to the harbour, where they'd get a good view of the fireworks at midnight.

"It was fun," Jess agreed as they hurried to keep up with the rest of their group. "I'm probably not staying out for long, by the way. I'm already freezing."

"We'll grab a drink in the pub down on the harbour. A bit more alcohol in your system will warm you up."

"I don't want to drink more. I'll watch the fireworks, then I'm off home for an early night."

"We'll see," Ava said with a mischievous glint in her eyes.

"I'm serious. Tomorrow is a new start for me. I want to be fresh and well-rested, not a hungover wreck. That's definitely not how I'm starting the year."

"Okay." Ava flashed her a teasing grin. "Whatever you say."

Down at the harbour it was clear a lot of people had had the same idea as them about watching the fireworks. There was a lot of bustle beneath the glow of the streetlights.

"Are we going to duck into the Ship Inn and grab a drink before the fireworks?" Chris asked, as he and Heather sidled up to them.

"It seems as though they'll give you beers to take away," Ava said, looking pointedly at a group nearby holding pint glasses. "You get drinks and Jess and I will find a good spot to watch the fireworks."

"Where did everyone else go?" Jess asked.

"In the pub," Heather said, as she and Chris headed in that direction.

"It's absolutely freezing," Jess complained as Ava pulled her along the road until they found a space beside the railing at the harbour wall. Looking down at the boats bobbing on the water, Jess was reminded of her romantic evening with Gary. She shook the thought away and stamped her feet to try and warm her toes.

"I need a wee," Ava said. "I'm going to run in the pub. Save this spot and I'll be right back."

Jess opened her mouth to complain, but Ava was already striding away from her. With no one around to protest she briefly contemplated slipping away home. Watching the fireworks from the living room window with a cup of tea in her hand was very appealing. Except she'd never hear the end of it from Ava.

She smiled at an older couple nearby, then rubbed her gloved hands together. When none of her group had appeared after five minutes, she set off to find them. She'd only taken a couple of steps towards the pub when a hand caught her elbow. Twisting around, she fully expected to see Ava.

"Sorry," the familiar face said. "We haven't really met properly. I'm Isla."

Jess flashed her a nervous smile. "Hi."

"I noticed you were on your own. Why don't you come and join us to watch the fireworks?"

"My friends are around here somewhere," Jess said, looking towards the pub. There was no sign of any of them.

"It's almost midnight," Isla said. "You shouldn't be on your own."

"I'm fine, thanks. I'll just go in the pub and find my friends."

"Then you'll miss the fireworks." She was surprisingly forceful when she pulled on Jess's arm. "Come with me. Logan and Gary are just over here."

Jess's heart rate went through the roof. "I can't," she said as Isla dragged her along. "It's awkward between me and Gary."

"It's Hogmanay. Everyone's tipsy. It won't be awkward. Promise."

"But …" Her excuses died on her tongue as she came face to

face with Gary. "Hi," she said as confidently as she could manage.

"Hi." He swallowed hard and forced a smile. "How are you?"

"Fine, thanks."

"Did you have a good Christmas?"

"Yeah. How about you?" The conversation couldn't have been more stilted. It was difficult to chat when she felt as though her heart was about to crash through her chest.

"The usual family stuff," he said. "I survived."

As people along the harbour began to count back from ten, Isla grinned at Jess and moved over to Logan.

"Ava and some other friends are around here somewhere," Jess said, raising her voice over the sound of people counting down around them.

He smiled and nodded just as the countdown reached "one" and shouts of Happy New Year rang around them. Seconds later the sky exploded with a loud crack and a shower of red light rained down and reflected off the water.

Automatically, Jess moved to the railing, clutching at the top bar as she craned her neck to watch the fantastic light display. Aware of Gary beside her, she leaned slightly so her arm touched his.

"I wanted to tell you something," he said, without taking his eyes from the sky.

"What?" she asked when he didn't continue.

His gaze fell to her and he waited for the crackle of fireworks to fade before he spoke again. "I just wanted you to know that I'm sorry for how things ended between us. I know it won't make you feel any better, but I really am sorry."

"It's okay." She paused as an almighty bang rang out in the sky. "Actually, it's not really okay, but I'm not angry with you any more. You did the best thing for Paige."

His eyebrows drew together. "This probably just makes

things worse, but I really wish things had worked out differently."

"Me too," she said, forcing a smile. "But things don't always work out as we want." Remembering her resolve to start the new year on a more positive note, she smiled up at him. "Happy New Year!"

"Happy New Year." He bent to hug her, and as his arms wrapped around her, she buried her cheek against his neck, savouring the warmth of him and the wonderfully familiar scent. When he relaxed his hold, she inhaled one last time, then drew back slightly. With her hands on his shoulders she fought a mental battle with herself; the part of her telling her to back away was quickly drowned out by the part of her that wanted to kiss him.

His warm lips against hers sent an electric shock though her body and it felt like the most natural thing in the world. Gently, he drew back and broke the moment.

"I'm sorry," he said, with a pained expression. "Paige has been much more settled the last few weeks. When I said I wished things were different, I only meant …"

Shaking her head, she stepped away from him. "I know what you meant," she said on a sigh. "I shouldn't have kissed you. I'm such an idiot."

"No. You're not. And it's not as though I don't want to kiss you … I'm just not sure it's the best idea."

"It's not. Let's forget this happened." She glanced around and caught sight of Ava and the rest of the gang huddled together near the doorway of the pub. "I have to go. I'm really sorry." She rushed away and didn't look back.

"There you are!" Ava said, embracing her tightly and wishing her a Happy New Year. "We were looking for you."

"I saw Gary," Jess told her, keeping a little distance from the group.

Ava's eyes widened. "How was it?"

"I kissed him! What the heck is wrong with me?"

"I thought you wanted to get over him and move on?"

"That's the plan, yes! That's got to be the quickest anyone has ever broken a New Year's resolution."

"It's New Year!" Ava said brightly. "You can kiss anyone. I kissed Chris," she said quietly, glancing in his direction.

"That's not a great surprise." She scanned the crowd, but Gary was nowhere to be seen. "I'm going home."

"Wait a while and I'll come with you."

Jess shook her head. "You stay and have fun. I really want to go."

"I'm coming with you," Ava said triumphantly. "No way I can leave you to walk home alone. Besides, I'll thank you in the morning when I don't have a hangover."

"I hate to break it to you, but I think it's too late for that." They waved to the others and shouted Happy New Year before they set off up the road, arm in arm.

Jess sighed loudly. "New Year's resolutions only start when you wake up on New Year's Day, right?"

"Sure. Why not!"

"Good. Tomorrow I'm putting my plan to get over Gary into action."

The kiss had been a goodbye kiss. Now she could move on.

CHAPTER TWENTY-SIX

"I'm really bored," Lexie complained as she lumbered into the living room where Nick had his nose in his laptop. "Dad definitely won't let me work any more."

"You're thirty-nine weeks pregnant," Nick said. "I think you can give up any ideas about working now."

She lowered herself onto the couch. "I invited Dale over for dinner."

"Tonight?"

"Yeah, but he's not coming. He said he was busy, but he's been weird with me ever since Christmas Day. He knows I'm onto him."

Nick closed the laptop and tilted his head to one side.

"I know you don't want to hear about this any more." Lexie dragged an imaginary zip across her lips. For the sake of a stress-free homelife, she'd agreed to drop the subject of Dale and the robberies.

"I have all my students set up with remote learning for the next few weeks," Nick said, changing the subject.

"You're still going into work sometimes, aren't you? I'll feel a lot of pressure on me if you're at home all the time, waiting for me to go into labour. First babies are usually late, you know."

"Yeah, I know." He shifted on the couch to face her. From the serious set of his features, she had the feeling he was gearing up to say something she wouldn't like.

"What's wrong?" she asked.

"The weather forecast for the next couple of weeks is terrible."

"It's January. That's normal."

"Heavy snowfall is expected." He winced. "And I know that you have your heart set on giving birth at the clinic on Skye but—"

"No!" She let out a humourless laugh as she interrupted him. "We have a plan and we're sticking to it."

"Maybe we could think about changing the plan."

"There's no need to change the plan. It's unlikely that the roads will be so bad that we can't make it to the hospital."

"That's not what worries me." Nick took her hand. "The hospital on Skye is only equipped for normal birth with no complications. If there are any problems they'd transfer you to Inverness."

"Yeah, I know." They'd been through all this with the doctor and the midwife.

"But if the weather's bad we wouldn't be able to get to Inverness. The air ambulance can't fly in a snowstorm."

"Don't do this," she said as a lump swelled in her throat. "You always have to jump to worst-case scenarios. The doctor said I have no risk factors, so there's no indication that there'll be any complications. But if you stress me out by telling me every possible scenario for things going wrong, then the stress is likely to cause problems."

Nick massaged his temples and inhaled a steady breath. "You're right. I'm sorry." He kissed the side of her head, then picked up his laptop.

"Where are you going?"

"I've got a bit of work to do. Give me a shout if you need anything."

As she listened to the creak of the stairs, she stared into the fire and mulled over his concerns. Of course now he'd put the ideas in her head, all she could focus on was what could go wrong. After ten minutes she trudged upstairs in search of Nick.

Predictably, he wasn't working at all but lying on their bed, staring at the ceiling. Perching beside him, she took his hand.

"Now you've got me worried," she said.

"Sorry." Concern was etched in his features as he sat up and pushed a tear from the corner of his eye. "I'm just freaking out a bit. But you're right – everything will be fine. The medical team at the hospital on Skye are great. There's no reason to be worried."

"I'm mostly worried about you," she said, smiling lightly. "Catastrophising everything isn't good for you. You'll give yourself a heart attack at this rate."

"It's my curse. I can't help it."

"I know. But maybe you also have a point. It probably wouldn't hurt to look at other options."

He gave her that look again, as though he was working up the courage for his next suggestion.

Lexie laughed. "I hope you're not going to suggest we go and camp outside the hospital in Inverness?"

"Not camp, obviously. I found a nice hotel nearby …"

"Oh, no," she said, pouting dramatically. "That's really your plan?"

"It'd be like a holiday."

"No one goes on holiday when they're full term in their pregnancy. What if the baby's late? We could be living in a hotel for weeks. It sounds like hell."

"Only if you go with that mindset. If you see it as a time to relax and for us to spend quality time together before the baby arrives, it might be fun."

"It's going to cost a fortune."

He shook his head. "The hotel isn't *that* nice. And we're

always sensible with money. We have savings. And there's the money from your grandad."

Lexie squeezed her eyes shut as she tried to get her thoughts in order.

"It's only an idea," Nick said, rubbing her lower back. "I'll support you with whatever you want. If you want to stay here that's fine."

"I haven't been to Inverness since Grandad's funeral," Lexie said sadly. "I'm not sure how I'll feel going back there. All my memories of Stephanie are wrapped up in Inverness too. Whenever I'm there, I walk around worried I might turn a corner and bump into her."

"I thought she was living down in Manchester."

"She probably is, but I don't know for sure. I'll still wonder." She puffed her cheeks out. "I really don't want to think about her." It was hard not to though; all the love Lexie had for her unborn child made the hurt of being abandoned by Stephanie even worse.

"We'll stay here then," Nick said decisively. "I wanted us to consider all options, but we need to do what you're most comfortable with."

"Show me the hotel," she said, nodding wearily towards his laptop.

Nick chewed on his thumbnail while Lexie looked over the website for the hotel.

"Okay," she finally said. "Let's have a holiday in Inverness."

"Are you sure?" Nick asked, trying and failing to hide his relief.

"Yes. But I'm also fairly sure this is going to guarantee this baby arrives way after her due date."

"That just means a longer holiday!"

His smile was infectious, and she couldn't help but laugh.

Jess and Ava were eating breakfast on Saturday when the post arrived. They eagerly opened their matching envelopes.

"I love weddings," Ava remarked. Her eyes were bright as she held the invitation in her hand. "Are you okay?" she asked, snapping her attention to Jess. "Is it weird for you that Rory's getting married?"

"No. I'm happy for him." She also enjoyed weddings, but the invitation had made her heart sink as soon as she'd laid eyes on it. Not because of anything to do with Rory, but because it highlighted the lack of forward motion in her own life.

"Have you heard anything from Gary?" Ava asked hesitantly.

"No. He's not going to get in touch."

"I thought he might after Hogmanay. You guys kissed, after all."

"I kissed him. He made it clear that nothing had changed and there couldn't be anything between us. It's better that he hasn't been in touch. I need to put it all behind me. Sitting around pining won't get me anywhere."

"You should go on some dates. That would be the best way to get over him."

"No." Jess chuckled and took a sip of her coffee. "I'm definitely not going on dates. I don't need a man to be happy. In fact, recent times have shown me that men make me miserable."

"You've had a bit of bad luck, that's all."

"I'm definitely not going to start dating random guys." Jess shook her head. "I don't want to be in a relationship with just anyone. I want to be with Gary, but that can't happen."

"It's such a stupid situation," Ava growled. "I've a good mind to tell Paige exactly what I think of her."

"Stay away from Paige," Jess said seriously. She'd put a lot of effort into staying professional and treating Paige like any other student, so the last thing she needed was Ava interfering and stirring things up. Thankfully, Paige had been keeping her head down in Jess's lessons. She'd half expected her to be smug about the fact that she'd come between Jess and Gary, but there was no trace of attitude from her.

"So, are you going to go to the wedding?" Ava asked, turning over the invitation again.

"Yes." Jess was thankful they were only invited for the evening do. That felt much more manageable than a whole day. Especially as she suspected Gary would be there.

It was a couple of months away, so she had plenty of time to get herself into a more stable emotional state. In two months, she'd probably be completely over him and being in the same room as him wouldn't affect her at all.

At least she hoped that would be the case.

CHAPTER TWENTY-SEVEN

The drive to Inverness left Lexie stiff and aching. As she walked into the hotel room, she was torn between lying down for a nap or soaking in a warm bath.

"The bathroom better be nice," she said, as Nick set their bags down. "Lying in the bath is the only place I'm comfortable these days. My bladder's pretty useless too." After a quick scan of the hotel room, which was perfectly fine but nothing fancy, she made her way to the bathroom and closed the door behind her.

"You're not going to believe this," she said when she opened the door again a couple of minutes later.

"Is it a jacuzzi bath?" Nick paused from browsing through the complimentary tea and coffee selection to look at her.

She shook her head. "My waters just broke."

He gave her a bemused smile. "You're right – I don't believe you."

"I'm soaked." She grabbed a towel from the rack beside the door and threw it on the floor to try to absorb the worst of it.

"Are you serious? Your waters have broken?"

"Yes."

"But we only just arrived."

"I know."

"You're not due for five days."

"Tell *her* that," Lexie said, pointing at her belly.

Nick was frozen to the spot and staring at her.

"Take a breath," she said slowly. "You're not allowed to freak out, because if you freak out, I will too. Okay?"

He nodded. "Yeah, okay."

"Pass me some fresh clothes. I'll get changed and you can call the hospital."

"Are you in pain?" he asked as he opened up her bag.

"No. I'm uncomfortable, but no more than usual."

"Good. You're not panicking, are you? Because everything's going to be great."

"*I'm* not panicking," she said, amused. "Can you remember to breathe please?"

"Yeah, I am." He pulled clothes from the bag and walked over to her. "How come you look so calm?"

She put a hand on his cheek and kissed him softly. "I'm excited. We're going to have a baby very soon."

"I'm excited too," he said, not quite managing to disguise the panic in his voice.

The middle-aged woman at the reception desk looked up when they arrived back in the lobby fifteen minutes after they'd checked in. The hospital had said Lexie could go straight over and get checked out but there didn't seem to be any urgency, other than the fact that Nick was panicking.

"Is everything okay for you?" the receptionist asked.

"I'm having a baby," Lexie told her brightly.

"Now?"

"Her waters broke," Nick said. "We're going to the hospital."

"How exciting," the woman said. "Good luck."

"Thanks." Lexie grimaced. "I made a bit of a mess of the bathroom, I'm afraid. I mopped it up as best I could …"

"I'll send housekeeping up," she said with a professional smile.

"Tell them we'll tip them well!" She smiled at her again. "I really like your earrings."

"Thank you." She beamed and fingered the dangling blue teardrop at her left lobe. "They're new."

"Let's go," Nick said, taking Lexie's arm and ushering her towards the door.

As the automatic doors slid shut behind them, a bolt of pain hit Lexie and she stopped dead, clutching at Nick's hand.

"It's okay," he said, giving her a reassuring smile. "Just remember to breathe. You'll be fine."

Gradually, the pain subsided and she let out a long breath.

"Are you okay?" Nick asked. "Shall I drive the car around to you?"

"No. I'm okay. Get my hospital bag from the car and we can walk over there. It'll be easier than trying to find a parking spot."

"Are you sure?"

"Yes. I don't think we're in any rush. It's not far, is it?"

"No. It's really close. I'll get the bag."

"Wait!" Lexie's eyes widened.

"Are you having another contraction?" Nick asked.

"No." She shook her head. "I just … oh my God! Come with me …"

"Where are you going?" He rushed after her as she walked back into the hotel.

"Excuse me," she said to the woman behind the reception desk. "Can I have a look at your earrings?"

She looked at Lexie like she was crazy but leaned towards her nonetheless.

"They're Isla's!" Grabbing at Nick's arm, she pulled him close. "Look! They're Isla's earrings."

"I bought them last week," the woman said with a nervous smile.

"They're made from sea glass," Lexie told her. "I have a similar pair. They're very distinctive." She nodded firmly. "They're stolen."

"No," the woman said, then gave a nervous laugh. "I paid for them. Bought them from a market stall in town."

"I'm not saying *you* stole them," Lexie said. "I'm saying you bought stolen goods."

"I don't think so," the woman said, drawing back.

"Definitely. Aren't they Isla's?" she asked Nick.

"Maybe," he said with a shrug. "But do we really need to have a conversation about this now?"

"Can I take a photo of them?" Lexie asked. "I can send it to Isla and check if they're one of the pairs that were stolen. If they are, we could get the police involved …"

"Lexie!" Nick said loudly. "Can you stop playing Sherlock and focus on having a baby?"

"I just need a photo. Where's your phone? Take a photo of the earrings and then we can go."

"I'm really sorry," Nick said to the woman. "Would you mind?"

After a moment, she took the earrings out and laid them on the desk for Nick to photograph.

"Can we please go now?" he said to Lexie.

"Yes." They thanked the woman and set off to the door again. "Send that photo to Isla, will you?"

"No! We have better things to think about at this moment."

"Fine, but we're definitely looking into this later. Do you believe me that they're Isla's earrings?"

"I've got no idea, but we'll look into it. Just not right now."

"I can't believe I've tracked down the stolen goods!"

"*If* they're Isla's earrings, at least you can finally stop pinning the blame on Dale."

"He could've sold them on. It'll be good to find out what happened though." She stopped and squeezed Nick's hand as another contraction hit.

She could definitely save the detective work for later.

As it turned out, twelve hours of labour made Lexie forget all about stolen earrings, and when that was over with, all she could think about was the baby girl in her arms. Grace Mary Stewart was absolutely perfect.

Exhausted after being in labour all night, Lexie spent the following day dozing on and off.

"You should go to the hotel and get some sleep," she told Nick when she flicked her eyes open late in the afternoon. He was sitting in a chair beside the bed, gazing down at Grace as he had been for most of the day.

"I'll stay a bit longer."

"You should go and sleep so you're fit to drive us home tomorrow. You'll also need to speak to someone at the hotel about us checking out earlier than we expected."

He came over to the bed and perched beside Lexie with Grace nestled in the crook of his arm. "The trip to Inverness was a bit of a waste of time, wasn't it? You're welcome to have a go at me for worrying too much."

"It's okay. I think it saved me some stress knowing that if anything went wrong we were in the best possible place."

"I should have known you'd breeze through childbirth."

Smiling, she rested her head on his shoulder. "I'm glad I made it look like a breeze. That's not how it felt."

"She's amazing, isn't she?" he said, stroking Grace's cheek with the back of his finger.

"We did a good job there," Lexie agreed, her chin twitching as she looked at Nick with their daughter.

"Are you going to start crying again?"

"I can't help it!" She wiped tears away. "I'm so happy. And my hormones are all over the place."

He passed Grace to her and kissed them both. "Are you sure you're okay on your own?"

"Yes. We're fine. There are lots of nurses around if I need anything."

"I still don't like leaving you."

"You look exhausted. Go and sleep or you're going to be useless tomorrow."

"Okay." He pushed her hair behind her ear and kissed her deeply. "I love you so much."

She told him she loved him too, then sank back onto the cushions when he left. As she stared down at Grace, tears filled her eyes again.

"I love you, Gracie," she whispered, her voice breaking on the words.

Nick reappeared in the doorway. "You'll call me if you need anything, won't you?" He stopped dead when he saw she was crying, then strode across the room. "What's wrong?"

"I don't understand why she didn't love me," she said, her voice brittle as her chest heaved.

"Who?" Nick asked, taking Grace and placing her in the crib by the bed.

"Stephanie," she said, her throat so tight it was difficult to speak. "How could my own mother not love me?"

Nick sat beside her on the bed and wrapped his arms around her, not attempting to answer the question but holding her tightly as she sobbed.

It took a while for her to calm down enough to speak again. "Sorry," she sniffed. "I don't know why I keep thinking about her."

"Do you think it would help to call Mary?"

"Probably. But I don't want her to know I'm thinking about Stephanie. Mary's always been such a great mum. It's not as though I'm lacking anything. Stephanie doesn't deserve my thoughts or tears."

"You can't help how you feel," Nick said, resting his cheek

on the top of her head. "And Mary won't be upset if you speak to her about Stephanie. She'll know the right thing to say and make you feel better."

Lexie put her ear against Nick's chest so she could hear the steady rhythm of his heartbeat. "You always know the right thing to say too," she told him. "Can you pass me my phone and I'll call Mum? Then you should really go back to the hotel and sleep."

"I'm not going anywhere," he said, giving her a squeeze before moving to get her phone.

~

"Anyone would think it was him who'd had the baby," Angus grumbled, tipping his head towards Nick, who was fast asleep on the couch beside Lexie. They hadn't been home long before the doting grandparents had descended on them.

"Leave him alone. He missed a full night's sleep while I was in labour, and last night he refused to leave the hospital, so he only managed a few hours sleeping in a chair."

Mary dragged her gaze away from the baby in her arms to look affectionately at Nick. "He's a good man. You chose a good husband."

"I'm glad he was looking after you," Angus agreed. "I was slightly concerned he was too busy solving crimes."

"What are you talking about?" Lexie asked.

"He led the police to catch the couple who'd been knocking off the gift shops."

Lexie's eyes widened and she automatically nudged Nick's leg. "What happened with the police?" she asked when he fought to open his eyes. She felt slightly guilty at dragging him out of what was clearly a deep sleep, but her curiosity was all-consuming. "Did you tell the police about the woman at the hotel?"

"Yeah." He yawned and blinked his eyes. "You kept falling asleep in the hospital, so I thought I'd look into it. Isla said the earrings were definitely hers so I called the police station in Portree. They were going to get in touch with the police in Inverness. That's all I know."

"Isla had a call about it this morning," Angus said. "Apparently the police in Inverness spoke to the woman at the hotel. The thieves were selling stolen goods on a market stall. They caught them red-handed. Some middle-aged couple. They'd already sold a lot of the stuff, but whatever the police recovered will be returned to Isla and the gift shops."

Lexie grinned. "I knew they were Isla's earrings. That poor woman at the hotel. I swear she'll be telling people about me for years – the crazy woman who was in labour but stopped to take a photo of her stolen earrings."

"I was pretty embarrassed," Nick said, then yawned and rested his head on Lexie's shoulder.

Mary reached over and patted his knee. "Why don't you go up to bed for a bit?"

"Are you going to hang around and look after my girls?"

Lexie gave him an affectionate shove. "We're fine. I can take care of things for a while."

"I'm staying," Mary said to Nick. "I'll cook you a nice dinner later."

"Thank you." He went along the couch, kissing all three of them before shaking Angus's hand and heading upstairs.

"I ought to get back and check on the pub," Angus said, five minutes later. "I left Dale on his own."

Lexie rolled her eyes. "He'll be running the place before long."

"The place was dead. And he might be young, but he's very capable. Didn't I tell you I had an instinct for staff? I was right about Dale – he's an asset to the place."

"I have to say, I'm surprised he worked out so well," Lexie said. "I had my doubts."

"I think we all know that." Angus hovered over Mary, looking down at wee Grace. "You weren't exactly subtle."

Lexie had a sinking feeling. Now she knew it wasn't Dale who'd carried out the thefts, she felt bad for ever suspecting him. The rest of the community had been so warm and welcoming, while she'd been hostile and suspicious.

Once she'd settled into a routine with the baby, she'd make more effort to be nice to Dale, if only to appease her own conscience.

CHAPTER TWENTY-EIGHT

By the middle of February, Elspeth had the wedding plans well underway. It had come together much easier than she'd expected and had certainly been easier to organise than Logan had led her to believe. Her excitement was building by the day, and it couldn't come around quickly enough.

She was busy decorating a cake on Saturday morning when Isla wandered into the cafe.

"I brought more paintings," she called, then appeared in the kitchen. "Are you practising your wedding cake?"

"No. I have it all designed though. Did I already show you the drawings?"

"Yes. Logan still can't get over the fact that you're making your own wedding cake."

"How come he's so stressed about my wedding?"

Isla shook her head. "I think organising our wedding has scarred him for life. Anyway, what are you making? It looks yummy."

Elspeth added individual peaks of meringue to the top of the freshly iced cake. "It's lemon meringue cake. For a teenager who loves lemon meringue pie."

"That sounds like a special order," Isla said drearily. "Which means I can't have a slice."

"I'm afraid not. It's for Gary's niece. He called last night in a panic. I think he forgot her birthday or something. He'll be here to pick it up any minute."

"I don't think he had any idea what he was getting himself into when he agreed to let Paige stay with him." Isla leaned against the counter. "I think it's done him good. He seems much more settled. Although that could be the situation with Jess too. I've never seen him smitten like he was with her."

"Are they still not together?"

"No. He hasn't been in touch with her since Hogmanay. I still feel a bit bad about that. Trying to play matchmaker wasn't my best idea. I think I made things worse."

"I don't understand it. If he likes her so much, why doesn't he do something about it."

"Because of Paige. He's taking his responsibility to her very seriously. Whenever Logan meets up with him, he only stays for one or two drinks then has to get home."

The sound of someone walking into the cafe shut them up, and they both shouted hello in response to Gary.

"I've just finished the cake," Elspeth called. "Come and have a look."

He loped into the kitchen and peered over her shoulder. "That looks amazing."

"It's lemon sponge with a layer of cream and lemon curd in the centre. I glazed the top with more lemon curd, then crumbled meringue over it and added mini meringues for decoration."

"Paige will love it." He gave her shoulder a squeeze. "Thanks so much. Hopefully it will go some way to salvaging her birthday."

"I'll box it up for you," Elspeth said.

"How did you manage to forget her birthday?" Isla asked. "I'd have thought she'd have given you plenty of reminders."

"I didn't forget. I expected her to be with her mum, so I didn't plan anything. Donna was supposed to come up and take her for this spa weekend in a hotel, but she called yesterday to say she's got flu so they'll have to postpone." He paused and blew out a breath. "I know she can't help being ill, but it feels as though she constantly lets Paige down."

"Poor Paige," Elspeth murmured as she slid the cake into the box.

"She won't leave her room," Gary said. "I told her to invite her friend over today but she refused."

"Why?" Isla asked.

"She thinks my house is a massive embarrassment."

"It's not that bad," Isla said.

"Apparently it is when you're fifteen and your best friend lives in a nice house with a perfect family. She says this will be the worst birthday ever and she's going to stay in her room until it's over." Gary shook his head. "I thought I could book a spa day for her and her friend, but it costs an absolute fortune and you have to book way in advance. At least she'll have cake."

"Have you got her a present?" Elspeth asked.

"Yeah. A pair of trainers that she wanted."

Isla's eyes lit up. "I bet she'd love some jewellery. You know, I have a lovely range of sea glass jewellery … It'd make a lovely gift."

Gary laughed. "Go on then. Choose something for me. She'd probably like a necklace or earrings."

"I have a set with a necklace *and* earrings."

"I'm sure you do," he said, amused. "Choose whatever you think she'll like and tell me how much I owe you."

They wandered into the cafe and Isla browsed the jewellery cabinet beside the counter. Since the thefts, they'd upgraded to a locked cabinet rather than having the jewellery out on the counter.

"What about a home spa day?" Elspeth said.

Gary quirked an eyebrow. "I hope you're not suggesting I paint her nails."

"No." Elspeth laughed. "Get her friend to come over and they can do facials and manicures and stuff. I can get you a load of beauty treatments."

Isla swung around and grinned at her. "Leana's stash?"

Elspeth nodded and pulled her phone out. She filled Leana in on the situation and asked what she could donate. When she ended the call, Gary was staring at her.

"What's going on?" he asked.

"Alasdair's mum's always buying all these pampering beauty treatments for Leana and she never uses any of it. She'll be here in ten minutes."

Gary looked sceptical. "Paige doesn't want to invite Sophie over to the house."

"Call Sophie's mum," Elspeth said. "Explain the situation and tell her that Paige is sensitive about the house because it's being renovated. Don't ask Paige, just arrange to pick Sophie up on the way home and you can surprise Paige with the pampering afternoon."

"That's actually not a bad idea." He scratched the back of his head. "It's probably better than my idea of getting her a dog."

Isla squinted at him as she gift-wrapped the jewellery. "A dog?"

"Yeah. She's wanted a dog for as long as I can remember. Her mum would never let her have one. She asked me for one for her birthday … found a breeder and everything." He brought up a picture of puppies huddled together in a dog bed. "She said any of these golden retriever pups would be fine. I told her there was no chance, but I can't stop thinking about it. I quite fancy having a dog myself."

Elspeth took the phone from him. "They're gorgeous."

"They are, aren't they?" He took the phone back and looked thoughtful. "Sod it. I'm going to call and see if there are any still available. I'll be back in a minute."

Elspeth and Isla stared after him as he strode out of the cafe. He paced the path at the front with his phone to his ear.

"Is he seriously going to get her a puppy?" Elspeth asked, coming to stand beside Isla.

"It seems like it."

Elspeth tilted her head to one side. "There's something different about him …"

"He doesn't flirt any more," Isla said. "He used to be incapable of talking to any women without flirting."

"Oh, yeah." Elspeth laughed. "That's it."

"I'm not sure whether it's Paige or Jess," Isla said. "But one of them has had a big effect on him."

"He and Jess are both coming to the wedding," Elspeth said, a smile tugging at her lips.

"Are you thinking of matchmaking?"

"Maybe. If the opportunity comes up."

"I already told you that I tried at Hogmanay and it didn't go well."

"It's such a shame they're not together," Elspeth said, sure she wasn't going to be able to resist a bit of matchmaking.

Ten minutes later the door swung open and Gary stepped inside with a huge grin on his face. "There are two puppies left. We can drive down and have a look tomorrow. I also spoke to Sophie's mum. She was really nice. I'm going to pick Sophie up on the way home. Apparently she wanted to bring a present around for Paige anyway."

"I guess it's not going to be the worst birthday after all," Isla said.

Elspeth beamed. "I can't believe you're getting her a puppy."

"Technically, it'll be my dog," he said.

"You know the dog's going to cost you an absolute fortune," Isla said. "Not just buying it, but food and vet bills?"

"Aye. I realise that. I've had to listen to Logan complain about how much he spends on Jasper often enough. It'll be great to have a dog though. I can take him to work with me."

Elspeth moved to open the door at the sight of Leana lumbering along with two big shopping bags.

"That's not all for Paige, is it?" Gary asked as Leana set the bags at his feet.

"Yes. And I can't tell you how happy I am to get rid of it."

"What the hell is it all?" Gary asked, peering into one of the bags.

"That box is a foot spa thing. You fill it with water and put some aromatherapy drops in it and it massages your feet while you soak them. The instructions are in the box. I've never used it." She pushed things around in the other bag. "There are manicure and pedicure sets, face masks, eyebrow shaping kits, nail art …" She held up a hand. "Do I look like someone who could be bothered with nail art? I have no idea why Clare always gives me all these beauty products."

Isla chuckled. "Maybe she thinks you need them."

"Shut up," Leana said lightly.

"I bet Paige will love all of this," Elspeth said. "She'll probably end up being glad that her mum cancelled."

"I really hope it cheers her up." Gary pulled his wallet out and handed Elspeth his credit card. "Try not to clear me out completely. I need money left to buy a dog."

"You're getting a dog?" Leana asked.

"Aye. I think so." He showed her the photo on his phone. After he'd paid for the cake and jewellery, he looked down at Leana's bags. "Should I give you something for all this?"

"No, it's fine." Leana smiled sweetly. "You might be able to do me a small favour in return …"

"Something up with your car by any chance?"

She grimaced. "It's been making a weird knocking sound."

"Bring it over to the garage sometime and I'll have a look."

"Thank you." She held the door for him and they all shouted goodbye at once.

"There was something weird about him today," Leana mused after he'd left.

"He's stopped flirting," Elspeth said.

"That's it!"

Isla took a seat. "It's because he's in love with Jess."

"I thought they weren't together."

"They're not." Elspeth grinned mischievously. "Not yet anyway."

CHAPTER TWENTY-NINE

The first month of parenthood left Lexie in a zombie-like state. Sleep began to feel like a precious commodity, as did time to herself. During the day, Grace would only take naps when out for a walk in the pram. It meant Lexie didn't get a moment of peace while Nick was at work. Half the time she didn't even manage to shower.

That Wednesday afternoon, she was just arriving home from a walk when Nick pulled up at home.

"How was your day?" he asked, kissing her cheek before peering into the pram.

"Fine," Lexie said unenthusiastically.

Nick slipped an arm around her waist and pulled her close. "Are you okay?"

"Yes." She nodded. "Just tired."

"I'll make dinner."

"Thanks."

Nick manoeuvred the pram along the path and Lexie glanced along the road.

"I might wander over and speak to Mum. I'd told her I wanted to start working a few shifts at the pub when Grace was six weeks, but that's coming around quickly and it's clearly not going to happen."

"I'm sure Mary knows that. Go and speak to her and I'll see what I can rustle up to eat."

"I won't be long." She ambled up the road and into the pub.

The warmth of the place enveloped her as soon as she was in the door. A low fire crackled in the grate and the familiar scent of oak and woodsmoke hung in the air. A few tables were occupied and a couple of customers sat along the bar.

"Hi!" Dale said. "How's Grace?"

"Good, thanks," Lexie mumbled through a forced smile. Her plans to befriend Dale hadn't been effective. There was a good chance it was the sleep deprivation, but any time she saw him he seemed to rub her up the wrong way. He might not be the dodgy character she thought he was, but that didn't mean she had to like him. Mostly, she tried to stay out of his way.

"Is my mum around?" Lexie asked.

"Yeah. I'm not sure if she's in the kitchen or upstairs."

A man waved from a table nearby and Dale went over to take their food order.

Lexie was about to go in search of her mum when she was distracted by the light of a phone on the shelf behind the bar. Instinctively she checked the display. It was Dale's dad calling him.

She was about to return it to the shelf but stopped and stared at the display. After glancing at Dale, who was engrossed in chatting with the customers, she swiped her thumb across the phone screen, accepting the call. With her eyes firmly fixed on Dale, Lexie brought the phone to her ear.

"Hello?"

There was a brief pause. "I think you have my son's phone. Who is this?"

"Lexie," she said weakly. What the heck was she doing? "I work with Dale. He's busy now. Maybe you can call back later."

"He won't answer … don't hang up, please … where is he working?"

Lexie's heart rate increased. She should end the call and put the phone back where she'd found it.

"Please," the man whispered.

"He works at the Old Inn in Lannick." As soon as the words were out, her stomach twisted to a tight knot.

"Where is that?"

"I have to go," Lexie said.

"Wait," he said frantically. "I need to know where he is."

"He's your son. If he wanted you to know where he was, he'd have told you himself."

"He ran away. Completely out of the blue. Are you a friend of his?"

"More of an acquaintance." She panicked as Dale set off walking in her direction. "I'm sorry, I have to go," she whispered into the phone, then ended the call and returned the phone to the shelf.

"I didn't know you were here," Mary said, walking out of the back.

Lexie tried to breathe evenly and get her heart rate under control. "I only just got here," she said, her eyes on Dale as he walked to the kitchen.

"Is everything okay?" Mary asked. "You look wiped out."

"I'm tired … So tired. I feel as though I'm losing my mind half of the time." She swallowed hard. "I wanted to let you know that I won't be coming back to work as soon as I thought."

"That's okay. I assumed you might decide to take more time. Dale's been brilliant, so we're covered anyway."

"What are you saying about me?" Dale asked, grinning as he joined them behind the bar.

"Saying that you're a natural at working in a pub," Mary said, giving his arm a gentle pat.

"It's fun." He smiled at Lexie. "You were so lucky to grow up here."

"Yeah." Guiltily, her gaze darted to his phone on the shelf. What on earth had possessed her to answer it? She should tell him he'd missed a call from his dad. That was the least she could do.

A customer at the end of the bar asked for another pint and Dale moved to pour it.

"Are you hanging around for a while?" Mary asked Lexie. "Do you want something to eat?"

She shook her head. "Nick was going to cook. I should get back." Slowly, she walked around the bar, pausing before she reached the door.

Dale caught her eye and beamed at her.

She opened her mouth to say something but couldn't find any words. "Bye," she mumbled, before walking quickly away.

The phone call played on her mind all evening. She wanted to tell Nick about it but suspected it would end in an argument and she was too tired. It wasn't as though she'd done anything terrible. Answering someone else's phone was hardly a crime.

That's what she kept telling herself, but the guilt that niggled deep in her gut wouldn't go away. Every time she got up with Grace in the night, her mind replayed the phone conversation and her guilt intensified.

By the time Nick was about to leave for work the next morning, she couldn't take it any more.

"I did something," she said, as he took a final swig of his coffee. "It'll sound bad, but if I don't tell someone I might go mad."

His smile fell away as he sighed. "What did you do?"

"When I was at the pub yesterday, Dale's phone rang and I answered it."

"Who was it?"

"His dad."

"And?"

"And I told him that Dale was working." She winced. "He said Dale had run away. He wanted to know where he was ..."

"Please don't say you told him."

She winced again. "It just slipped out."

"Does Dale know you told his dad where he is?"

"No."

He looked at her in confusion. "What were you thinking?"

"I *wasn't* thinking. But he sounded like a nice guy, and he was clearly worried about Dale."

Nick shook his head. "Maybe he just sounded worried to get information from you. Have you ever stopped to wonder why Dale moved hundreds of miles and took refuge in a remote village on a Scottish island?"

"You have no idea why he ran away. Maybe he'd done something really bad and didn't want to be found."

Nick tipped the last of his coffee into the sink. "Are you going to tell Dale what you did or am I?"

"You're being very condescending."

"Clearly you wanted me to be the voice of reason or you wouldn't have told me. If you don't tell him, I'm going to. But I guess you already knew that."

"Fine," she huffed. "I'll tell him."

He gave her a quick kiss before he left. After picking up the phone to call Dale, she immediately set it aside again. It would probably be better to go over to his place later and speak to him in person. That would be easier than telling him over the phone.

As usual, the day went by in a blur of feeding and nappies and trying to get Grace to sleep. When Nick called in the middle of the afternoon, Lexie was pacing the living room with Grace cradled in the crook of her arm.

"Did you speak to Dale?" Nick asked.

She rolled her eyes at the predictable question. "Not yet."

"Lexie," he said, exasperated.

"I haven't had a chance," she said defensively. "Grace has only had a twenty-minute nap all day, and I decided to use that time to eat and have a cup of coffee. I'll talk to Dale when I see him. I'm sure you're making a mountain out of a molehill anyway. So what if his dad knows where he is?"

The silence down the line was unnerving. When Nick chose to say nothing, it was much more effective than arguing.

"I'll see you later," he finally said.

She stopped pacing and felt a stab of anxiety in the pit of her stomach. "This is a really stupid thing for you to be angry with me about," she said after swallowing the lump in her throat. "Why is some random guy who we barely know causing issues between us?"

"Because you treat him like he's some sort of criminal, and I honestly can't understand why."

Her throat burned and tears stung her eyes. "I always had a bad feeling about him," she said, knowing she sounded irrational. "Every instinct I have tells me not to trust him. But I also know you'll say I'm hormonal and neurotic because I just had a baby." She lowered herself onto the couch and gazed down at baby Grace. "And maybe I am, but I can't ignore my gut feeling. I hate that you don't believe me."

"It's not that I don't believe you," he said softly. "I just don't understand it. Dale's a nice kid. He hasn't done anything wrong. How long can you think someone's a bad person based on no evidence?"

Lexie stared at the giraffe motif on Grace's blanket. "I don't like him," she said sadly. "I've tried to give him a chance, but at the end of the day, I just don't like him. I can't do anything about that. Can you tell him about me taking the call from his dad? I don't think I can face it."

"I've got a class now but I'll try and speak to him later."

Lexie felt restless after she'd hung up. She put Grace in her sling and set off for a walk with her snuggled against her chest. She'd hoped the fresh air and exercise might help her clear her head, but her thoughts continued to race as she walked on the path around the loch.

The rational part of her brain couldn't disagree with Nick; Dale really hadn't done anything wrong. But no matter how hard Lexie tried, she couldn't get past the feeling that there was more to him than he'd let on. She just couldn't make sense of him. Previously he'd told her that he hated his dad, but if he was so bad, Dale would have blocked him and not still have him listed as "Dad" in his contacts. Wouldn't he?

She consoled herself with the fact that Nick was going to speak to Dale. If he really had a good reason for not wanting his dad to know his whereabouts, at least he'd be warned that he knew where he was.

Grace stared up at Lexie for almost an hour and a half as she trudged around the loch. Her little eyes only drooped closed as they were returning to the house. Lexie debated whether to keep her in the sling before deciding to risk transferring her to the cot. It was the first time she'd managed to put her down in her own bedroom, and as she crept out of the room, she decided she'd try for a quick shower while she slept.

Lexie was lathering shampoo into her hair when Grace began to cry. She hadn't fully closed the bathroom or bedroom door, but even so, she must've been wailing loudly for Lexie to hear it over the running water. Tipping her head back under the spray, Lexie's shoulders slumped. She stared longingly at the bottle of conditioner for a moment before Grace's cries became even more insistent. Nick called out to her just as she was about to turn the water off, and she called back to say she wouldn't be long before grabbing at the conditioner as though it was a prized treasure. The crying stopped almost immediately. Grace had probably fallen straight back to sleep in Nick's arms. Taking her time, Lexie basked in the warm spray before finally stepping out to get dry and dressed.

In their bedroom, she put the folded washing away, then followed Nick's murmuring voice to Grace's room.

"How was work?" she asked, then froze as she realised the

figure in the rocking chair wasn't Nick. Her heart pounded as she looked at Dale with Grace in his arms. "What are you doing?" she managed, her throat feeling as though it was being squeezed.

"Nick wanted to talk to me about something. He told me to come over." He looked down at Grace resting happily on his forearms. "She's really cute."

Lexie took a few quick steps towards him. "Give her to me," she said, a quiver to her voice. Her hands trembled as she reached for her baby.

"I heard her crying," Dale said, whipping his gaze up to Lexie. "I only wanted to check everything was okay. The front door was open so I came in to check."

Lexie scooped Grace up, hugging her to her chest. "You don't walk into someone else's house and pick up their baby. What's wrong with you?"

"I just heard her crying." He looked genuinely surprised by Lexie's harsh tone. "I was only trying to help. I called out to you when I came in. You shouted back ..."

"I thought you were Nick." Through the window, she caught sight of Nick stepping out of his car and greeting the neighbour in the garden next door.

"Please leave," Lexie said firmly.

"Nick wanted to talk to me."

Lexie inhaled deeply. "I answered your phone yesterday. It was your dad. He asked where you were and I told him. Nick thought you should know. That's all he wanted to tell you. Now you can leave."

He stood in the centre of the room, staring at Lexie. "You told my dad where I am?"

"Yes," she said, wishing he'd leave.

Dale's shoulders tensed and the colour drained from his face. "Why?" he whispered.

"He asked. I didn't realise he wasn't supposed to know. He sounded worried about you."

He cast his gaze to the floor and took a few slow steps to the doorway. "You've ruined everything," he said quietly.

"I don't understand what the problem is."

Dale shook his head sadly. "I'm sorry if I scared you – picking Grace up. I only wanted to check she was okay." He took a step away, then turned back, his eyes shining with tears. "And I'm sorry if I did something to make you hate me."

"I don't hate you," she murmured, feeling as though he was about to disappear from Lannick as quickly and mysteriously as he'd appeared.

"Every time you look at me it feels as though you hate me. I don't know what I did wrong. Everyone else was so nice."

Nick shouted up to her and she called back to say she'd be down in a minute.

In the silence that followed, she stared at Dale with the feeling that she was missing some vital pieces of a puzzle.

"I'm sorry for telling your dad where you are. I shouldn't have done that."

"It's okay." He forced a smile before walking away.

"Maybe you could stay for dinner and we can talk?" Lexie followed close behind him. "If there's a problem with your dad we might be able to help."

"You can't help," he said as he reached the bottom of the stairs. "I need to go."

"Go where?" she asked, not sure if he was talking about leaving their house or leaving Skye.

"I need to think," he muttered. "Figure out what to do."

"Hey," Nick said in the kitchen, looking slightly confused.

Dale kept his head down, saying a quick goodbye as he slipped out of the front door.

"You told him about the phone call?" Nick asked Lexie.

"Yes." She rubbed Grace's back.

Nick laid a gentle kiss on the top of Grace's head and another on Lexie's cheek. "Why was he upstairs?"

"I was in the shower. Grace was crying and he let himself in.

When I came out of the shower he was sitting in the rocking chair with her. I'd heard him come in but thought it was you."

"What?" Nick asked, screwing his face up.

"It was really creepy. Then I told him about calling his dad and he bolted."

Nick rubbed her arm. "Wait here. I'll be back soon." He headed out of the door, ignoring Lexie when she shouted after him.

When he returned a couple of minutes later, she'd moved to the couch.

"He was driving away," Nick told her. "And he's not answering his phone."

Lexie's jaw tensed. "Why are you more concerned about him than us? He freaked me out, and you didn't bother to ask if I'm okay."

"I'm not more concerned about him," Nick said, his forehead creased.

"But I told you that he let himself into our house and you ran off to check he's okay."

"No. I was going to tell him to stay away from you. It's definitely not okay for him to let himself into the house. I can't believe he went upstairs and picked Grace up." He rubbed at his temples. "He always seemed trustworthy, but clearly something's not right. Are you okay?"

"Yes. I'm fine." She leaned her head against his shoulder while Grace drifted back to sleep in her arms. "He scared me for a minute, but I don't actually think he had any ill intentions. He heard Grace crying and wanted to check everything was okay."

"You're not sticking up for him now, are you?"

"When I mentioned his dad he looked scared. And he started talking as though he was going to pack up and leave." She looked up at Nick. "I'm worried I did something terrible when I told his dad where he is."

"It's partly Dale's fault for being so secretive. But there's no point in worrying. He didn't take any of his stuff with him. Just got in the car and drove. He'll be back. And we don't know that his dad will even turn up here. Or if it would be a bad thing if he did. You said he sounded nice."

"Yes." That's what she kept telling herself. "But I also don't trust my instincts about people at the moment."

CHAPTER THIRTY

On Saturday morning, Lexie woke with a tightness in her chest. It radiated to her stomach when Nick tried to call Dale and got no answer. Even though she'd lost faith in her gut feelings, something told her that trouble was brewing, and worry niggled in every part of her.

Late in the morning, Nick went over to the bunkhouse but there was no answer at the door. Dale was due at work soon, but when Lexie called her mum to see if he was there, she said he hadn't arrived yet.

"Where the hell is he?" Lexie grumbled, pacing the kitchen and keeping an eye on the window for his car.

"He'll turn up," Nick said confidently. "I looked in the windows at the bunkhouse and everything looks normal. No signs of him having done a midnight flit."

"I have a bad feeling," she murmured, glancing out of the window again.

When Nick took Grace for a nappy change, Lexie rummaged in a kitchen drawer until she found her old key for the bunkhouse. Maybe she could pop in and check everything was okay. There was no real harm in it. Nick would probably argue otherwise, so she shouted that she was going over to the pub and would be back soon.

After pressing the doorbell at the bunkhouse, she waited on the doorstep with her key poised in her hand. Her phone vibrating in her pocket almost made her jump out of her skin. Wandering away from the door, she answered the phone to her dad.

"You haven't seen Dale, have you?" Angus asked.

"No."

"He's supposed to be working," he said. "I haven't heard anything from him. Which I thought was strange in itself, but I've also just had some guy looking for him and claiming to be his dad."

Lexie's heart rate went through the roof. "What did you say to him?"

"Sent him packing. Told him I don't give out details of my employees and pointed out that if he's his dad, he should probably know where his son is."

"What was he like?"

"Just your average fella. Seemed a bit on edge. More so when I wouldn't tell him anything. He reckoned he'd spoken with another staff member on the phone who'd told him Dale was working here."

"That was me," she admitted, then stopped dead when she caught sight of a man sitting hunched over on the wall at the other side of the car park. "How long ago did this guy leave?"

"A couple of minutes ago. Why?"

"No reason. I'll let you know if I see Dale."

"Any chance you can come in and cover his shift? Just over lunchtime."

"I can't." Her gaze was fixed on the guy with his head in his hands. "I'll call you back later." She hung up without saying goodbye and glanced at the bunkhouse before walking slowly across the car park.

The man looked to be in his forties. He wore jeans and a

dark jumper under a grey jacket that didn't look anything near warm enough. Lexie shivered looking at him. He hadn't noticed her, so she purposely disturbed the gravel with her shoe. His head shot up and he looked at her questioningly with piercing blue eyes. His salt and pepper hair looked recently cut. She hadn't been sure what to expect from Dale's dad, but nothing about him unnerved Lexie. The hint of stubble at his jaw and dark circles under his eyes made him look weary.

Realising he was waiting for her to say something, Lexie cleared her throat. He might not even be Dale's dad. For all she knew, he was just another tourist.

"Is everything okay?" she asked.

"Fine, thanks."

Registering his mobile in his hands, she tipped her head at it. "I'm local. If you're lost I can probably help you out."

"I'm not lost." He unlocked the phone screen and an image of Dale appeared. "I'm looking for my son," he said, holding the phone out. "Maybe you've seen him? I think he's been working at the pub here. His name's Dale." His finger swiped the photo to bring up another. This time it was the two of them grinning. Lexie couldn't take her eyes off it.

"Do you recognise him?" the man asked. "I really need to find him."

Lexie pulled her shoulder blades together as she stepped back. "Maybe he doesn't want to be found."

"You know him?" he said in a rush.

"Yes. I also know that he doesn't want to see you." She shuffled back another couple of steps. "He's got a lot of friends around here. If you've come to cause trouble, people aren't going to take that well."

He sprang up from the wall. "I haven't come to cause trouble. I just need to find Dale."

"I already told you he doesn't want to be found."

He dragged his teeth across his bottom lip as he shook his

head. "Why? I don't understand it. He was a normal, happy kid. We were close."

"There must be some reason he wanted to get away from you."

His brow furrowed as though he was trying to figure that out for himself. "He started to go off the rails a bit, but I thought it was the usual teenage stuff. Then he stole my car and vanished without a word. All I've had since then is the odd message to let me know he's alive. I need to know what's going on."

Lexie was torn. He seemed genuine, but maybe he was just a good actor. "When I see him, I'll let him know you're looking for him."

"Wait," he called as she began to walk away. "It was you I spoke to on the phone, wasn't it?"

She stopped and turned slowly back to him. "I shouldn't have answered the phone, never mind tell you where he was. I don't know why I did that."

"I'm really grateful that you did. Thank you."

"I can't help you any more than I already have. I'm sorry."

He swallowed hard. "I understand. Thanks anyway."

As she was about to leave, Lexie paused and looked over at the bunkhouse. Things weren't adding up. "It doesn't make any sense," she murmured.

"What doesn't?"

"Nothing makes sense." Taking a step towards him, she held her hand out. "Can I have another look at those photos?"

"Of course." He unlocked the phone and passed it to her. On the camera roll were rows and rows of photos.

"Is it okay if I look through them?"

He pressed his lips together as he nodded.

As she flicked through, Lexie moved to sit on the wall.

Dale's dad hovered over her. "What are you looking for?"

"He looks happy," she said, taking in the goofy photos. Even on the ones where he clearly didn't want his photo to be taken, there was still a glint of affection in his eyes. Lexie glanced up. "You really like taking selfies, don't you?"

"It was a bit of an inside joke." He sank onto the wall beside her. "It was always just the two of us, so I got good at selfies of us. At some point Dale decided it was embarrassing, which is why it looks as though I've got him in a headlock in half of them."

She smiled at one where Dale was obviously squirming to get away. "How old was Dale when his mum died?" From the way his eyes widened, she knew immediately that she'd over-stepped the mark. "Sorry. I didn't mean to pry."

"It's not a problem. But Dale's mum isn't dead."

"Oh." Confused, she passed the phone back. "Dale said she'd died not long ago."

"She wasn't around for most of his life, but she's definitely alive. Dale had been spending some time with her before he took off. He didn't tell her where he was going either."

"That's weird." Lexie rubbed her hands together to warm her fingers. If there was something dodgy about this guy, then pregnancy hormones had definitely wrecked her instincts. "He's been staying over there," she said, pointing at the bunkhouse. "He's not there now though. When I told him that I'd spoken to you he freaked out and no one's seen him since. That was last night. He's supposed to be working at the pub now, but he didn't turn up.

"Wait!" she called when he strode away from her in the direction of the bunkhouse. Hurrying after him, she caught up to him at the door. "He's not answering the door or his phone. And his car's not here. There's really no point in banging on the door," she said, raising her voice over the hammering of his fist. "Hey." She put a hand on his arm to stop him. "What's your name?"

"Matthew," he said, his shoulders slumping.

"I've got a key," she told him. "I shouldn't really use it, but we could go in and quickly check that everything's okay. You need to calm down though."

"Okay." He took a deep breath and stepped aside to let her get to the lock. "Thanks."

As she opened the door, Lexie called out to Dale but got no reply. It briefly occurred to her that neither Nick nor her parents would approve of her going into a house alone with a man whose son seemed to be terrified of him. Ignoring the thought, Lexie stepped inside and hoped that her instincts weren't completely off. The kitchen was tidy enough, and a quick glance into the living room didn't reveal anything obviously out of place. Upstairs, Dale's bedroom looked like that of a typical teenage boy. The bed wasn't made and clothes were strewn across the floor and on the chair in the corner.

"Everything looks normal," Lexie said. "It definitely doesn't look as though he's not intending to come back."

Matthew stayed in the doorway, scanning the mess while Lexie moved across the hall to check the spare room.

"Did you report him missing?" she asked, standing in the doorway. The room was empty apart from the furniture.

"Yeah. But since he messaged me to say he was fine, the police wouldn't do anything. Legally, he's an adult and can do what he wants. My only option was to report the car stolen, but I didn't want to do that."

Nodding, Lexie pulled the door to the spare room closed but stopped when a box beside the desk caught her eye. "That's weird," she mumbled, moving closer and registering Stephanie's name written across the top of the box in her grandad's distinctive wobbly scrawl. Pulling a flap back revealed an assortment of old photographs and papers. A few more photos were laid out on the desk.

"What is it?" Matthew asked.

"Nothing." She shook her head. "Just old family photos. My dad must have stored them here. I'm not sure why."

Matthew moved past her and touched one of the photos on the desk. "I don't understand," he whispered.

"It's a load of junk," she said through gritted teeth as she glanced at the variety of photos of her with her grandparents and Stephanie when she was a kid. The colour drained from Matthew's face as he sank onto the chair.

"We'll find Dale," Lexie said sympathetically. "I'm sure he's fine, wherever he is. And he'll definitely be back. He made loads of friends here, so there's no way he'd leave without saying goodbye."

Matthew's eye shifted to the photos on the desk. "I really don't understand what's going on."

"Why don't I get you a glass of water?" Lexie suggested. "Then we'll figure out what to do about Dale."

When she returned a couple of minutes later, Matthew had pulled more photos out of the box and was spreading them out across the desk.

"What are you doing?" Lexie asked.

He glanced up at her. "I don't know."

"I had a thought," Lexie said, ignoring the fact that he was acting so strangely. "Maybe Dale thinks you're angry at him for taking your car. It might have been an impulsive teenage stunt that he took too far and then didn't know how to fix the situation …"

"I told him in the messages that I didn't care about the car. That I didn't care about anything as long as he was okay." He took the glass from her and set it on the desk without drinking any of it. "That's not the problem anyway," he said, picking up one of the photos. "Is this you?"

"Aye. With my grandad." Stephanie was in the picture too but standing a little away from them, looking as though she was there under duress.

Matthew's finger went to Stephanie. "And this is …?"

"That's Stephanie. My mother."

"So, you weren't …" He trailed off and squeezed the bridge of his nose.

"I wasn't *what*?"

"This will sound strange … you weren't adopted, were you?"

"Yes, I was. Probably not long after this photo was taken. I was five at the time. My biological mother wasn't very reliable, so my grandparents had been taking care of me. Then my gran got ill so I went to live with my grandad's brother and his wife. They adopted me a little while later … sorry, I don't know why I'm telling you this."

"Because I asked," he said wearily. "I don't even know your name."

"Lexie," she said, slightly puzzled as to how he could possibly know she was adopted.

He looked at her with such intensity that she took a step back. "I think I know why Dale ran away," he said. "But I'm also more confused than ever."

"Why did he run away?"

His brow creased. "I think he was looking for you."

"Why would he be looking for me?" Lexie asked, smiling through her confusion.

Matthew's gaze went to the photo in his hand, his thumb beside Stephanie. "This is Dale's mother."

"I don't think so," Lexie said, her bemused smile stuck in place. "Stephanie doesn't have any other kids. I'm sure I'd know if she did." As soon as the words were out, she realised they probably weren't true. She'd seen Stephanie sporadically through her life, but there were massive chunks of time when she hadn't seen her. Of course she could have had more kids. It's not as though she ever really told Lexie anything about her life.

Her chest felt tight and she took a few steps backwards and lowered herself onto the bed. "Stephanie's Dale's mother?"

He nodded slowly. "I watched her give birth to him."

"Right …" A lump formed in her throat, making it difficult to breathe. "Okay … but that would mean that Dale is …" She trailed off, her mind feeling as though it were spinning at about a million miles per hour.

"That would make Dale your brother," Matthew said gently. "I guess he found out about you when he was spending time with Stephanie."

"Dale came looking for me because I'm his sister?" Lexie's hands shook as she pushed her hair behind her ears. "I was awful to him. I mean, he didn't tell me who he was, but even so, I was pretty rude to him. I thought he was secretive and suspicious. Which I was right about – he did have a secret." She snapped her gaze to Matthew. "Why the hell didn't he tell me who he was?"

"Maybe he thought you'd freak out," he said with a hint of a smile.

"I think it's quite normal to freak out when you find out you have a brother that you knew nothing about. I could bloody kill Stephanie. Why the hell didn't she tell me I have a brother? How many more siblings do I have hidden away?"

"None that I know of." He stood when she did. "Where are you going?"

"To find Dale. I snapped at him yesterday. He thinks I hate him."

"Why don't you wait a few minutes and let this sink in? Your head must be spinning. I know mine is." He hurried down the stairs behind her.

"I don't want to sit around. I need to find Dale."

"Just wait a minute."

"I can't," she said, ploughing on towards the door. "If he's my half-brother, I need to find him and talk to him."

"Please will you listen to me?" Matthew said in a tone that stopped Lexie in her tracks. "I don't think he is your half-brother."

CHAPTER THIRTY-ONE

Lexie stared at Matthew, sure she'd never been so confused in her life. "If we have the same mother, I'm fairly sure that makes Dale my half-brother."

"Maybe not." Matthew swallowed hard and took his wallet from his back pocket. He opened it to reveal a couple of passport-sized photos of Dale when he was younger. From behind them, he retrieved a baby photo and held it out to Lexie.

"What's this?" she asked, staring down at it.

"I'm not sure." The skin around his eyes crinkled. "I think … maybe … is that you?"

"Me?" She stared at the photo again, then turned it over and found her date of birth written neatly on the back. Her heart thudded against her ribs as she examined the baby again. She'd seen the same photo at her grandad's house. "Yes," she finally said. "It's me. Why do you have it?"

He gave her a crooked smile and tipped his head towards the kitchen table. "Maybe we should sit down."

She shook her head, her chest feeling as though it was being crushed. "I'd rather you just tell me why you have a photo of me in your wallet."

"I need to speak to Stephanie. I'm not quite sure what's going on."

"Tell me what you do know," Lexie said, as tears blurred her vision. "Please."

His eyes shifted to look at the photo in her hand, then he moved to a chair. "Stephanie and I had two children. The first, our daughter, was adopted at birth."

"If you're thinking that was me, I already told you I wasn't adopted until I was five."

"Yeah." He ran his hands through his hair. "And you were adopted by family, so Stephanie knew where you were the whole time?"

"Yes."

"Has she been in contact with you a lot?"

"No." She thought back to the time she'd lived with Stephanie when she was a teenager. "Whenever she has been in touch, things turned out badly. I'm better off without her."

Matthew tilted his head to one side as he searched her features. It was the same way that Dale looked at her sometimes.

"We're not related," Lexie snapped, roughly pulling out a chair to sit down. "My biological father was some loser who left as soon as Stephanie found out she was pregnant. She definitely didn't go on to have more kids with the guy."

"But the date on that photo is your date of birth?"

She idly turned the photo over again. "Yes."

"In that case, I'm almost certain you're my daughter."

She let out a humourless laugh. "So you're claiming to be the loser who left as soon as you found out about my existence?"

"I think Stephanie lied to us both," he said sadly. "I'm not even sure why I'm surprised. I should try and get hold of her." He took his phone out and wandered towards the living room as he held it to his ear.

Lexie's mind raced and her heart was working overtime. She listened while Matthew left a message for Stephanie, calmly asking her to call him back.

"None of this makes any sense," Lexie said when he hung up. "I honestly don't understand how you could be my father. And why you think I was adopted at birth."

"I don't even know where to start. This is all very surreal." He sat back down and rested his forearms on the table. "Stephanie and I had been together for six months or so when she found out she was pregnant …"

"And you ditched her and took off?" Lexie asked through a lump in her throat.

"No. She ditched me. Told me I'd ruined her life and that she didn't want anything to do with me. I tried to tell her we'd figure it out and that everything would be okay, but she wouldn't listen. She wouldn't even discuss it with me."

Sadness flashed in his eyes. "One day she called and said she'd had an abortion. She said the problem was solved and that we could get on with our lives, but she didn't want to see me again. I only found out years later that she went ahead with the pregnancy without telling me." His eyes pleaded with Lexie, as though he was desperate for her to believe him.

Lexie shook her head, unable and unwilling to entertain the idea that the guy opposite her might be her biological father.

"You would have been about six when I found out about you," he went on. "I'd moved down to Manchester. Stephanie got in touch out of the blue and would turn up and stay with me for a few weeks, then disappear again. After her mum died she came to live with me permanently."

"That's when Angus and Mary adopted me," Lexie put in.

"I still didn't know that Stephanie had gone through with the pregnancy. Things were pretty good with us for a year or so. I wanted to get married, she didn't … that was always an issue. Then Stephanie got pregnant again. That's when she told me that she'd gone through with the first pregnancy. I was going to doctors' appointments with her so I guess she realised it would probably come out that it wasn't her first child." He paused and took a breath. "Everything fell apart between us after that. I was furious with her. I couldn't seem to get past it."

"But if you were upset, why didn't you try and find me …" She closed her eyes, still not ready to believe that they were talking about her. "If you knew you had a child … why wouldn't you look for them?"

"Stephanie told me it was a closed adoption and that she hadn't put my name on the birth certificate. As far as I was concerned, there was nothing I could do. I looked into it with the adoption agency but hit a wall immediately."

"So what happened then? You forgot about me and got on with your life? I presume you and Stephanie split up?"

"I didn't just get on with my life," he said, pain evident in his features. "Stephanie and I stayed together until Dale was born. I wanted Dale to have a normal family life." He frowned, as though reliving events in his head. "He was two weeks old the first time she took off. I had no idea where she'd gone or if she was ever coming back. She came and went for the first year of his life. Sometimes she'd disappear for a few days, or sometimes a few weeks. In the end, I said she had to decide whether she was in or out. I couldn't cope with not knowing when she was going to be there and worrying about where she was when she wasn't."

"She chose to leave?" Lexie guessed.

"Yes. Which was actually a relief. My parents were living in Leeds and I found a place near them so they could help with Dale. Stephanie would call or message me occasionally, but she stayed away. When Dale was a teenager he became curious about her and we arranged for them to meet."

"I presume that was a disaster?"

"For me it was," he said with a reluctant smile. "They got on really well and I hated it. I was the one who was always there for him, and suddenly she was the one he wanted to hang out with. It didn't seem fair, especially because if I complained about him spending time with her, I ended up looking like the annoying, nagging parent."

"She did the same to me," Lexie said, fingering the edge of the photo in her hand and trying not to think about the fact that he'd been carrying it in his wallet for all these years.

"How do you mean?"

"I went to live with her when I was sixteen. I thought she was so cool …" She chewed on the inside of her lip. "Until I actually needed her to be a parent and then she completely let me down."

"I'm sorry."

She shrugged. "It doesn't matter. Like I said, I'm better off without her. I guess Dale figured that out too, considering he told everyone here that his mother's dead."

"The last time I saw him, he was going to stay with her for a few days. It was last October. He was studying for his A levels and doing well. Then he went to visit Stephanie and didn't come back. Stephanie said he was there for a couple of days and then disappeared. I guess he found out about you and set off to find you. I just don't understand why he couldn't tell me that." He dropped his head to his hands and rubbed his temples.

"I'll help you find him," Lexie said. "You can talk to him and figure everything out."

"Thank you."

Lexie nodded. "I can't do anything more than that though."

"What do you mean?"

"I mean, if you really are my biological father, it doesn't make any difference to me. I already have parents and they're great. I don't need a brother or another dad. I have all the family I need."

When he reached for the photo of her and slid it back into his wallet, she felt like snatching it from him. It was creepy that he had a picture of her.

"I just want to find Dale," he said quietly.

CHAPTER THIRTY-TWO

Lexie left Matthew in the bunkhouse and walked home in a daze. As she entered the living room, Nick started talking about dinner. He was sitting on the floor beside Grace, who was wriggling on her play mat. Stunned, Lexie stood over them, not registering a word Nick was saying.

Finally, he nudged her leg and called her name. "What's going on? You're miles away."

"Something happened." She squeezed her eyes closed. "I was looking for Dale."

"Did you find him?"

Her legs felt like jelly and she moved to the couch. "I think he's my brother."

"What?" Nick let out a confused laugh.

"I can't get my head around it, but Stephanie's his mother. So that makes him my brother."

"What the heck are you talking about? Dale's mum's dead …"

"That was a lie," Lexie said, chewing the corner of her thumbnail. "I don't know why he lied about it, but he did."

"I don't understand." Nick came to sit beside her. "Have you spoken to Dale?"

"No. His dad's here. I spoke to him. I used my key to get into the bunkhouse and there was a box of Stephanie's things … old photos of me and her with my grandparents." Her chin wobbled and her chest heaved as a rush of emotions swept through her.

"So that's why Dale came to Lannick?" Nick asked, his brow wrinkled. "To find you?"

"It seems like it."

"That's crazy." They sat in confused silence. "What did his dad say?" Nick asked eventually. "Did he know that was why Dale was here?"

"He had no idea. He only figured it out when he saw the photos of Stephanie and me." Emotions squeezed at her windpipe and tears spilled down her cheeks. "He has a photo of me," she spluttered.

"Who?"

"Matthew. Dale's dad. He has a photo of me in his wallet from when I was a baby."

Nick's eyes widened. "I'm really confused."

"Me too," she said in a shaky voice. "He thinks he's my biological father."

Nick screwed his features up. "What?"

"He and Stephanie had another child. Stephanie didn't tell him about me until after Mary and Angus had adopted me. And she told him it was a closed adoption."

Nick's jaw hung open. "He really thinks he's your dad?"

"Yes. He seemed genuine. And I don't see any reason for him to make that up. Plus he has a photo of me, with my date of birth on it." More tears came and she leaned into Nick's embrace as he folded his arms around her.

"I guess you were right about there being something off about Dale," Nick remarked, rubbing her back as she calmed down.

"I can't believe he has a photo of me," Lexie sniffed, reaching for a tissue. "Whenever I imagined my biological father, I thought he was some selfish idiot who wasn't even worth thinking about. I never cared about him." She blew her nose. "But he's been carrying a photo of me in his wallet for years."

"What's he like?"

"I don't know. He seemed nice. Normal. But that can't be right if he was in a relationship with Stephanie. He can't be that normal."

"Is he still with her?"

"No. Apparently she hasn't really been in Dale's life. He only met her recently. That's how he found out about me."

"What a mess."

"I feel terrible for being suspicious of him."

Nick sighed. "You were right to be suspicious of him."

"Except I was suspicious for all the wrong reasons. And now I don't know where he is." Reaching for her phone, she scrolled to his number and pressed dial, not quite sure what she'd say if he answered. When he didn't, she looked sadly at the phone. "Should I send him a message? Tell him I know everything and ask him to call me?"

"I don't know. He might panic and leave."

"That's what worries me." She shook her head. "If he was spending time with Stephanie before he came here, I presume she somehow traumatised him. Especially since he's claiming his mum's dead. Knowing her, she probably said something to make him wish she was." Sighing heavily, she leaned back on the couch. "I don't know what to do. I need to talk to him. And I've left his dad at the bunkhouse. I'm not sure what to do about him either."

"Let's wait a while and see if Dale turns up. Maybe you should send him a message and tell him you'd like to speak to him. He might reach out."

She nodded and did just that, then almost leapt out of her skin when the phone rang five minutes later.

"Is it Dale?" Nick asked, rocking Grace in his arms as he paced the room.

"No. It's Tim. I guess the activity centre is falling apart without me and he wants me to come back to work." She smiled as she answered the phone and exchanged pleasantries.

"The old bids are missing you on the hikes," he said, getting down to business.

"I'm not ready to come back to work," Lexie said lightly. "I guess I won't come back for a few months at the earliest."

"That's fine. There's no rush. I thought I could get the hiking group to come for coffee and cake one morning and you could bring the baby along. They're dying to meet her."

"Oh, I'd like that. I'm free any day, so just let me know when."

"I'll set something up for next week and get back to you. I was sorry to hear about Dale leaving," he said, changing the subject. "He's been a good worker."

"He's leaving?"

"Yeah," he said slowly. "I assumed you'd know. He told me this afternoon … something about a family emergency and he needs to leave in a hurry."

"When did you see him?" Lexie asked in a rush.

"He was cleaning the cabins this morning. I asked if he could hang around and do a few extra jobs. As far as I know, he's still here."

Lexie leapt up from the couch. "Don't let him leave."

"What?"

"Don't tell him you've spoken to me. I've been trying to get hold of him. It's a long story but I need to speak to him. I'm on my way now. Don't say anything to him, but if he's going to leave, keep him chatting."

"What on earth's going on?"

"I'll explain later. I'm on my way now." She ended the call and looked at Nick. "Dale's at the activity centre."

"Will you be all right talking to him on your own?"

"Yes. I need to speak to him alone." She kissed Nick's cheek and gave Grace's tummy a tickle. "I have to go quick before he leaves."

"Good luck," Nick called after her as she rushed out of the door.

The walk to the activity centre had never felt so long. Her fitness levels were pretty low following the pregnancy and she wasn't completely healed yet, so she forced herself not to rush too much. Plus, she needed to be calm when she got there.

Tim was hanging around in his office doorway when she arrived.

"Where is he?" she asked.

"I asked him to check the climbing equipment against the inventory. What's going on?"

"I can't explain now. It's a long story." She paused and took a breath as the events of the afternoon made her slightly light-headed. "It's also a really strange story. I actually can't believe this is happening."

"Are you okay?" he asked, the skin around his eyes crinkled in concern.

"Yeah. Sorry to be so cryptic. I'll explain everything another time." She set off towards the equipment room and moved slowly inside. Dale was standing in front of the helmet rack with a clipboard in his hand.

"Hi," she said, feeling as though she was approaching a wild horse and wondering whether it would bolt.

He bit his lip as he turned to her. "I'm supposed to be at a shift at the pub," he said sheepishly. "I wanted to call and say I couldn't work any more, but I knew Angus would ask lots of questions and I wasn't sure what I'd say."

"Tim said you're leaving."

"Yeah. I think it's time I went home."

"Were you planning on telling me who you really are before you left?"

Panic flashed in his eyes and he froze to the spot.

"Your dad's at the bunkhouse. We found the box of Stephanie's things. He figured most things out from that."

"I'm sorry," he muttered.

"Why didn't you tell me?"

His shoulders slumped and he moved to sit on the wooden bench in the middle of the room. "I was going to … I didn't really think about what I'd do when I found you." He looked sadly up at her. "I also didn't expect to find you so easily. So when I did … I kept wanting to say something, but I didn't know how. Angus offered me the job and I thought maybe once you knew me a bit, it would be easier to bring it up. Except you didn't seem to like me. I thought you'd freak out if I told you we were related. After a while, it felt as though I'd left it too long. I thought everyone would hate me for not mentioning it earlier."

"You said your mum was dead," Lexie said, sinking onto the space beside him. "Why did you say that?"

"I panicked. I wanted to tell the truth, but everyone was looking at me … I didn't know how to explain. I blurted out the first thing that came to my head. It was so stupid. I felt terrible immediately, but I couldn't take it back."

Silence fell for a moment.

"I'm really struggling to take everything in," Lexie said. "I don't know what to think. Your dad thinks he's also my dad. Did you know that?"

"Yeah. Stephanie told me."

"And she told you where to find me?"

He nodded.

"Your dad's going to go mad at her. She told him she had no idea where you were."

"I asked her not to tell him."

"I got the impression that you don't get on with him, but he says you were really close."

"We were," he said, his voice thick with emotion. "I always thought I had the best dad in the world. He was always there for me and we could talk about everything."

"So why didn't you talk to him when you found out about me?"

"Because he'd known about you all along and he never told me. I always thought we were really honest with each other, but he kept this massive secret from me for my whole life."

"I'm sure he had his reasons," Lexie said, not sure why she was defending him.

Dale wiped his damp cheeks with his palms. "I'm so angry with him. But I miss him too."

"He's still at the bunkhouse. He's desperate to see you."

"Do you hate me?" Dale asked.

"No. Of course I don't hate you."

"It always felt like you didn't like me."

"I didn't," she said lightly. "I always had a feeling you were hiding something."

"You were right," he said with a shy smile.

"I can't believe all this."

"I kept asking you questions about your family," Dale said. "And you never mentioned being adopted. You always talk about Angus and Mary as though they're your real parents."

"As far as I'm concerned they are."

"But you remember Stephanie being around when you were little. And you're in touch with her, right?"

"I've been in touch with her occasionally over the years, but I'm not now."

Dale opened his mouth to speak, then paused and took a couple of deep breaths. "When I found out about you, I was annoyed that she'd kept you hidden … and then I realised it wasn't *you* who she'd kept hidden. It was me. She left when I was a baby, and she never even told her family I existed. Angus told me that you were close to Stephanie's dad – our grandad. But I never got to meet him. He didn't know anything about me." He paused again and tears spilled down his cheeks. "I don't understand why she never wanted anything to do with me. She's my mum and she doesn't care about me."

Lexie put an arm around his shoulders. “It’s not you,” she said, then couldn’t help the quiet laugh that escaped through her tears.

“What’s funny?”

“That’s what Nick always says to me when I’m upset about Stephanie. He says it’s her and not me, and I never really believe him. It’s true though. She’s awful … but the problem is her and not us.”

He shook his head. “At least she didn’t pretend you didn’t exist.”

“She once told me I was a huge mistake and she wished she’d had an abortion.”

His eyes widened. “That’s horrible.”

“She is. My advice is to stay well away from her.”

“That was my plan anyway.” He sighed. “I want to go and see my dad, sort things out.”

Lexie nodded slowly. “What’s he like?”

“Really cool … when he’s not keeping massive secrets anyway.” He smiled at her. “It must have been weird for you to meet him?”

“Just a bit,” she said with a smirk. “I’ll put that down as one of the most surreal moments of my life.”

“Did you ever wonder about your biological father?”

“Not really. So it really was a shock.”

He stood up. “You can come back with me and talk to him if you want?”

“I’ll leave you to sort things out. You’re not going to skip town though, are you? Tim said you’re leaving.”

“I’ll go back to Leeds with Dad. I can’t stay here now.”

“Why not?”

“I lied to everyone,” he said, as though it should be obvious. “Angus and Mary were so kind to me, and I lied to them the whole time. And that guy Logan keeps asking if I want to talk about my mum. He’s so nice and I feel like crap because he really lost his parents and I just made it up. Everyone will hate me."

"I'll talk to them. They'll understand."

"I don't think they will."

"They will, I'll make sure of it."

He tilted his head. "Do you even want me around?"

"Yeah," she said slowly. She'd told Matthew that she didn't want any more family, but that wasn't true. It felt completely unreal that Dale was her brother, but she definitely didn't want him to walk out of her life. "I'd like to get to know you better. And I'm sure Grace would like to meet her uncle properly."

Dale's smile came slowly and lit up his face. "She's really cute."

"So will you stay around?"

"I have to talk to Dad. I was supposed to take my A levels and go to uni. I've messed that up."

Lexie felt strangely disappointed. "You'll keep in touch though."

He nodded. "Definitely. Maybe I can stay around here for the rest of the school year, then go back to Leeds and finish my A levels next year. That's if Angus and Mary will let me work at the pub still. They probably won't trust me when they find out the truth."

"They'll be fine. Once they get over the shock anyway. They love having you at the pub. I think Dad will be delighted to hear you're related. In fact, he'll probably claim he always knew there was a deep connection and I'll never hear the end of it!"

"I hope so."

CHAPTER THIRTY-THREE

Blinking her eyes open the next morning, it took a few seconds for the events of the previous day to come back to Lexie. It felt completely surreal, but at the same time the fact that Dale was her brother didn't feel quite as shocking as it should have done. While her instincts had been slightly off about him, the strange feeling that she'd had about him suddenly made sense.

When she'd left him the previous afternoon, she'd come back and chatted everything through with Nick again. Then, with her thoughts in order, she'd gone to the pub at closing time and sat her parents down for a long chat. She'd known her mum would be calm and measured about it but hadn't been sure of her dad's reaction. Mostly, he'd been shocked. It was clear as they chatted that they both felt a lot of sympathy for Dale's situation, and she had no doubt that they'd continue to welcome him into the pub and their lives.

Now Lexie had to figure out what to do about Matthew. Having a sibling seemed pretty easy to accept in comparison. Her feelings for her biological father were much more complex, but one thing she knew for certain was that she wanted to speak to him again.

"Thanks for letting me sleep," she said to Nick when she went down to the kitchen after a leisurely shower.

"You're welcome. How are you feeling?" He kissed her softly, the taste of coffee on his lips.

"Like I had a really strange dream." She sank onto the chair. "Is Grace asleep?"

"Yeah. In the bassinet in the living room."

Lexie rolled her eyes. "How come she'll sleep in the bassinet when you're around, but only wants to be held when she's with me?"

"Maybe you smell better than me. Try wearing my after-shave – she might give you a break." He grinned at her. "What's the plan for today?"

"I guess I need to speak to my long-lost relatives," she said flatly.

"What are you going to do about Matthew?"

She pulled her hair into a ponytail, securing it with a hair tie from her wrist. "I don't know. I have very mixed feelings about him."

"I imagine he'll want to get to know you. He's been carrying a photo of you, so he's obviously thought about you."

"It's so bizarre," she said, resting her elbows on the table. "I was always perfectly content with the idea that he'd gone on with his life without a second thought about me. I can't get my head around the fact that he actually cared."

"I bet it was a shock for him to meet you."

"I told him I don't need another dad. Which is true. I'm an adult. I don't need anything from him."

Nick massaged her shoulders. "That doesn't mean you can't get to know him."

"I'm going to have breakfast, then I'll go over to the bunkhouse."

"It's almost lunchtime," Nick pointed out.

"I haven't slept so late in a long time." Not that she felt

particularly refreshed. She was mid-yawn when a knock came at the door.

Nick opened it and said a quizzical hello to the man on the doorstep.

"Hi," Lexie said, moving beside Nick and introducing him to Matthew. He looked vaguely surprised when she told him Nick was her husband but smiled as he shook his hand.

"Sorry to just turn up," he said. "I was hoping we might be able to talk a bit more …"

"It's fine," Lexie said, taking a step back to let him in. "I was going to come over to you later."

"Would you rather do that?" he asked quickly. "I don't want to intrude."

"No. It's all right. Come in."

He wiped his shoes on the mat and glanced around the kitchen.

"Go into the living room," Nick said. "I'll make coffee."

"I don't know about you," Matthew said as he followed Lexie through, "but I hardly slept. My brain wouldn't switch off."

"There was definitely a lot to think about," she agreed. "Did Dale tell you about the latest member of my family?" She went to the bassinet, where Grace's eyes slowly blinked open. "Good morning," Lexie whispered as she lifted her into her arms.

"She's yours?" Matthew asked, wide-eyed.

"Yes." She moved closer to him. "This is Grace Mary Stewart. Five weeks old."

"Wow." Gently, he touched her tiny fingers. "She's beautiful. Congratulations."

"Thank you."

His Adam's apple bobbed as he swallowed. "Could I hold her?"

"Yes." She passed her over and he sat on the couch, his gaze not shifting from Grace, who stared back up at him.

"Is it okay if I take a photo of her?" he asked, pulling his phone from his pocket.

Lexie perched on the arm of the couch. "Go ahead."

"My mum's going to go crazy when I tell her she has a great-grandchild." He took the photo and smiled down at Grace. "I can't believe I'm a grandad." His brow knitted together as he glanced at Lexie. "Sorry. I know you said you don't want a relationship, but Dale said you were keen for him to stick around, so I wonder if …" Tears pooled in his eyes and he switched his focus back to Grace. "I understand you don't need me to be your dad or anything, but I'd really like to get to know you."

"I don't think I really meant what I said yesterday. It was all such a shock. I'm still not sure what to think." Pausing, she chewed the inside of her cheek. "Do your parents know about me?"

"Yes. They've always known. I mean, as long as I've known."

"But you didn't tell Dale?"

"No." He stroked Grace's palm with his little finger until she wrapped her fingers around it and clung to him. "I always thought I was doing him a favour."

"How?"

He looked thoughtful. "Dale's like me. I knew he'd want to find you. I was sure that knowing he had a sister but not being able to find you would drive him crazy. I wanted to spare him the torture of sitting around hoping you might come looking for us."

Lexie bit down on her lip as her chin trembled. "Why didn't you look for me?" she asked, her voice brittle. "I know you thought it was a closed adoption but if you'd have asked Stephanie more questions, or dug around a bit …"

"I can't tell you how much I wish I had done. I even wish I'd told Dale about you. Maybe he'd have badgered Stephanie for information sooner … But I honestly thought I had no chance of finding you. I just clung to the hope that one day you might come looking for me."

"What do you mean?"

He wiped a tear that trickled down his cheek. "I believed Stephanie when she told me it was a closed adoption. In Scotland, the biological parents aren't allowed to contact the child they gave up … but when the child turns sixteen they can access the records and track down their birth parents."

He looked at Lexie with a pained expression. "On your sixteenth birthday, I didn't go to work. I knew that it was unlikely that you'd try and find us as soon as you turned sixteen. And I knew you'd have to go through Stephanie since my name wasn't on your birth certificate, but I made her promise to contact me if she heard from you. I was on edge for a long time. The more time went on, the more I told myself I should accept that I'd never get to meet you. But I couldn't quite let myself believe it."

"I had no idea," Lexie said. "I honestly didn't ever give much thought to my biological father. I was kind of glad that he'd left before I was born … I didn't take the abandonment personally like I did with Stephanie."

"She really hurt you, didn't she?"

"Yes," she replied quickly, not wanting to dwell on it.

"I'm sorry." He repositioned Grace when she wriggled, laying her on his thighs so her feet kicked at his stomach. "You're feisty, aren't you?" he said to her.

"She gets that from Lexie," Nick said, wandering in.

"That's probably true," Lexie agreed, smiling up at Nick. "I'm fairly sure no one's ever described you as feisty."

He raised an eyebrow and looked to Matthew. "I'm hoping it means she got my brains."

"Hey!" Laughing, Lexie gave his leg a gentle shove. "Weren't you making coffee?"

Nick asked Matthew how he took it, then came straight back with drinks for them all.

"I met Angus and Mary earlier," Matthew said. "They came over to talk to Dale."

"I spoke to them yesterday and explained the situation," Lexie said.

"They seem really sweet. Dale obviously thinks highly of them."

"They're great," Nick said. "Angus has a real soft spot for Dale. He lost his brother recently, and having Dale around perked him up."

"That was your grandad?" Matthew asked Lexie. "Stephanie's dad?"

"Yeah. Dale must have found out about me not long after he died. Stephanie would have been clearing out his house, so she probably had a lot of his stuff at her place. I bet that's how Dale stumbled on it."

Matthew chuckled as Grace kicked him repeatedly. "How did you choose her name?" he asked.

"We just both liked the name Grace, and Mary after my mum." Lexie realised it was probably the last name he was wondering about. "Nick took my name when we married so that made things easier. We didn't have to decide if she'd get a double-barrelled surname or anything."

He gave a soft shake of the head. "It's just that my mum's name is Grace."

"No way!" Nick said dramatically. "That's spooky."

"It's a coincidence," Lexie said, rolling her eyes.

"No," Nick said confidently. "That's the universe having fun. I'm telling you some things are just impossible to explain …"

"I already explained it!" Lexie laughed. "Coincidence!"

Nick reached over and stroked Grace's cheek. "This kid has more grandparents than anyone I've known." He looked at Matthew. "You'll have to bring your parents up to Skye for a visit. They'll love it. Everyone loves Skye."

"Nick!" Lexie said. "Slow down a bit, please."

"Sorry."

"They'd really love to meet you," Matthew said, looking at Lexie intently.

"I think I'd probably like to meet them too. When I've had more time to get my head around all of this."

"Of course," Matthew said, beaming down at Grace.

CHAPTER THIRTY-FOUR

The Lochview Hotel was an idyllic location for a wedding. Getting married in March may not have been the perfect choice, but Elspeth argued that you couldn't guarantee the weather on Skye at any time of year, and freezing cold was preferable to pouring rain. If she could only find the mute button for Isla, Elspeth could probably forget about the fact that it was a few degrees below freezing.

"I actually might die in a minute," Isla said, through chattering teeth. "I'll freeze solid, then topple off this jetty, into the dark waters of the loch and float away … I'll drift out to sea and become fish food."

"Hopefully that happens soon so we don't have to listen to you complaining any more," Leana said.

"I might push you in the water now," Lexie added. "We'd already be finished with the photos if you'd smile instead of going on about how cold you are."

"It's difficult to smile when I'm borderline hypothermic," Isla said.

"We're almost done," Elspeth said, standing tall in the middle of her bridesmaids. Their deep red dresses matched the roses in her bouquet. With the crisp blue skies behind them, she was sure the photos would be stunning. If their lips were slightly blue, the photographer could surely edit that out.

"Could you try not to look so cold?" Kyle called out to them. He was standing beside the photographer, having decided to be her unofficial assistant. "Maybe turn a little to the side, Elspeth. And if you could smile instead of scowling, Isla, I think that would be a better choice."

That made them all laugh and the photographer snapped away. As soon as she lowered the camera, Isla grumbled that she'd had enough and set off across the frost-covered lawn towards the warmth of the hotel, with Leana hurrying beside her.

"Can you manage?" Lexie asked Elspeth when she lifted the train of her dress.

"Yes, I've got it." Juggling her flowers and the hem of her dress, they set off up the gardens behind Kyle and the photographer, who were discussing who they should photograph next. "You're quiet today," she commented to Lexie.

"Sorry, I'm exhausted. Grace had us up most of last night."

"The sleepless nights feel as though they'll go on forever, but they don't. That feels like a lifetime ago with Arran." She smiled as she saw Rory chatting away with his two best men on the terrace at the back of the hotel. Alasdair and Logan looked highly amused by whatever Rory was saying, and they all looked fantastic in their kilts. The terrace was scattered with outdoor heaters and strung with an abundance of fairy lights giving it a magical feel. The warmth of the scene filled Elspeth with joy. "I guess I'll be going back to the sleepless nights before long too."

Lexie's eyes widened. "Are you …?"

"No." Elspeth laughed. "I'm not pregnant. But we've been talking about it a lot. I don't think we'll wait long."

"That's so lovely. I'm really happy for you."

"Me too. It took us a long time, but we finally seem to have things figured out." She shot Lexie a sidelong glance. "Which reminds me, we need a proper catch-up soon. With all the wedding preparations, I feel as though I don't know what's going on with you. Matthew came to visit last week, didn't he?"

"Yes. He came to visit Dale for a long weekend."

"And you, presumably?"

"Yeah. It all feels really weird still. I don't think it'll ever feel like a father/daughter relationship. I'm not sure I want it to. He's lovely though. And he's so sweet with Grace. His mum had knitted her a blanket and a little cardigan."

"That's nice."

"Yeah. They're going to come up the next time Matthew visits. I'm trying to go with the flow and not overthink it too much."

"That's a good idea. It's nice that Dale decided to hang around."

"For now. He'll go back to Leeds at the end of the summer. I'm not sure what will happen after that. Hopefully we'll keep in touch and they'll come back and visit sometimes."

"Of course they will." Elspeth dropped the dress, letting it drag on the ground so she could take Lexie's arm. "Dale's not just going to walk out of your life again … or Matthew."

"I hope not," Lexie said, her eyes shining with tears as she smiled.

"I think you'd struggle to get rid of Dale if you wanted to. He was at the cafe the other week and he couldn't stop talking about you and Grace."

"I know they'll stay in touch really. I think I'm just already dreading not having Dale around all the time. It's been good talking to him about Stephanie. Having someone who completely understands is great."

"You've got almost six months of him living next door, so just make the most of that."

"I intend to. I already have him taking Grace out for walks when Nick's at work and I need a break!"

They arrived at the terrace, where the wedding guests were sipping champagne and chatting away. It was all very relaxed and civilised, but there'd be an influx of evening guests soon to liven things up.

"Isla reckons you're trying to kill her," Rory said, appearing behind Elspeth and slipping his arms around her waist. She leaned back against his chest, soaking up his body heat.

"You'd think my lovely big sister could shut up complaining for one day!"

"It wouldn't be a proper celebration without Isla grumbling about something," Lexie remarked, then squeezed Elspeth's arm before wandering away in Nick's direction.

"Are you freezing too?" Rory asked, rubbing at Elspeth's upper arms.

"No." She turned to face him, draping her arms around his neck. "I have absolutely no complaints today."

"Glad to hear it." He kissed her nose. "I think I picked a good wedding venue."

"It's perfect."

Lightly, he kissed her lips. "I love you, wife."

"I love you too, husband! That sounds so weird."

He kissed her again, then glanced over her shoulder, where there was some commotion by the door. "The evening guests are arriving. We better go and be sociable."

~

Jess had been psyching herself up to the wedding for weeks. She'd known Gary would be there and had told herself repeatedly that she could manage an evening in close proximity to him. As soon as she stepped out onto the hotel terrace with the group of her colleagues, she clocked him standing to her left. The sight of him in his kilt caught her off guard, but she managed to smile when their eyes met, then moved to congratulate Elspeth and Rory.

She hoped no one would suspect how fiercely her heart was crashing against her rib cage, or how jelly-like her legs felt.

When she'd been mentally preparing for the evening, she'd envisioned making easy conversation with Gary as though they were old friends catching up. Clearly that wasn't going to be possible, so she quickly revised her plan, deciding she needed to avoid speaking to him at all costs.

It was easier than she'd thought. She mingled with her colleagues and sipped champagne. Not long after they arrived, the party moved inside where a buffet was laid out with finger foods. Speeches were made and champagne flowed. The dancing was in full swing when Rory nudged his way between Jess and Ava.

"Can I tempt you to a dance?" he asked Jess.

"I don't think I feel like dancing."

"Me neither," he said, his attention drifting across the room.

She laughed. "Why did you ask, then?"

"Instructions from my wife. Apparently I'm not allowed to argue with her on our wedding day."

"Elspeth told you to ask me to dance?"

"Yeah." He glanced over to where Elspeth was pulling Gary up to dance. "The plan was for her to dance with Gary, and I'd dance with you …"

"Then you'd switch?" Jess asked, twirling the stem of her wine glass. "So I'd end up dancing with Gary?"

"I told Elspeth that I'm not into the whole matchmaking thing, but once she gets an idea in her head it's difficult to sway her."

"It's a good plan," Ava said, beaming. "I like Elspeth's style."

Jess shook her head and was about to argue when her gaze was drawn to Gary, laughing as he attempted to squirm away from Elspeth.

"I'll dance with you," Jess said firmly, setting her wine on the table nearby, then taking Rory's hand.

"What?"

"I'll dance with you." She took his hand and led the way, ignoring the whoop of delight from Ava.

"So you *want* to dance with Gary?" Rory asked.

"Yes." She stopped. "No. I'm not sure. I definitely *want* to dance with him, but it's probably not the best idea. The alcohol's making me brave."

"You really like him, don't you?" Rory asked, leading her the final few steps to the dance floor.

"Yeah." She rested a hand on his shoulder and slotted her other hand into his. "Apparently I'm attracted to unavailable men."

He winced. "Apart from relationship drama, how's everything else with you? Are you still enjoying the job?"

"It's fine." She was only half concentrating as she glanced at Elspeth laughing with Gary and getting gradually closer. "Gary might not even want to dance with me," she said, suddenly desperate to be in his arms instead of Rory's.

"He'd be an idiot if he didn't," Rory said kindly.

"There you are!" Elspeth said to Rory as she and Gary appeared beside them. "I wondered where you'd got to."

"You saw me three minutes ago," Rory said with a teasing glint in his eyes.

"It feels like longer," Elspeth said, then looked to Jess. "Would you mind if we swapped partners?"

Jess flashed Gary a nervous smile as she told Elspeth it was fine and moved away from Rory. Hesitantly, Gary held a hand out to her. The scent of him was overwhelming as she moved into his arms.

"I think that might have been a set-up," Gary said quietly.

"It was."

"We don't have to dance if you don't want to."

A warm wave of longing swept through her as she looked up at him. "I want to, but if you don't it's fine."

"I want to," he whispered against her hair as he pulled her closer.

Neither of them spoke for the duration of the song, and they didn't break apart when it came to an end either.

"How've you been?" Gary asked halfway through the next song, which was thankfully another slow number.

"Pretty good," she said, hoping she sounded convincing. She'd rather he didn't know that her efforts to get over him and remove him from her thoughts had been spectacularly unsuccessful.

"I should have called you after Hogmanay," he said softly, his breath tickling her cheek. "I wanted to call you a million times."

Tilting her head slightly, she rested her cheek against his. If he was going to be so honest, she supposed she may as well be too. "That's about the same number of times I wished you'd call."

His arms tightened around her back. "I didn't think you'd want me to."

"I didn't really. Nothing's changed, has it?"

"No." The song came to an end and he took a step back. "Do you want a drink or something?"

"I've already got one." She nodded toward the table at the far side of the room. "We could sit for a while, if you want?"

As they walked across the room, his hand brushed against hers, and it was an effort not to weave her fingers with his.

"Aren't you drinking?" she asked after taking a long sip of her wine.

"No. I've got the car. I wasn't intending on staying late."

"Is Paige waiting for you?" Jess asked, hoping the bitterness wasn't evident in her voice.

"Yeah, but I got her a dog, so she doesn't mind being alone so much now."

Jess's eyes widened. "You bought her a dog?"

"Yeah." He stretched his legs out and smiled widely. "She's wanted one for ages. Donna bailed on Paige's birthday and she was gutted so—"

"You bought a dog to cheer her up?"

"Yes. Pretty much."

"What breed is it?"

"Golden retriever. He's called Bailey and he's gorgeous. Paige adores him. She's like a different kid since she got the dog."

A lump swelled in Jess's throat. "I heard she's doing much better in school too."

"She's doing really well. I should have bought her a puppy sooner."

"I'm fairly sure it's not the dog that made the difference." Jess reached for her glass as tears pricked her eyes. She was pleased that Paige was doing well, and it proved what she'd known all along – that Gary had been right to end their relationship. He'd put Paige first and that was what she'd needed. "Is she going to stay on at school next year and take her Highers?"

Gary tilted his head. "We don't have to talk about Paige if it's too weird for you."

"It's fine." She sipped her wine and took a deep breath. "I'm interested."

"She wants to get a job. I'm trying to persuade her to stay in school."

"What job does she want to do?"

Gary leaned back in his seat, propping his ankle on the opposite knee as a smirk played at his lips. "Try not to laugh …"

"Oh God. What is it? Nail technician?"

"No." He laughed. "About as far from that as you can get. She wants to work with me."

"She wants to be a mechanic?"

"Maybe someday." He smiled gently. "My dad keeps on about retiring, so she wants to take over the bookkeeping and office work for now. She's been driving my dad crazy with notions about increasing profits."

"That's not a terrible idea …"

"I worry she'll get bored and have no qualifications to do anything else."

"Could she study part-time and work at the garage too?"

"That's what I want her to do. But she's keen to get out of school." He nodded across the room. "I've been talking to Nick today. Do you know him? The one with the baby."

Jess shook her head. "Who is he?"

"He's married to Lexie, who works in the Old Inn. Anyway, he teaches Business IT at the college in Portree. He said he can have a chat with Paige and show her around the college. I figure that might be more appealing to her than staying on at school."

"It's a really good idea."

"I'm not sure she'll go for it, but it's worth a shot."

"If she thinks it's what you want I'm sure she'll do it."

He ran his teeth along his bottom lip as he looked at her intently. After a moment his gaze flicked away and he scanned the room.

"I get the feeling we're being talked about," he said.

Ava and Elspeth were standing with their heads together at the edge of the dance floor. They glanced in Jess's direction before Ava walked over to them.

"A bunch of people are going back to Chris's place to continue the party once things wind down here," she said to Jess. "Do you fancy it?"

"I don't think so. Who's going?"

"Me and Chris so far," she said, giggling.

"In that case I'll definitely pass."

"You don't mind me ditching you, do you?" She gripped the back of Jess's chair as she swayed. "I'll ask around and see who else is going back to Portree that you can share a taxi with." She tilted her head and smiled at Gary. "I suppose you're going in that direction. Are you getting a taxi?"

He raised his eyebrows and his lips pulled to an amused smile. "I'm driving."

"Can you drop Jess off then?"

"I can get a taxi," Jess said quickly. "It's fine."

"I don't mind." Gary sat up straighter. "I pretty much go past your door anyway."

"Thanks," she said, not sure whether to be annoyed with Ava's matchmaking or happy about it.

"When do you want to leave?" he asked, checking his watch.

"Whenever. If you want to leave already that's fine by me."

"You need to eat some cake first," Ava said.

"I already had cake," Jess told her.

Gary nodded. "Me too."

"Well, you need to eat more. Elspeth baked it herself and she's going to think people don't like it if there's some left at the end of the evening." She took Jess's hand to pull her up, then did the same to Gary. "Go! Eat cake!"

"Is it me or is she being weird?" Gary said out of the side of his mouth as they walked towards the buffet table.

"She's quite tipsy. But she's also being weird, even for her. I'm not going to complain about eating more cake though."

"Me neither." He took two plates and got them each a slice.

They quietly watched the dancing as they ate, then collected their things and said goodbye to a few people.

The half hour drive back to Portree was nowhere near long enough. The time flew by as Jess quizzed Gary about the progress he'd made on his house. When he talked more about Paige and Bailey, the affection in his voice made her heart yearn for him.

They pulled up outside her place before she knew it. Jess sighed as she looked out at the dark, empty house but made no move to get out of the car.

"It was good to catch up with you," Gary said softly.

"You too." She swallowed hard, trying to summon the willpower to get out of the car. Not knowing when she'd see him again felt unbearable. "I guess I'll see you around," she said hesitantly.

"I hope so. It was really good to see you."

"You just said that," she said, smiling.

"I know." He unclipped his seatbelt and leaned towards her. "This is probably a really stupid move," he whispered, his gaze flicking to her lips.

Her heart seemed to stop dead and butterflies whirled in her stomach. She licked her lips and felt the warmth of his breath on them just as her phone began to ring. Gary pulled back while Jess scrabbled to find the stupid phone.

"It's Ava," she said, scowling as she swiped to accept the call.

"Are you still with Gary?" Ava asked loudly, her voice full of mirth.

Jess glanced at him, trying to figure out if he could hear, but he was looking out of the windscreen with a blank expression. "Yes," she replied slowly. "Why?"

"There seems to be a small problem. I've just found your house keys under the table we were sitting at. They must have fallen out of your bag."

Automatically, Jess opened the small clutch bag and shifted a packet of tissues and her lip gloss around. "How can my keys have fallen out of my bag?"

Ava giggled. "I've no idea."

"Did you steal my keys?"

"No! They obviously just fell out of your bag. Do you want me to wait at the hotel while you drive back for them?"

"No!" Jess spat. "You'll have to come home so I can get in."

"I'm going back to Chris's place. Do you want to pick them up from there?"

"No. I do not!" Laughter rattled down the phone, and this time it wasn't only Ava's. "Who are you with?" Jess demanded.

"Elspeth," Ava said. "I think she has an idea … hang on, I'll put you on speaker …"

As she listened to yet more laughter down the line, Jess glanced at Gary, whose mouth had curved to an amused smile.

"Ask Gary if you can stay at his place," Elspeth called into the phone. "Problem solved!"

"I'm glad you two are enjoying yourselves," Jess said. "I'm going to hang up now."

"Have fun!" Ava shouted before Jess ended the call.

"It seems that I'm locked out," she said to Gary.

"So I heard." His eyes sparkled as he started the engine. "You can stay at my place."

CHAPTER THIRTY-FIVE

"Are you sure it's okay for me to stay?" Jess asked as they turned off the road and through the gap in the trees that led to Gary's house. "Won't it cause issues with Paige?"

"I'm not going to leave you on your doorstep in the freezing cold." He grinned. "If it was summer, maybe, but not in winter."

"I'll have to tell Ava never to steal my keys in summer then."

Gary cast her a sidelong glance. "Paige is probably asleep. And I don't think she'd have a problem with you staying over when you're locked out."

Jess hoped he was right, but even if Paige was fine with it, Jess wasn't sure she was. Spending time with Gary would only lead to more heartache. Her mind flashed to him almost kissing her, and she mentally cursed Ava for choosing that moment to call.

The car juddering over the uneven ground jolted her back to the present. "Are you ever going to get a driveway?" she teased.

"It's next on my list. I'll need to wait until spring, but once the ground thaws I'm getting a driveway. By the end of the year this place will look like a palace."

"That's ambitious."

"Well, maybe not a palace … but a house with a driveway!"

By the time Jess had stepped out of the car, Gary was already at her side.

"Be careful," he said, offering her his hand. "I'll feel really bad about the lack of driveway if you fall over."

"Thanks." Her fingers curled around his and it felt like a surge of electricity passing through her. She was definitely setting herself up for more heartbreak. Or Ava and Elspeth were.

They'd just stepped into the kitchen when a thudding sound came from the stairs, like multiple people running down them at once. Seconds later a yellow bundle of fur landed at the bottom of the stairs, then clawed at the tiled floor until he found his grip and bounded to Gary.

"You daft dog," Gary said, crouching and scooping the excited pup into his arms. "This is Bailey." He stroked the beautiful dog as he nuzzled his head under Gary's chin.

"Hello!" Jess said, running a hand over his soft coat. "He's gorgeous."

"It's a good job, because he's quite a handful."

There were more footsteps on the stairs before Paige appeared, looking childlike in a pair of fleece pyjamas.

"Hi," she said through a yawn, then blinked a few times when she noticed Jess.

"I'm locked out of my house," Jess said. "Gary offered for me to crash here."

Gary set the dog on the floor and moved to the stairs. "I'll make up the spare room."

"How was the wedding?" Paige asked, crouching to stroke Bailey but tilting her head to look at Jess.

"It was great. I had a good time." She shrugged her coat off and hung it over the back of a chair at the kitchen table.

"I like your dress," Paige remarked.

"Thanks."

"I've only been to one wedding. It was my mum's and I had to be a bridesmaid. My dress was gross … pale green. It was horrific."

"The bridesmaid's dresses today were gorgeous. I took photos." She pulled them up on her phone.

Paige commented on how amazing the bride looked, then yawned widely when Jess put the phone away. "I'm going back to bed. Goodnight."

"Night," Jess said, then took a seat and stroked Bailey as he bounced around at her feet.

It didn't take long for Gary to reappear. "The spare room is in about the same state as the rest of the house."

"It'll be fine," Jess said and followed when he led the way upstairs. At the top of the stairs he pointed out the bathroom, then walked to the bedroom at the front of the house. It was fairly bare, with a bed and a wardrobe and a load of cardboard boxes against one wall.

"I left a T-shirt out for you to sleep in," Gary said. "And I found a toothbrush for you." It was in the packet atop the folded T-shirt.

"Thank you."

"No worries." He hovered in the doorway. "Do you need anything else?"

She needed him not to walk out of the room and leave her to sleep alone, but since she couldn't say that she smiled and told him she was all set.

"Goodnight." He picked Bailey up as the dog appeared at his feet, then backed out of the room, pulling the door closed behind him.

~

Unsurprisingly, Jess had trouble sleeping. The bed in the spare room felt too big and too empty. As she tossed and turned, all she could think about was Gary, just across the hall. Knowing he was so close made her stomach twist every time she drifted between sleep and waking.

A lack of curtains meant she was awake early. Her instinct

told her to make her exit before Gary got up. For one thing, she'd rather he didn't see the state of her, with the remnants of the previous day's make-up no doubt smudged under her eyes and her bedraggled hair, which would be untameable after her restless night. There was also the fact that she wasn't sure she'd manage to drag herself away if she waited until he was awake.

When she crept downstairs she found Paige munching on a bowl of cereal at the table. Bailey sat by her feet with his tongue lolling out and his tail sweeping an arc on the floor.

"Morning," Jess said quietly, feeling self-conscious in her wedding clothes while Paige was in her pyjamas.

"Hi." She wiped milk from her lip. "How did you sleep?"

"Fine, thanks." Jess picked up her coat and put it on.

"Do you want breakfast or a coffee or something?"

"No, I'm good, thanks."

"Is Gary still asleep?"

Jess diverted her gaze to the puppy, who didn't move from Paige's side. "I guess so. I haven't seen him. I slept in the spare room."

"He'll probably be up soon," Paige said, moving to put her bowl in the sink. "I'm taking Bailey to his obedience class so I need to get ready. I'll wake Gary up."

"No, leave him," Jess said, heading for the door. "I have to go anyway. Tell him I said bye, and thanks for letting me crash here."

"You could wait a wee while …"

"Have a good day!" Jess called breezily as she stepped outside. In her haste she almost lost her footing on the makeshift brick step. She righted herself and was more careful for the rest of the way. It was only when she was halfway home that she realised she had no idea if Ava would be back yet. There was a good chance she might still be locked out. She shivered as snowflakes fluttered on the icy breeze. It wasn't ideal conditions for waiting on the doorstep, and she wasn't appropriately dressed for killing time in a cafe.

With her phone to her ear, she bunched her shoulders up.

"You better be at home or be able to get home in the next ten minutes," she grumbled when Ava answered the phone with an unintelligible grunt.

"I'm at home," she said.

"Good. I'll see you soon."

Ava was looking more than a little worse for wear when she opened the door for Jess. Her skin was pasty and her hair was sticking up all over the place.

"I hope I don't look as bad as you do," Jess said as she stepped inside. If she did, the decision to leave before Gary saw her was a good one. Glancing in the hallway mirror she found she looked surprisingly fresh – at least in comparison to Ava.

"I feel terrible." Ava walked to the kitchen and dropped into a chair, her head sinking to the tabletop.

"What happened with Chris?"

"Nothing. A few of us went back to his and played poker and drank more. I passed out on his couch and he gave me a lift home early this morning."

"I thought you'd have finally got together with him."

"I don't think it's going to happen. We're probably better as friends." She yawned loudly. "How did it go with Gary?"

"It was all a bit embarrassing. I can't believe you stole my keys."

Her shoulders shook as she laughed, then she winced as though it was painful. "I think that was Elspeth's idea. Did you sleep with him?"

"No." Jess poured them a glass of water each and sat down. "We almost kissed, but you called and ruined the moment."

"Did you sleep in his bed?"

"No. I slept in the spare room."

"Was Paige there?"

"Yes." Jess pondered their encounters the previous evening and that morning. "She seemed surprisingly fine with me being there. I also got the feeling that she assumed I'd slept in Gary's bed."

"And she was okay with that?"

Jess shrugged. "It seemed that way."

"Surely you can get back together if she's fine with it."

"She's doing well in school and has really settled down. Gary won't want to rock the boat, and I understand that."

"Do you? I'd be livid at the whole situation. You like him and he likes you. You ought to be together!"

"I think so too." She took a few long swigs of water. "But there's not much I can do about the situation."

CHAPTER THIRTY-SIX

On Wednesday morning the noise of pupils filing out of the classroom was dying down, and Jess picked up the sponge to clear the whiteboard when she caught Paige hovering by her desk.

"Everything okay?" she asked.

"It's none of my business, but I was wondering if Gary called you?"

"I haven't spoken to him since Saturday night. Why?"

"He was upset that you'd already left when he got up on Sunday, so I told him he should call you."

Jess turned her back and got on with wiping the board. "He didn't call," she said, hoping her voice didn't give away her disappointment.

"Idiot," Paige muttered.

"This isn't really an appropriate conversation for us to be having in school." Jess did her best to sound authoritative.

"Do you hate me?"

Jess sighed and turned to face her. "No. I don't hate you."

"I didn't tell Gary to break up with you. You probably don't believe me, but it's true."

"I believe you. Not that it matters."

"It does matter," she said firmly. "I honestly had no idea he'd split up with you."

"*That* I don't believe." Jess moved to stand behind the desk, trying to make herself feel more in control of the conversation than she was. "You might not have asked him to end things with me, but you knew he would if you made enough of a fuss about it."

"No!" She shook her head adamantly. "I thought that if I got in the way you might decide it was too much hassle to be with him and you'd end things. I swear I never thought *he* would."

Jess dropped into her chair and folded her arms over her chest. "Why did you have such an issue with us being together anyway? Were you embarrassed about being seen with a teacher outside of school?"

Her gaze fell to her feet. "I thought if you were together he wouldn't want me around any more. My mum was always like that – whenever she got a boyfriend she didn't have time for me. When she married Scott I felt like I was in the way all the time. I thought it'd be the same with Gary. And if *he* didn't want me around, I didn't have anywhere else to go. I'd have had to move down to Glasgow with my mum, and I really don't want to do that."

"I'm sorry," Jess said. "That's a crappy situation to be in."

She lifted a shoulder. "I think Gary really misses you. You could get back together with him. It's fine with me. I'd rather he was happy. And I don't think he'd ditch me like Mum did."

"He'd never do that."

"So you'll get back with him?"

"It's not that simple."

"Why not?"

That was a good question. She wasn't really sure why, other than that Paige had clearly given him her blessing and he'd failed to do anything about it.

"It's just not. Thank you for speaking to me though."

"I'll talk to him again … get him to call you."

"You don't need to do that. Things will either work out or they won't. Don't push him."

"He's a man. Sometimes they need pushing!"

Jess couldn't help but laugh. "I have work to do. Off you go."

"Maybe I should message him," Jess said on Friday night. She'd thought Gary might put in an appearance at the pub, but there'd been no sign of him. At this rate she'd have neck ache from checking the door every time it opened.

"The pub's closing soon," Chris said from beside Ava.

"I don't mean message and invite him out, just a general message to see how he's doing."

"At this time on a Friday night that's going to look suspiciously like a booty call." Chris shrugged. "Not that I'm saying you shouldn't message him, just telling you how he's going to interpret it."

"Maybe he's not like you," Ava said.

Chris knocked his shoulder against hers. "He's a guy."

"I'd actually be fine with him interpreting it as a booty call," Jess said. "But he lives with his niece, so booty calls aren't really possible." She took a swig of her beer and was surprised to find it was the last sip. "I wish he'd get in touch with me."

"I think he will," Ava said. "You need to be patient."

"I've been very patient. Now I think Paige might be right that he needs a push." Staring down at her phone, she tried to work up the courage to contact him. She tapped out a message but ended up deleting it without sending it.

The following morning, she did the same again, then gave herself a mental shake and told herself to put the phone away and forget about Gary.

Predictably, she failed in the endeavour and was thinking

about him as she cleaned the kitchen after dinner. Her thoughts were broken by someone at the door. Ava went to answer it, then shouted to Jess.

Walking down the hall, she caught sight of Gary on the doorstep.

"I'll be upstairs," Ava said and made herself scarce.

"Hi." Gary stepped inside, holding out a scarf. "You left this at my place last weekend."

"I didn't," she said, shaking her head. "It's not mine."

His brow creased as he looked at it. "Paige said it was yours."

"I'm guessing Paige was just giving you a reason to come over here." Jess tipped her head to indicate they should move into the living room. "She thinks we should get back together."

"Did she tell you that?" he asked.

"Yeah." Jess sat at the end of the couch. "I got the impression she'd said the same to you."

"She did." He swallowed hard and sat beside her.

"And yet you didn't feel like getting in touch?" She couldn't keep the annoyance from her voice.

"I definitely felt like it," he said. "I just didn't know if I should."

"Surely it's not that difficult to figure out. Do you want to be with me or not?"

"Of course I do." He reached for her hand, caressing her palm with the pad of his thumb and sending goosebumps rippling up her arm. "I didn't know if you wanted to be with me."

"I thought I'd made it pretty clear at Hogmanay and at the wedding."

"I wasn't sure. You disappeared before I got up last week, so I wasn't sure what to think. When we split up you were adamant that it was definitely over and you had no intention of waiting around for me."

"Because I was upset. I still want to be with you." His thumb continued to trace soft circles on her palm, but the faraway look in his eyes was disconcerting. "Why do you look so uncertain?"

"I'm not." He snapped his gaze to her. "I want to be with you. That's completely certain. But Paige is going to be staying with me for the foreseeable future. And I know she says she's fine about us now, but that might change …"

"And then you'd have to split up with me?"

"No. I can't let her dictate my life. But she is going to be in my life and that would affect you too. Sometimes Paige is going to freak out about something and need me to stay home with her, or call for a lift home when we're out. She's going to disrupt my life and I'm fine with that … but I understand if you're not."

"I'm okay with it." She threaded her fingers through his. "I think it's great how much you do for Paige. And I understand that she comes first for you at the moment."

He shook his head. "It's not that black and white. It's not as though I'll always put her before you. I want to be there for you both. You might just need to be a bit patient sometimes."

"I can try." She smiled mischievously. "I haven't been very patient this week though when I was waiting for you to call."

He rubbed at his temple with his palm. "I'm sorry. Maybe I can take you out for dinner this evening and make it up to you?"

"I already ate, but we could go for a drink."

He nodded and leaned close. Her stomach flipped as his lips brushed lightly against hers. His fingers untangled from hers and slipped around her back to pull her closer still. "I've missed you so much," he murmured as he broke the kiss.

"I missed you too."

"I'm really sorry about everything."

She grazed her fingers along his troubled brow. "You did the right thing for Paige. Which was probably the right thing for us in the end. Let's just try not to let anything get in the way from now on."

Smiling, he cupped her cheek and sank his lips against hers again, kissing her until she was breathless.

"Ava is upstairs," she reminded him through gentle laughter as he coaxed her to lying on the couch and covered her body with his.

"Don't remind me." He dotted kisses up her neck and nibbled her earlobe. "I really wish we didn't both live with someone."

"I thought we were going to the pub?" she said, beaming as his hands strayed under the hem of her T-shirt.

"I suggested that before I remembered how much I enjoy kissing you. The pub is much less appealing since I can't do this …" Gently, he caught her bottom lip between his teeth while his fingers quivered over her ribs.

She tilted her hips to meet his, then pulled back and sucked in a quick breath at an unexpected pressure at her thigh. Gary quirked an eyebrow as he pushed himself off her and onto his knees. "It's my phone ringing," he said with amusement, struggling to remove it from the pocket of his jeans.

Jess covered her mouth as she laughed. "Is it Paige?" she asked, catching the look on his face as he went to answer it.

"Yeah." He put the phone to his ear and said hello.

Jess couldn't hear what Paige was saying and couldn't concentrate enough to try to eavesdrop the conversation since Gary remained between her legs and nudged her top up to draw circles along the skin at her hip. Whatever it was that Paige was asking him he agreed to before ending the call.

"I have to go," he said, getting off the couch and pulling her up.

"Is Paige okay?"

"Yes. She's going for a sleepover at Sophie's house. Bailey will trash the house if he's left alone for too long, so I need to go home. I'm afraid we'll have to abandon our plans to go to the pub." A flirty smile crept onto his lips. "How about drinks at my place instead?"

She draped her arms around his shoulders. “You have the house to yourself all night?”

“Yes! And I don’t think we should waste it standing around here chatting! Grab whatever you need for our own sleepover and let’s go.”

She gave him a chaste kiss, then did as she was told.

CHAPTER THIRTY-SEVEN

It was mid-morning when Jess padded downstairs in search of coffee. Gary had fallen back to sleep, while she was riding a wave of blissful ecstasy. Her happy bubble was stretched so big she was in danger of either floating away or exploding.

The stupid grin on her face faded quickly at the sound of the front door opening. She tugged helplessly at the hem of Gary's T-shirt as Paige walked into the kitchen. No matter what she did she couldn't make it do more than only just cover her bum cheeks. She had underwear on but even so, the sight of her half-naked teacher in the kitchen on a Sunday morning might make Paige rethink whether she was really okay with having Jess around.

"Morning," Paige said, her eyes filling with laughter as her brows rose slowly towards her hairline. "I see you don't feel the cold like I do. I always have to bundle up."

"I … erm …" Jess bent her knees to give the illusion of the T-shirt covering more of her than it actually did. "Did you have a good time with Sophie?"

"Yes. Thanks." After ruffling the top of Bailey's head, Paige took an apple from the fruit bowl and bit into it. "I take it you and Gary figured things out?"

"Yes."

"Good." Her smile was genuine and filled with warmth. "I have to take Bailey to the dog training class. I'll take him for a walk too, so I'll probably be gone for a couple of hours. Will you still be here when I get back?"

"I'm not sure." With her arms rigid by her sides, stretching the T-shirt to the longest possible length, she searched Paige's face for clues as to what the right answer might be. Was she hinting that Jess should be gone by then? Were they going to be on some sort of bizarre rota for Gary's time?

"We can have lunch together if you're still here," Paige said. "I could do with your help with something."

"Okay." Jess tried to hide her surprise. "I'll hang around."

"You really ought to wear more clothes." A teasing glint flashed in Paige's eyes. "You'll catch your death."

Once Paige had grabbed the dog lead and hustled Bailey out of the door, Jess let out a long breath. Then she returned to the task of making coffees and took two mugs upstairs.

"That smells good," Gary groaned into the pillow without lifting his head.

Setting the drinks on the bedside table, she sat beside him, her back against the headboard and her legs stretched out in front of her. As she threaded her fingers into Gary's hair, he turned his face to look up at her.

"You look good in my T-shirt," he told her.

"Paige was worried I might be cold."

He spluttered a laugh. "Did she get photos? Imagine having that kind of ammo to blackmail your teacher with. When she gets an A in chemistry I'll know why."

"I'm really embarrassed."

"I bet Paige loved it. She's probably already on the phone to Sophie having a good laugh about it."

Jess gave his bicep a shove but he only wrapped an arm around her thigh and snuggled up like she was his own personal pillow. His words tickled her skin when he spoke.

"I suppose we should get up if Paige is home. I don't want to make her uncomfortable."

"She's gone out again. Taken Bailey to dog training."

"I'm glad she remembered that. I completely forgot." He reached behind Jess's back and pulled her down the bed until she was level with him. "I'm also glad we don't have to get up yet."

"Me too," she whispered, pulling his face to hers until their warm lips melted together.

~

"I need you to help me convince Gary that my business ideas for the garage are good."

Jess leaned back on the couch after finishing her bacon sandwich and raised her eyebrows at Paige, who sat eagerly on the edge of the armchair. "I'm not sure business plans are really my speciality."

"It doesn't need to be. This is just common sense." She picked a notepad from the coffee table and began writing. "I'm going to give you a scenario. Pretend you're a customer and let me know what you think."

Jess looked to Gary beside her.

"I don't think we should involve Jess in this," he said.

"Why not? I need an ally since you and Grandad are too pigheaded to listen to my ideas."

"I don't remember having any choice but to listen to you. We said we'd think about it."

"There's nothing to think about. If you implement my ideas, you'll be instantly more profitable." She slipped off the chair and knelt beside the coffee table, sliding the notepad towards Jess. "Imagine you need an MOT. You call around the local garages and these are the prices you're quoted. Which one do you go for?"

"No one makes a choice purely on the price," Gary said wearily.

Paige glared at him. "Let's pretend they do for now."

"I wouldn't go for that one," Jess said, pointing. "Or that one. I'd pick one of the others."

From Gary's extended sigh and Paige's grin, it seemed she'd just put herself squarely on Team Paige.

"Why?" Paige asked eagerly.

"This one's too expensive. I'd feel like I was being ripped off. That one's too cheap, so I'd assume they don't know what they're doing. I'd choose one of the middle ones."

"Good choice," Paige said, grinning. "Unfortunately you haven't picked Gary's place, so it won't be him doing your MOT."

"I know what I'm doing," Gary grumbled.

"Are your prices really that low?" Jess asked.

"These are real prices from local garages," Paige told her. "I called around and got quotes."

Jess nodded approvingly. "Nice work."

"We get our customers through word of mouth," Gary said. "Not from random people calling for a quote."

Paige rolled her eyes. "Because you quote them too low!"

"We have a loyal customer base. Most of our customers have been coming to us for years."

"This is another issue," Paige told Jess. "Half the time they're not even charging this much ..." She tapped her pen against the paper. "They give mates' rates to almost everyone."

"Not everyone. Just friends."

"Who was that woman who brought her car in last week and you only charged her for parts and not labour?"

"Leana Mackenzie. Who I've known forever. The Mackenzies are Logan's family and Logan's pretty much family to me. Of course I don't charge them full price."

"There are loads of them," Paige said. "Practically every other week there's a Mackenzie bringing their car in for something. I'm sure they don't expect you to work for cheap."

"If we increase the prices, our long-standing customers aren't going to be very happy with us."

"They won't care," Paige protested. "I reckon most of them wouldn't even notice. But they definitely wouldn't go elsewhere because of it."

"She's right," Jess put in. "Loyal customers keep coming back because they know you and trust you. They'd happily pay more because of that. I know I would."

Gary narrowed his eyes and gave her a look that said she was a traitor. "The thing is, neither me or Dad have ever cared about making loads of money. If I have enough to pay the mortgage and a bit extra I'm fine. I'm quite happy with my simple life. There's no stress."

"There's also no driveway to your house," Paige said cockily. "The postman won't deliver here."

"Seriously?" Jess asked. "The postman won't drive up to the house?"

"He got stuck one time when it was muddy," Gary muttered. "But he brings my post to the garage so it's not an issue."

"All you have to do is increase prices and stop charging mates' rates." Paige rocked back onto her heels, then sat on the chair again. "Profits will increase immediately. This isn't rocket science."

"I feel bad charging people I know well."

"I don't see why. Did you pay Elspeth for making my birthday cake?"

"Yes."

"Did she charge you mates' rates?"

His shoulders hitched. "I've no idea."

"Exactly. You didn't care. You just handed over the money without a thought. Would you expect her to only charge for the ingredients and not the time it took her to make it?"

"I think you've made your point," he said resignedly.

"This is a lot of fun." She grinned as Bailey jumped into her lap.

"It's not as though I'm going to start charging Logan. He might decide to charge me for all the work he's done on my house."

"I agree that you shouldn't charge Logan," Paige said. "Or your mum. But everyone else …" She paused as Jess cleared her throat. "You can also do any work on Jess's car for free. And obviously when I'm old enough to drive and you've bought me a car you should work on that for free … but everyone else you can charge properly."

"I'll think about it," Gary said.

"Whatever!" Paige scratched the top of Bailey's head. "Soon it'll be my job to send out invoices and I'll be in charge of pricing. When Nick showed me around the college last week, he said that if I take a business course he can tailor it so I'm learning exactly what I need to know to run the garage. Everything I learn I'll be able to implement immediately."

"That sounds great," Jess said, then patted Gary's thigh. "I should probably get going."

He hooked a thumb into the waist of her jeans, pinning her to the couch like a tent peg as he gave a quick shake of the head. "Hang around a bit longer."

"I've got some work I need to do for tomorrow." She wasn't actually keen to go anywhere but didn't want to outstay her welcome.

"You could stay and watch a film with us," Paige suggested. "That's got to be better than work."

"I guess I could." Jess looked questioningly at Gary. "If that's okay?"

Paige chuckled. "He can't stop staring at you and he pinned you to the couch when you mentioned leaving, so I'd say it's probably fine with him."

A bashful smile hit Gary's lips and he removed his hand from Jess's waistband. "Are you two going to gang up on me and make me watch something soppy?"

"Yes," Paige and Jess said at once.

Paige stood up and headed to the kitchen. "I'll make popcorn."

"You can run away if you want," Gary said, then shuffled closer and kissed Jess as though he'd been dying to get a moment alone with her.

"I don't want to go," she said, a hand at his chest. "I just don't want Paige to get sick of having me around."

"I think she likes having you around."

"For now. I'd like it to stay that way, which probably means easing into things and not forcing my presence on her."

"Don't tell me we need to take things slow. I'm not sure I'm capable of it at this stage. I want to be with you all the time."

She put a hand to his cheek. "Are you going to be a clingy boyfriend?"

"Yes. Is that a problem?"

Her chest swelled and she shook her head. "Not at all."

EPILOGUE

FIVE MONTHS LATER …

"Why are you so stressed?" Nick asked when Lexie stepped outside and banged the front door shut behind her.

"I'm not."

He turned on the path to look at her. "We had the afternoon to ourselves and you spent it stomping around the house with a face like thunder."

"Can we just go to the pub and get this over with?" She tried to get past him, but he snatched at her waist to stop her.

"You're not saying goodbye to Dale forever. He'll finish school and be back before you know it."

"You don't know that." She felt her shoulders tense. "He might decide he doesn't want to come back."

"He's going to be in your life no matter what happens," Nick said, circling his arms around her. "I guarantee it."

"That's not the only problem," Lexie whispered. "I don't know how it will be with Matthew now."

"What do you mean?"

"He's been coming up once a month to visit Dale …"

"And *you,*" Nick said. "He'll still come to visit you."

"Will he?" Lexie asked, swallowing her emotions.

"Yes. Of course."

"I suppose he'll probably want to see Grace."

"And *you,*" Nick said in earnest.

"Maybe."

"Definitely."

"Do you think that will be an issue for Dad?"

"Why would it?"

"Because so far Matthew has been coming to visit Dale. That makes things easy for everyone. How will Dad feel about Matthew visiting when Dale isn't here?"

"I honestly can't imagine it will be a problem. Angus and Matthew get on well. And nobody other than you thinks Matthew has only been coming up to visit Dale. His visits were always about you. Probably more so than Dale."

"I hope you're right." Lexie couldn't quite let herself believe she could end up having a positive, healthy relationship with her biological father.

Nick kissed the side of her head, then took her hand and set off towards the pub. "Did you speak any more to Angus and Mary about taking on more shifts again?"

"It's Dad's favourite topic. He keeps blethering about me taking more of a managerial role so he can work less."

"Has he spoken to you about that in more detail?"

"Not really. Why? It's okay with you, isn't it? They know I have to work around your teaching schedule. Mum seems keen to help out with Grace, so it shouldn't be a problem."

"Whatever you want is fine with me."

"It's not as though Dad's actually going to work any less. He's such a control freak. I don't think he'll really cut back at all."

"He might surprise you."

Lexie shot him a sidelong glance. "Did he talk to you?"

"Not really." From the quiver in his voice, it was clear that wasn't true.

"What did he say?" Lexie demanded.

"Just that he'd like to cut down. Exactly what he said to you."

Lexie opened her mouth to quiz him further but was distracted by Dale walking out of the bunkhouse.

"I thought you'd already be in the pub," she told him. "You're late for your own leaving party."

"I was waiting for you. I wanted to talk to you without everyone else around."

"Sounds serious," Lexie said, keeping her voice light. She was determined to avoid any emotional goodbyes.

"You transferred five thousand pounds into my account," he said accusingly.

"Oh, that." She grimaced and caught Nick's small smile as he untangled his fingers from hers and told them he'd see them in the pub. "It's not a big deal," Lexie said, continuing slowly across the car park. "It's half of the money that Grandad left me. I told you I was going to share it with you."

He fell into step beside her. "I didn't realise how much it was. I feel bad taking it."

"If Grandad had known about you, he'd have left you something. Stephanie cheated him out of a grandson like she cheated us all."

"It's too much." He tugged on her elbow, forcing her to stop and face him. "I don't even know what I'll do with it."

"I'm sure you'll think of something. And you'll never be able to say you don't have petrol money to come and visit."

"I'll be back to visit all the time," he said, enveloping her in a hug.

Her breath hitched. "Promise?"

"Promise," he replied. "Thank you for the money."

"You're welcome."

As they entered the pub, Mary was walking in from the beer garden with a tray of empty glasses in her hands.

"The Mackenzies are all outside," she said, looking at Dale. "You better get out there since you're the guest of honour."

"Is Matthew here?" Lexie asked while Dale wandered towards the back door. "He took Grace out for a walk after lunch and I haven't seen them since."

"Yes. He's been here a while. Go outside and join everyone."

"Where's Dad?" The pub wasn't busy but she'd expected him to be behind the bar.

"He nipped upstairs for a bit while it's quiet."

"I'll go and say hi."

After taking the back stairs two at a time, she let herself into her parents' flat, where she found her dad sitting in the armchair in the living room, staring into space.

"What are you doing, hiding away up here?" she asked.

"Just enjoying the peace for a few minutes."

"You call this peaceful?" Lexie wandered to the window which overlooked the beer garden. "Logan's got the loudest laugh of anyone I know."

The group of her friends and family had pulled two picnic tables together and converged around them. Dale was being bombarded with hugs from the Mackenzie women while Matthew sat with Christine and Keith, bouncing Grace on his knee. Down by the loch, Arran was throwing stones, causing ripples to spread out over the still water. Jasper wandered by the shore too, barking occasionally at any seagulls brave enough to venture too close.

Lexie smiled as she watched Rory walk up behind Elspeth and slip his arms around her to rest his hands protectively on her emerging baby bump. As he bent to say something in her ear, Elspeth's face lit up.

"I take it Logan's been here a while," Lexie said as his distinctive laugh drifted up to them again.

"Aye. He and Alasdair and Rory are doing a fine job of keeping us in profit today." Angus closed his eyes and the lines on his face seemed more prominent. Lexie was hit with a wave of affection for him. "Shouldn't you be down there joining the party?" he asked when she took a seat on the couch.

"Are you coming down?"

"In a bit."

She relaxed into the old familiar couch cushions, trying to make out the voices that drifted from the beer garden.

"Is it hard for you, having Matthew here?" she asked eventually.

Angus smiled lightly. "No, love. It's fine."

"It must be weird for you."

He shook his head. "If anything, I feel guilty that we got to raise you while he missed out. I'm glad he's making so much effort to get to know you."

"You'll always be my dad," Lexie said, her voice brittle.

He leaned forwards, resting his elbows on his knees. "The more family you have the better, as far as I'm concerned. Plus he's twenty years younger than me so the chances are he'll be around long after I'm gone. I like the idea of you still having a dad to look out for you."

She glared at him. "Don't be so morbid."

"Well, it's true. I'm getting on."

"I don't see Matthew as my dad anyway. You're my dad."

He gave her a stern look. "You don't have to keep him at arm's length because you're worried about upsetting me."

"I'm not keeping him at arm's length."

"Yes, you are."

She stared at the worn green carpet for a moment. "I'd hate to upset you."

"You're not going to upset me." He tipped his head towards the door. "Now get downstairs and join the party."

"You have to come too. Don't sit up here being all morose."

He stood when she did. "I was only hiding up here because I don't like the thought of saying goodbye to Dale."

"Neither do I. But he'll be back." At least she hoped he would.

"I'm going to be a bit short-staffed without him," Angus said as they descended the stairs.

"I told you I can work more shifts."

"You didn't seem overly enthusiastic," he remarked.

"Only because I've had so long off work that it's hard to get back into it. You being short-staffed is just the motivation I need."

The pub was still quiet when they arrived downstairs. Lexie caught her dad wink at Mary, who was chatting to Douglas by the fire.

Outside, boisterous chatter filled the beer garden. Lexie said a few hellos to the Mackenzies before heading over to Matthew.

"Has she been good?" she asked, taking Grace from him.

"She's always good. She slept for a couple of hours in the buggy, then woke up in a great mood and ate a jar of baby food. We've had some fairly epic conversations too."

"I'm sure you have," Lexie said, as Grace nestled against her collarbone. She shifted her cuddly baby in her arms as her stomach lurched the way it often did around Matthew. The flutter of anxiety made her swing between wanting to hug him and wanting to run away from him. Her feelings about him wouldn't settle.

He looked at her intently. "If there's a quiet five minutes later, can we have a quick chat? We'll hit the road early tomorrow, so I might not get a chance to see you in the morning."

"Yeah, okay." She forced a smile in an attempt to hide the nerves that bounced around her stomach.

"Nothing bad," he said as though reading her mind.

All she could manage was a curt nod. As Nick had pointed out, Matthew had never done anything to suggest he was about to disappear without a trace. But that was how she felt. Every time he left Lannick she wondered when he'd be back. *If* he'd be back. Surely, it couldn't be long before he got sick of travelling up and down the country. That's probably why he wanted to talk to her.

"I'm going to grab a drink," Matthew said. "Do you want anything?"

"No thanks." She called him back when he'd taken a couple of steps away. "Can we talk *now?*" That would save her from spending the evening worrying about what he wanted to say.

His eyebrows rose upwards. "Yeah, if you want."

Since Dale was closest, Lexie passed Grace to him, then led the way towards the shore where they could talk more privately. Arran darted past them, heading up to the beer garden with Jasper close behind him.

"What did you want to talk about?" Lexie asked bluntly once they were away from the crowd.

Matthew shoved his hands in the pockets of his jeans and shifted his weight. "I wanted to sound you out about something …" He paused and cleared his throat. "I've been wondering how you feel about my visits. I feel as though it's worked well with me coming up for a long weekend once a month, but I was thinking about work … and how it's such a long way to come for a few days …"

"It's fine if you're here less," Lexie said quickly, jutting her chin out. "I expected you wouldn't be here as much once Dale left. It's not a big deal." Pressing her lips together she looked back towards the pub, where Nick was standing beside Dale, blowing raspberries on Grace's neck. The younger of the Mackenzies sat around the picnic tables, while Christine and Keith talked to her parents.

Lexie inhaled a deep breath as she focused on her mum and dad. She had fantastic parents, the best husband, a beautiful daughter and wonderful friends. She absolutely didn't need Matthew in her life. The fact that they shared DNA didn't mean they had to be close.

"You want me to visit less?" he asked uncertainly.

"I'm just saying it's fine." She tried her best to sound ambivalent. "I know it's a long way to come and inconvenient with work. You don't need to feel duty bound to visit."

"I don't." His eyebrows pulled together. "That's not why I visit. I want to be here."

"Do you?" she asked, hating how desperate she sounded.

"Yes. Of course."

Lexie drew her shoulders back and willed herself not to cry. "But you need to visit less because of work?"

"That's not what I was going to say. I was trying to ask if it would be okay for me to be here more. My job is pretty flexible and I can work remotely a lot of the time, so I thought about coming for a week sometimes. I was nervous about suggesting it in case you think it's too much."

"You want to be here *more?*" she asked, looking him in the eyes. "Even though Dale won't be here?"

"Yes." He smiled weakly. "It'll mean leaving him home alone, but I figured he's done all right living alone here … and my parents can keep an eye on him. But if it's too much for you just say so."

"It's okay with me," she said as her eyes welled up.

"I didn't mean to upset you."

"You haven't." She sucked in a breath. "I keep thinking you'll disappear from my life again. I daren't let myself get too attached."

"I really want to be a part of your life," he said. "I want to be here for you, in whatever way you're comfortable with."

"I like having you around," she told him honestly. "But I also worry about upsetting Dad … Angus," she clarified.

"I'd never want to come between you." He paused and glanced towards the pub. "I wanted to give Angus some money for letting me stay at the bunkhouse. I know Dale hasn't been paying him any rent either, so I wanted to give him something, but he refused."

Lexie nodded. "He wouldn't want your money."

"He also told me he'd keep the place empty so I can use it anytime I want to visit."

Lexie managed a small smile. "I guess that means he really is fine with you being here."

"I get that impression." Matthew looked at her seriously. "I'm just not sure what *you're* okay with."

"I'd like you to be here more," she said, tasting salty tears on her lips.

His lips twitched to a slow smile and he took a tentative step towards her. She gave him the usual awkward hug, but this time when she felt him loosen his grip, she held tighter and let herself relax into the embrace.

When they headed back to join the party, she caught Nick looking at her in concern and smiled to let him know she was okay.

Grace squirmed in Dale's arms when she saw Matthew approaching, and he happily took her for a cuddle.

"You're so cute I could eat you," he said, then made her giggle when he pretended to gobble up her fingers. When he managed to drag his attention from her, he looked at Dale and then Lexie. "I still want to get a selfie of the three of us before the end of the evening."

"You got one yesterday," Dale said, shaking his head.

Matthew screwed his face up. "You both went cross-eyed and looked ridiculous."

"It's not our fault if we got our looks from you," Dale said cheekily.

"I only want one decent photo."

"Why does it have to be a selfie?" Dale asked, rolling his eyes.

"Tradition," Matthew said firmly, then pulled his phone from his pocket. "Just let me take one, then I'll shut up about it."

Before he could get his photo, he was interrupted by Angus calling everyone to attention and moving to stand at the head of the table. Lexie slipped her arm around Nick's waist as they gravitated closer to the tables. She hadn't been expecting her dad to make a speech, especially not so early in the evening. Maybe after a few drinks.

"I'm not usually one for speeches," he announced, as Mary

moved beside him with a couple of gift bags in her hand. "But I thought I ought to say something. I promise to keep it brief.

"I think you all know how much Mary and I have enjoyed having Dale around. He's promised to come back and visit and we'll hold him to that." He shot Dale a warm smile. "In the meantime, we've got a little something for you to remember us by." Mary handed over the present, which Lexie knew was a framed photo of Dale and the rest of the staff behind the bar. There was also a card which had been signed by all the locals.

"Thank you." Dale beamed at the picture as he pulled it from the gift bag, then hugged both Mary and Angus.

"I'll be back begging for a job before you know it," he said.

"As far as I'm concerned there'll always be a job for you at the Old Inn," Angus said. "But I reckon it'll be up to Lexie by then."

Lexie stood up straighter at the sound of her name. "Are you planning on putting me in charge of hiring staff?" she asked, with a smirk. "Is this part of your plan to work less?"

"Aye. Part of it." He swallowed hard and looked around for Mary.

"We've got a little something for you too," she said, walking over to Lexie with the gift bag in her outstretched arm.

"Are we *all* getting presents?" Alasdair asked jokily, a slight slur to his words.

"I'm afraid not," Mary told him.

Lexie stared at the gift bag until Nick gave her an encouraging nudge and she sifted through the tissue paper inside. Her hand landed on something cold. Drawing it out, she stared in confusion at the shiny gold plaque, which was almost identical to the one above the front door of the pub.

"I don't understand," she said as she read the engraved words – which declared her to be the licencee of the Old Inn.

Angus cleared his throat. "Your mum and I have decided we'd like to retire – or semi-retire. There's no one else we'd trust to take over the pub." Lexie caught his eye and saw the raw emotions. "If you want to?"

"You're giving me the pub?" she asked slowly.

Angus cleared his throat. "You said you needed some motivation to get back to work. Having your name over the door ought to help."

Lexie put a hand over her mouth as she looked again at the plaque in her hands. When she raised her head, Isla, Leana and Elspeth were staring at her in surprise.

"Lexie's the landlady of the pub?" Elspeth asked in disbelief.

"We have to do some paperwork to make it official," Angus said, "but that's the idea."

"I can't," Lexie blurted out as it started to sink in. "How can I look after Grace and run the pub?"

"I'm sure you'll manage," Angus replied blithely.

"You will," Nick agreed, resting his hand at the small of her back.

"Angus and I can help with Grace when Nick's at work," Mary said.

Matthew jiggled Grace in his arms. "I'm happy to help when I'm here too."

"Which seems to be *all the time*," Angus said, with a small shake of the head.

An uncomfortable silence fell and Lexie's head shot up, searching Angus's features. There was a hint of amusement in his eyes, but she still wasn't sure if it was a joke.

"If you'd stop stealing my kids I wouldn't need to be here so much," Matthew retorted, causing Lexie's eyes to flick to him. The tension in the air felt like an electric current.

"That was a joke," he said, the corners of his mouth pulling downwards. "Did I go too far?"

Angus snorted a laugh and Lexie breathed a sigh of relief as the tension vanished. "The point is," he said. "You'll have plenty of help with Grace. And growing up around a pub didn't do you any harm ..."

"Debatable!" Logan jeered.

"It won't do Grace any harm," Angus finished. "If you want to run the pub, there's no reason why you can't … but only if you want to?"

As Lexie looked at the plaque again, a flutter of excitement whirled inside her. Running the pub had always been her dream. She hadn't expected it would happen so soon, but it was absolutely what she wanted.

"Are you sure?" she asked her dad, her chin wobbling as her emotions got the better of her.

He nodded firmly.

"We're going to have to start being nice to Lexie, aren't we?" Rory said, making her laugh and breaking the serious atmosphere.

"We're always nice to Lexie," Logan put in. "Weren't we saying earlier how good she looks recently?"

"Great personality too," Alasdair said loudly.

"Brilliant sense of humour," Rory added.

"And intelligent," Logan said, nodding. "She's the whole package."

"Exactly how much have you three clowns had to drink?" Elspeth asked.

"We were just celebrating," Rory said.

"Celebrating *what?*" Isla shot back.

"Elspeth and I are having another baby." He tutted as though it should be obvious. "Does anyone want to see the ultrasound picture?" As he pulled his phone from his pocket, there was a collective groan.

"I think everyone's seen it," Elspeth told him affectionately.

"Several times," Logan said.

"Twenty weeks pregnant is an odd time to celebrate," Isla said. "You're just a bunch of drunks with no excuses!"

"Hang on a minute!" Logan bellowed. "We came here this afternoon to support a local business. I don't think we should be getting grief about it."

Leana laughed loudly. "So you were doing Angus a favour by sitting in the pub all afternoon?"

"And *you,*" Logan pointed out. "It's your livelihood we're protecting."

Leana put a hand over her heart. "My heroes!"

"It's going to end up being a busy day," Alasdair said. "We'll have to have a drink to celebrate Lexie's news, then later we'll need to drown our sorrows over Dale leaving."

As the banter continued, Lexie went over to her parents with the plaque still in her hands. "You're really giving me the pub?" she asked.

"If you want it," Angus said.

"Of course I want it. I'm also terrified."

Mary put an arm around her shoulders. "We're not going anywhere. We'll be here to help you."

"Aye," Angus agreed with a wink. "Whether you like it or not!"

Lexie groaned. "You're going to interfere in everything, aren't you?"

"That's my plan," Angus said, grinning.

Logan's laugh drew Lexie's attention and she turned to find him looking at her. "I reckon you might need to crack open some bubbly so we can toast the new landlady!"

"I realise you're just angling for a free drink but that's not a bad idea." She was about to go in search of a bottle when a thought occurred to her. She glanced at her parents beside her, then at Leana sitting with her sisters. Dale had moved to sit with the boys ...

Her head shot to the pub. "Who's working?" she asked loudly. Everyone stared at her, but no one answered. "There's no one behind the bar!" she said to her dad.

"I'm sure it'll be fine," he said with a shrug.

"Have you seriously left the bar unmanned?"

He shrugged again. "It's your place now. Your problem."

"Dad! It's not officially mine yet, and I'd prefer it if you didn't run the place into the ground before we get to that point."

"He's winding you up," Mary said. "I asked Charlie to come out of the kitchen and cover the bar for a wee while."

"Why don't we all move inside?" Lexie suggested, shaking her head at her dad's teasing. When no one seemed keen to relocate, she tried again. "Everyone go inside! Champagne's on the house."

"Did I not teach you anything?" Angus grumbled loudly as the entire group moved eagerly towards the door. "We don't give free drinks."

"We do today!"

As everyone filed in through the back door, Lexie lingered outside with Nick. The sun had dropped below the mountains and the last of the daylight danced on the surface of the water. When she managed to drag her eyes away from the familiar view, she gazed up at the pub and slid an arm around Nick, resting her head on his shoulder. It dawned on her that he didn't seem surprised by the evening's revelation.

"Did you already know Dad wanted me to take over the pub?" she asked.

"Angus asked if I thought you'd want to."

"So you've been having secret chats with him?"

Guilt flashed in his eyes. "My late-night walks with Grace when she wouldn't settle might've ended up in the pub."

Lexie laughed. "I knew your walks only went as far as the pub, I just didn't imagine them involving deep conversations with Dad."

"He also asked if I wanted to be the landlord. He thought maybe we'd want to run the place together."

Lexie couldn't stop beaming. "Are you serious?"

"Yeah. I told him I was quite happy with my job and couldn't imagine switching careers." He gave her a playful poke in the ribs. "You can stop laughing. It's not that funny."

"Sorry. It's just hard to imagine you as a pub landlord." She turned to face him. "I love you, you know?"

He nodded gently. "I love you too."

She gave him a slow kiss before leading him inside. As soon as she opened the door, the noise of their friends and family hit her. Everyone had congregated by the bar and Angus shouted for her to do the honours with the bottle of champagne in his hands.

The front door opened before she'd even taken a step and her heart plummeted when Tim stepped inside. In all the excitement about taking over the pub she hadn't even considered her job at the activity centre.

"What's wrong with you?" he asked when he caught her eye.

She opened her mouth a few times without finding any words. Tim had been such a brilliant boss; the thought of leaving him in the lurch made her stomach clench. "I'm so sorry," she said. "Mum and Dad asked me to take over the pub … I told you I'd come back to work next week. I don't know how I can do both …"

Tim stepped closer and planted his hands firmly on her shoulders, the lines around his eyes deepening as he smiled. "I already know. Angus spoke to me about it. I'm happy for you."

"I'm going to miss working with you," she said as she embraced him. "Can I still take the old bids out for a hike now and again?"

"I was hoping you might." He squeezed her hard before he released her.

The door opened again and Gary and Jess arrived to a flurry of greetings. Now that Gary had a girlfriend who the Mackenzie women approved of, he was around a lot more. Jess made a beeline for Elspeth, giving her a big hug and making a fuss of her bump. The two of them had become close in the previous months.

"Hurry up with the drinks!" Logan jeered as Lexie finally made her way behind the bar. "We'll die of thirst."

"That seems highly unlikely." She took the bottle of chilled champagne from her dad, easing the cork out and letting it shoot up to the ceiling. Dale sat across from her as she poured the foamy liquid into glasses. "Sorry," she said. "It's supposed to be your leaving party but it seems to have been slightly overshadowed."

"It's more fun this way," he said, taking a glass. "Congratulations!"

"Thank you." It hadn't fully sunk in that she'd soon be the landlady, but she couldn't stop grinning as glasses were passed around, then raised in her honour. After taking a sip, she caught Matthew's eye. "Come around here," she instructed, then told Dale to do the same, before motioning for Nick to bring Grace around the bar too. "We need a family photo. How many people can you get in a selfie?" she asked Matthew.

"I've no idea." He held his phone aloft as they huddled together, pulling Angus and Mary in with them.

"I reckon it'd be easier if you took a normal photo," Isla pointed out.

"Selfies are a family tradition," Lexie explained, exchanging a knowing look with Matthew.

"I hate to tell you," Logan called out, "but I don't think you've got me in."

"Sorry." Matthew lowered the phone. "I think I got the family, but that's all I can manage."

Logan's eyes widened with mock offence. "I don't know if you realise, but your son-in-law is my wife's ex-boyfriend. In my opinion that makes us family."

Matthew took a second to digest the information. "Wait, what?"

"Nick and I used to date," Isla told him. "A long time ago."

"I didn't know that."

"There's probably a lot you don't know," Elspeth remarked with a mischievous glint in her eyes. "Did anyone tell you about the time Nick asked Mary out on a date?"

Matthew blinked rapidly as the rest of them fell about laughing. “I feel like I’m missing a joke.”

“It was *a dare,*” Nick called out. “Will you ever let me forget that?”

Lexie moved to kiss his cheek, which blazed bright red.

“I reckon I know how to get a selfie of the whole family ...” Logan hauled himself up onto the bar amid Angus's half-hearted protests. “Everyone move close and look up,” he instructed.

“Maybe I should get one of those selfie sticks,” Matthew said, as they all leaned into shot.

“No!” Dale’s voice was filled with mirth. “You’re embarrassing enough as it is.”

“I think I’ve got you all in,” Logan said proudly. “Everyone shout ‘Lannick family’!”

“You’re such a numpty!” Isla grumbled. “Take the bloody photo and get off the bar.”

He stopped and raised an eyebrow at her. “For once in your life can you just smile and do as you’re told?”

She managed to keep a straight face for a moment before she broke into a wide grin.

A chorus of “Lannick family” went up as Logan snapped a bunch of photos. Lexie doubted he’d be able to get a decent one, but as she looked around at all her favourite people, her heart swelled. If Logan managed to get them all in a photo it would be one to treasure.

As it turned out, with the phone at ceiling level it was easy to get everyone in the shot. One photo in particular captured the warmth and happiness in the room perfectly.

It ended up hanging on the wall of the Old Inn, as well as adorning the mantlepiece of several Lannick homes.

A NOTE FROM THE AUTHOR...

The idea for the Loch Lannick series was hatched early in 2019 when good friends invited me and my family to stay with them in their beautiful home in Broadford on the Isle of Skye.

Skye was one of my mum's favourite places so I loved the idea of using it as the setting for a series of books.

The week we spent there was wonderful. We got very lucky with the weather and explored the gorgeous island in bright sunshine. We even got a little sunburnt … at Easter!

I distinctly remember getting up early most mornings – while the rest of the house was still asleep – and sitting outside to watch the sunrise while jotting down story ideas in my notebook.

Very soon, I had a host of characters providing constant chatter in my head. Back at home I planned out the first three books in the Loch Lannick series. Then I came up with ideas for two more books, but was fairly sure I'd stop at five…

Obviously, that didn't happen.

It's slightly strange how the characters become so real to me. To say I've enjoyed working with the Mackenzies doesn't make a lot of sense, but that's how it feels. I'm going to miss these characters, but after nine books I think it's time to leave the Lannick residents to live happily ever after.

Maybe I'll go back and revisit them at some point in the future, but for now I have a new project to work on, with new characters who I hope will also end up feeling like wonderful old friends… just like the Mackenzies.

Thanks so much for sticking with the series and for all your kind messages and lovely reviews. I really appreciate your support.

If you'd like to hear about the new series I'm working on, you can sign up to receive emails updates on my website: www.authorhannahellis.com/newsletter

ALSO BY HANNAH ELLIS

The Hope Cove Series

The Cottage at Hope Cove (Book 1)

Escape to Oakbrook Farm (Book 2)

Summer at The Old Boathouse (Book 3)

Whispers at the Bluebell Inn (Book 4)

The House on Lavender Lane (Book 5)

The Bookshop of Hopes and Dreams (Book 6)

Winter Wishes in Hope Cove (Book 7)

There's Something about Scarlett (Book 8)

The Loch Lannick Series

Coming Home to the Loch (Book 1)

The Castle by the Loch (Book 2)

Fireworks over the Loch (Book 3)

The Cafe at the Loch (Book 4)

Secrets at the Loch (Book 5)

Surprises at the Loch (Book 6)

Finding Hope at the Loch (Book 7)

Fragile Hearts by the Loch (Book 8)

New Arrivals at the Loch (Book 9)

Always With You (Standalone novel)

The Friends Like These Series

Friends Like These (Book 1)

Christmas with Friends (Book 2)

My Kind of Perfect (Book 3)

A Friend in Need (Book 4)

The Lucy Mitchell Series

Beyond the Lens (Book 1)

Beneath These Stars (Book 2)

Hannah has also written a series of children's books aimed at 5-9 year olds under the pen name, Hannah Sparks.

Books in the Land of Stars series:

Where Dragons Fly (Book 1)

Where Stars Fall (Book 2)

Where Penguins Party (Book 3)

ABOUT THE AUTHOR

When she's not writing, Hannah enjoys spending time with her husband and kids. She loves to read and also enjoys yoga and jogging. And tea … she really loves a good cup of tea!

Hannah can be found online at the following places:

Twitter: @BooksEllis

Facebook: @authorhannahellis

Instagram: @authorhannahellis

Website: www.authorhannahellis.com

Feel free to contact Hannah at any of the above or email her at this address:

authorhannahellis@gmail.com

If you'd like to be kept up to date with news about Hannah's books you can sign up to her mailing list through her website:

www.authorhannahellis.com/newsletter

Printed in Great Britain
by Amazon

39597026R10189